Praise for The Tally Stick

"*The Tally Stick* is made of the stuff of nightmares. It spoke
to my deepest fears, and is written with such clarity that it
made me feel as if the story were really happening."
PILAR QUINTANA, author of *The Bitch*

"From its first sentences, *The Tally Stick* by Carl Nixon
swept me up and carried me away to a world I never knew
and a place I've never been: New Zealand's West Coast,
a rough and rugged place where after just five days in the
country the Chamberlain family completely disappears.
But more than the impeccably described landscape, it's
the complicated moral choices the characters must
confront that makes this novel so much more than a
gripping story of loss and survival. Richly drawn, intensely
atmospheric, and absolutely stunning, I loved this book!"
KAREN DIONNE, author of the #1 international bestseller *The
Marsh King's Daughter* and *The Wicked Sister*

"There's a steady relentlessness to the action in the bent
fairy tale of Carl Nixon's fourth novel. Nixon sketches in
aspects of his characters' lives deftly."
Newsroom

"The writing in *The Tally Stick* is evocative, you can smell
the native bush, see the birds, feel the soggy forest floor.
There is much that the reader must fill in for themselves.
It is a read full of conflict, violence, and dread, but there
is also beauty and kindness, and the switching back and
forth gives it an inevitability that puts the characters in
the frame of a morality play."
ALYSON BAKER, Nelson Public Libraries

"Carl Nixon is one of my favorite New Zealand writers. I love his stuff. This latest novel is very cinematic. I would place it firmly amongst what's called a literature of unease. Very ominous, very foreboding, it's all about the atmosphere. The writing is very powerful."
Radio New Zealand

"I like that the novel tests this Eurocentric notion of 'the wild,' and that it clearly looks to other dominant forms of narrative, not least the ambivalence of New Zealand Gothic. But it challenges our expectations of genre, and in doing so engages with thorny questions about the nature of our relationships with one another."
The Spinoff

"*The Tally Stick* is an efficient, gripping story, a Kiwi Gothic thriller that is confidently and economically told. It is probably Nixon's strongest novel."
PHILIP MATTHEWS, Academy of New Zealand Literature

"*The Tally Stick* unravels a yarn of acceptance, denial, love and resentment. There are many subtle investigations into why people behave as they do, and how simple but necessary choices affect everything. Every event and every conversation is essential to the plot with the things left unsaid and unexplained as the most powerful moments that will leave the reader thinking about the moral rights and wrongs of this story for some time to come. This is the best kind of novel: complex, contemplative, upsetting, written with an ease and flow that makes it a compelling read."
LOUISE WARD, Wardini Books

"*The Tally Stick* is a novel of character and edge-of-
the-seat suspense, with the landscape and weather of
the West Coast of New Zealand given a prominent role."
Weekend Herald

•

Praise for The Virgin and the Whale

"He's a contender, Carl Nixon. He's an acclaimed play-
wright, has won significant awards for his short stories
and he's come close with his novels, too. This book
offers us fragmentary insights into the way our national
memory constructs our national identity. With all that
self-consciousness going on, *The Virgin and the Whale*
is an ambitious project. But Nixon is no mere fashion
victim. This is an intelligently constructed novel and,
best of all, a beautifully told story."
NZ Herald

"This novel is wonderfully accomplished, beautifully told
and a delight to engage with."
NZ Listener

"This story is about battles of wills and ideologies as well
as the healing power of love. Yet Nixon's novel is also, and
equally, about the healing properties of storytelling itself.
Above all, those who can listen to a story and hear the
surface and subtexts are upheld over those whose minds
are not open to the riches and alternative ways of thinking
that stories can bring. Nixon brings home to us why
literature is highly placed among the humanities."
Otago Daily Times

"It is a story which is powerful, yet gentle. It is evocative and poignant. But most of all it is beautifully written and clever and kept me hooked to the last."
Timaru Herald

"I was literally hooked from the first eight words—just wonderful, storytelling at its most sublime. I'm going to do the unheard of for me and turn around and read it again."
Afternoons on *Radio New Zealand*

"Places Nixon firmly as one of our leading writers—complex narrative, beautiful prose and compelling characters make this book absolutely sing."
Radio New Zealand

"All lovers of Christchurch should read this book. It is as gripping and well written as Carl Nixon's first two novels."
The Press (New Zealand)

•

Praise for Rocking Horse Road

"Intensely atmospheric, it strongly evokes 1980s New Zealand—dairies, summer, the beach, teenage boredom and sexual yearning—*Rocking Horse Road* is also a powerful exploration of maleness, and of grief and the impossibility of articulating grief."
The Dominion Post

"The whodunit is just a small part of what makes this book such a joy to read."
Australian Women's Weekly

"This is a book of illusions, one of those works crafted by a magician, skilled at subtly directing your attention away from the real story until it's too late and you're suddenly given a whole new picture of all that has gone before. Told in a laconic, almost languid way, never missing a beat, nor the opportunity to quietly set you up for what's coming, the book is gripping and forthright. Though it started as a short story, it never feels forced or stretched. It is detailed and full and written with such attention and verve that it feels that it is the right length."
The Press (New Zealand)

"I enjoyed Carl Nixon's short stories, so dived into this novel eagerly, and it didn't let me down—Nixon's writing conjures vivid pictures of that place and period, allowing the reader to step back into a familiar New Zealand of 27 years ago. While the timing of the story is a growing and turning point for the boys involved, it is also a similar point for the country as a whole. More than that, as the boys grow into men their fixation on the murder remains. To me the book also hints at a subconscious longing in us all for a time when things seemed simpler and more cohesive."
Waikato Times

"Nixon captures well the calculus of suspicion in this type of murder—its circling and descent: the way its mass builds around a man before, with cruel fickleness, it moves on to menace someone else. This, and the parallel he offers between the boys' trapping and killing of a dog and their revenge on a young 'Don't Stand So Close To Me' teacher, show Nixon to be a writer of talent."
Sunday Star Times

"Carl Nixon has skillfully recreated provincial 1980s New Zealand—I hope Nixon writes many more novels."
Herald on Sunday

"Nixon's teenage voice never loses character, and he has perfectly realized the burning emotion and slightly befuddled sense of discovery of the teenage boys—it would be a crime if it doesn't make it on to the reading lists for senior English classes throughout the country."
Nelson Mail

"Nixon writes beautifully. He gets the style and timbre of the teenagers just right. He uses their language. Something easy is 'a piece of piss,' a lazy-training member of the 1st XV 'needs a fire lit under his arse.' Is there anyone who's played rugby at any level in New Zealand who hasn't heard that expression? What a pleasure then to read *Rocking Horse Road*. Carl Nixon has fulfilled the promise he showed with last year's stories, *Fish 'n' Chip Shop Song*. He is a major talent and this is a very good book. You should read it."
North & South Magazine

"Both chronicle and investigation, sociological fiction and morality tale, *Rocking Horse Road* is a beautiful impressionist novel."
Telemara Magazine

"Carl Nixon tells this story, and that is what is outstanding about it, from a we-perspective: the crime and the efforts to solve it are reported from the boys' perspective—later: the men's—furthermore, the country and its people are characterized, families and relationships are dissected, so that, at the end, a panorama of New Zealand's society

over the last two decades evolves. The result: a very distinct and exceptional crime novel, which is brilliantly constructed and passionately narrated."
Funkhaus Europa

"Nixon interprets the classic coming-of-age motif in a stunning manner."
Die Welt

"Carl Nixon wrote a clever, multilayered and extremely thrilling novel, in which we get to know a lot about New Zealand along the way. He does not establish a causally determined connection between the individual crime and the authoritarian conditions during the 1981 Springbok rugby tour but mirrors the one in the other. In a knowledgeable and subtle fashion, he tells us about a few teenagers, in whom a sense of justice and a restrained sensuality are mixed together into a highly explosive brew. And he provides us with an eventful image of a New Zealand suburb which tries to seal itself off from the big world, while everything that is happening in this world is reflected in it nonetheless."
Die Presse

The TALLY STICK

CARL NIXON

The TALLY STICK

WORLD EDITIONS
New York, London, Amsterdam

Published in the USA in 2022 by World Editions LLC, New York
Published in the UK in 2022 by World Editions Ltd., London

World Editions
New York / London / Amsterdam

Copyright © Carl Nixon, 2020
By agreement with Pontas Literary & Film Agency.
Cover image © plainpicture/cgimanufaktur
Author portrait © Stephanie Nixon

Printed by Lake Book, USA

World Editions is committed to a sustainable future. Papers used by
World Editions meet the FSC standards of certification.

Library of Congress Cataloging in Publication Data is available

ISBN 978-1-64286-098-6

First published by Penguin Random House New Zealand, 2020

Twitter: @WorldEdBooks
Facebook: @WorldEditionsInternationalPublishing
Instagram: @WorldEdBooks
YouTube: World Editions
www.worldeditions.org

Book Club Discussion Guides are available on our website.

For Rebecca, Alice and Fenton.

TALLY STICK *historical* a piece of wood scored across with notches for the items of an account and then split into halves, each party keeping one.

FAMILY a set of parents and children, or of relations, living together or not.

THE CAR CONTAINING the four sleeping children left the earth. From the top of the wooded bluff, where the rain-slick road had curved so treacherously, down to the swollen river at the base of the cliff, was easily sixty feet. There was no moon that night, only low, leaden cloud clogging the sky. As if suspended, the car hung in the air for a fraction—of a fraction—of a moment. Very soon the children would begin to fall. Towards the tops of the trees. Towards the headlong water rushing between the boulders. Into the future.

The only person awake was the driver, the children's father, John Chamberlain. His long, narrow face was visible in the dashboard light. He was staring forward at the headlights as they shone east over the seemingly endless forest; fat, diamond drops of rain slanting through the beams. His expression was, more than anything—even more than fearful—disbelieving. Both hands still grasped the wheel as if he remained in control. Perhaps he believed there might, even then, be a manoeuvre he could perform, a secret lever known only to a few he could search for, yank; something—anything—he could do that might save his family. Behind him, one of the children groaned and shifted in their sleep.

"Julia." John's voice was a dry whisper.

The children's mother was next to him, her chin tucked bird-like into her shoulder, head resting on a cardigan pressed against the door. Earlier, she had unbuckled her seat belt—it had been uncomfortable—now it coiled loosely across her shoulder and down into the shallow pool of her lap. She was dreaming about horses. Three brindled mares were wheeling in formation in a dry, barren field. White dust rose around them, swirling higher and higher. Faster and faster the horses ran, as if trying to escape the dust they were throwing into the air. In Julia's dream, the horses' hooves were impossibly loud.

John wished there were time to apologise to his wife. He wanted to say sorry for many things: the long hours he'd been keeping at work; that petty argument about the wallpaper; the woman in Tottenham Julia still knew nothing about. Mostly he was sorry for bringing the children to this country. Julia hadn't wanted to leave London. He'd pressured her: that was the right word to use, pressured—he could admit it now. He'd insisted that this job was a stepping stone. A place to land lightly before moving on. He'd promised her a future with postings to the New York office, perhaps even Paris. They would hire a nanny once they had settled into the new house in Wellington. A picturesque little city. "It's only two years at the bottom of the world," he'd said. "Think of New Zealand as an adventure." In the end Julia had come around to his way of thinking. She was a good wife. A fine mother.

Hours earlier, the family had stopped at a small village to eat a dinner of steak and chips. Julia talked about getting a room for the night. Perhaps they could walk up the valley the next morning with the other tourists to see the face of the glacier? Excited by the idea, the children looked up from their meals.

"It's just a wall of dirty ice," he told them, pushing

aside the plate with his thumb, his food half-eaten. "There'll be nothing to see. Besides, I'm sure this rain isn't going to stop, not before morning. We should push on."

John had been told this part of the country was a natural wonder, a remnant of prehistory, but all they'd experienced in the three days they'd been travelling was relentless rain and grey coastline, mountains hidden behind cloud, and undercooked chips. If they'd bought a ticket, he would have asked for his money back.

It had been dark when they left the restaurant. As they made the bowing dash to the car, the neon vacancy sign outside a motel was smudged to the point of illegibility by the downpour. He'd never seen anything like it. Drops as big as marbles. Monsoon rain.

He had driven down the coast, heading for the only pass through the Alps this far south. Even on full, the wipers fought to clear the water from the windscreen. The three eldest children had cocooned themselves in the back seat with pillows, sleeping bags and a woollen blanket. Lulled by the vibration of the engine and the timpani of rain on the roof, they'd quickly fallen asleep. The baby, Emma, had taken longer to settle. She was lying at his wife's feet in a portable bed, a sort of fashionable, hippy papoose that zipped up to her chin. It had been given to them by Julia's sister, Suzanne, as a going-away present. At the time John had believed the bed to be a waste of precious space, but it had proved surprisingly useful. Emma's grizzling had dissolved into soft snuffling and then silence.

The map claimed they were following a highway, but to John it seemed more like a side road. There were no more towns, no streetlights, not so much as a lit farmhouse window in the distance. The road eventually led them away from the coast. For miles at a time, trees grew right up to the edge of the chipseal, their branches sometimes draped with moss, all of it flashing into existence in the headlights before vanishing behind. Everything was drowning beneath the incessant rain. No headlights loomed bright in the rear mirror. No cars going north passed him.

John hadn't seen the water on the road until the last moment. It was flowing in a broad fan at the end of a straight, along which he had unwisely accelerated. His foot jabbed at the brake and he felt the car begin to slide as he fought the drift. Wrestling the steering wheel achieved nothing; the car had its head and would not be persuaded. Still travelling fast, they left the road. The tyres bit into the narrow strip of mud and shingle at the same time as the bonnet thrust into the soft folds of the forest. By rights, they should have hit a tree and halted in a jolting mangle on the side of the road, where they would have been found in a matter of hours. Instead, the car slipped between the trunks like a blade. The only noises were the engine, the rain and the long scrape of twigs on metal. Onwards they ploughed, down a steep slope, crushing ferns and snapping saplings, to where the cliff above the river had been hidden from the road. Avoiding the last significant impediment—a granite rock as big as a washing machine—by only a few inches, the car pushed eagerly on.

Sprang.

Found the air. Where it hung.

For a fraction of a moment, the headlights shone east over the forest. Diamonds glittered in the white light. One of the children shifted and sighed in their sleep as the windscreen wipers began their downward arc. It had all happened so quickly that John had not yet made a coherent sound.

It's true, he thought. *Everything does slow down at the end.*

"Julia."

Pulled by the weight of the engine, the car leant forward. The headlights angled down, revealing white water and shadow boulders.

They began to fall.

When Julia finally turned her head to look at him, John could see fear filling her eyes, like water into a blue-tiled pool. He tried to reach out his hand to her. He wanted to reassure her, but moving had become too difficult. If only the seat belt didn't press so hard across his chest. He could *almost* reach.

The way John said her name frightened Julia even more than the untranslatable expression on his face. Seen over his shoulder, the world outside the car was a nightmarish kaleidoscope rushing up at them. Unbidden, a prayer flashed through her mind. It was to a God she had not believed in for years, not since she was a girl. The rejected God of her mother. In a fleeting invocation—really just a wish—Julia implored someone more powerful than her to save them. *Please make it that I haven't woken up after all. Let me still be dreaming.*

The car fell faster. It began to pitch and yaw.

Julia Chamberlain did not notice when her husband finally succeeded in gripping her arm. Her last thought before she died was for the baby lying at her feet.

John Chamberlain's last thought was also about the children. He hoped they were still asleep. He didn't want their final moments to be filled with fear. Most of all, he didn't want them to know he had failed them.

Water rocks spinning white light
the car
fell
Almost
fe ...

* * *

Up on the highway, the only evidence that the Chamberlains had ever been there was two smeared tyre tracks in the mud leading into the almost undamaged screen of bushes and trees. No other cars passed that way until after dawn. By that time the tracks had been washed away by the heavy rain, which, despite John Chamberlain's prediction back in the restaurant, eased shortly before morning. It was a magic trick. After being in the country for only five days, the Chamberlain family had vanished into the air.

The date was 4 April, 1978.

PART I

ONE

4 APRIL 1978

Katherine was ripped from sleep into darkness and chaos. Wrenched, jolted, shaken, tumbled and pierced, with no sense of front or back, down or up, this way or that. From inside an unfolding explosion, she couldn't tell where she ended and the world began. In this place-less confusion, *before this started* and *after it stops* meant nothing. There was only *noise and pain*. How long it went on she couldn't tell.

Until ...

Her first shuddering breath. And another. Heavy darkness through which she drifted, barely conscious. What was that sound? Wind? Water? Perhaps that was it, yes—water. Water gushing from the taps into the long, white curve of the bath in the upstairs bathroom at home in Hornton Street. Much louder than that, though, as though she had her ear right up to the tap, or maybe there were many baths all being filled at the same time? She could also hear, inside the roar of the perhaps-water, metallic creaks and groans, as if a train were slowing into the station. She must have fallen asleep on the Tube, on the way home from Saturday shopping with Mother. *A train crash*, she thought without any emotion. *I'm on the Tube, that's why it's so dark, and the train has come off the rails.* Or maybe someone had set off a bomb. She'd once overheard her parents talking about bombings in the city. Some people had died. *The Irish, they were the ones who were blowing things up*, although she didn't know why. Mother had sounded worried. Father told her it wasn't something they should discuss in front of the children.

"Katherine."

Someone was calling her name from far away.

"Katherine. Wake up."

She opened her eyes. Closed them. Tried again. Her eyes felt like doll eyes that would roll open only when her head was lifted. A little light was coming from somewhere, milky and cold. Something was squeezing her chest. It hurt when she breathed, sharp stabs that she could see as red flashes even when her eyes were shut. Her neck also hurt, when she turned her head. Everything was painted in oily shadow and her eyes slipped off the shapes pressing around her. All she could tell was that she was in a small space.

Her head suddenly spun and she felt her stomach push up into her throat. Her mouth opened by itself and she felt the vomit gush warm down her front and smelt the acid tang. She felt ashamed and wondered what Father would say.

"Katherine."

She thrust a hand in the direction of Maurice's voice.

"Don't! That hurt."

She felt something soft.

"Stop it!"

She could see her brother's face now, although his body was still lost in the dark. He wasn't far away, as she'd thought, but very close. And Tommy too. He was right there, blinking up at her.

"We've been in a crash," Maurice said, sobbing.

"What?"

"We've been in a crash," he repeated, louder. "My leg's hurt."

"What happened?"

"A car crash."

"The car? What happened to the car?"

"You're not listening! You've got to wake up properly."

Despite everything, Katherine felt angry. Why did Maurice have to talk to her like that? Did he always have to act so superior? Besides, he was the one who was talking too quietly. She could barely hear what he was saying over that constant shushing sound.

"The car crashed," she said slowly, unravelling the idea as she spoke.

"Yes, while we were asleep. There's water. You have to help me. My leg's stuck."

She understood now. They'd crashed in the night. They were all jammed in together, in the back of the car.

"Mummy," she said. And then, louder, "Daddy."

She tried to shift herself so that she could see past the front seats with their high headrests, but the pain in her chest stabbed and flashed when she moved. She gasped and sank back. All she could see was part of the windscreen. It was cracked in a thousand places, crazed white. The light was coming from outside, leaching through the glass.

"Daddy!"

"Stop shouting," said Maurice angrily. "He won't wake up. *You* have to help me."

"I can't see."

She could smell poo mixed with the reek of her vomit and taste blood in her mouth.

"The water's cold." Maurice made a choking sound that scared her.

What was he talking about? How could there be water? They were *inside* the car. She remembered it had been raining very hard as they drove. Did he mean that rain was coming into the car?

"Stop closing your eyes. You have to wake up properly. Look at me, look down here."

Down? Yes, she understood. Maurice wasn't sitting next to her after all. He and Tommy were *down*. She was *up*. Blindly her hands moved over her body. Her seat belt was there, still buckled. It was holding her in place, stopping her from falling. Which must mean ... the car was ... on its side.

"Daddy!"

"Stop it!"

Maurice moved, before he screamed.

"What's the matter?"

He whimpered.

"Maurice? Mo?"

"My leg's stuck. We have to get out. The water's freezing and I think it's getting deeper."

She stared into the shadows that had been hiding everything except her brother's head and shoulders and they transformed into water. It was flowing through the inside of the car. Katherine saw the baby's bottle, still half full of milk, roll and bob. She recognised a waterlogged pillow, a sodden blanket, a bloated copy of *Five Go Off to Camp*, which she'd borrowed from the family they'd met in Wellington on their first night. *A river. That was the noise she'd been hearing all along. The car had crashed into a river.*

Katherine groped for the buckle on her seat belt. The catch clicked open. She felt herself slipping, and then the strap was under her chin. As she turned her head, it scraped painfully across her ear. She slid, legs first, to the door of the car, which was now the floor. The freezing water gripped her and she gasped. It reached to her knees.

"Get off me!" Maurice tried to push her away.

Tommy's elbows and shoulders jammed into her and he groaned, the first sound she'd heard him make.

"Tommy? Are you hurt?"

He didn't speak. He was standing up and was mostly out of the water.

"It's going to be all right," said Katherine, in their mother's voice. "Maurice, you have to try to pull your leg free."

"I told you, I can't. It's stuck."

She reached beneath the water and with one hand felt along her brother's leg. The water was to her shoulder by the time she found his shoe. Her fingers were already going numb.

"Don't!" he yelled, into her ear.

"I need to feel."

"It hurts."

She tried to ignore him. There; that was Maurice's running shoe. And, that; a metal part of the seat—the track thing that let the seat slide backward and forward. Her hands fumbled for understanding of how her brother's leg was trapped.

"I need to undo your shoelace."

"Be careful."

It took a long time. With the shoelace finally untied, she gave a tug. Her brother's leg came free. Maurice screamed again and hit her across the face with the back of his hand.

"Don't!" she said.

He felt cold and clammy as she pulled him from the water. He stood on one leg as the three children pressed together, shivering in the small space of the side-on car.

Now that she was standing, Katherine could see her

father. He was a shadow slumped over the wheel, his face turned towards where Mother should be sitting, but for some reason she wasn't there anymore.

She must've already escaped. She's climbed out and gone to get help. Of course she's taken baby Emma with her.

"Daddy," said Katherine.

Reaching between the seats, she tugged at her father's shirt. He didn't move.

It's all right, this happens in the movies all the time. When someone gets a bang on the head they're unconscious, just for a little while.

Soon Father would groan and sit up and shake his head. He'd have a headache and an egg on his forehead from hitting the steering wheel. The lump would probably need a bandage, though before that happened he would help them all out of the wrecked car. Then Father would find Mother and Emma. After that he would go and get help.

"Stop it," said Maurice. "We have to get out. You need to open that door."

Reaching above her, Katherine grabbed the handle and pushed as hard as she could. The door groaned and shifted a few inches.

"Help me."

Together, they pushed and the door flopped outwards with a metallic squeal. Maurice and Katherine both raised their hands above their heads, expecting the door to fall back, but it stayed open. Heavy rain fell onto their upturned faces.

Katherine was the first to scramble up. Only when she was balancing on the door did she realise her glasses were gone. Not that they would've helped much in the dark and rain, but she had worn them since before she started school.

This much she could see: one headlight, only just out of the water, was still glowing. That was the only light. Below her a white-capped wave was pushing into the roof, holding the car against a large rock. All around her the river was churning and frothing between the rocks. The roar of rushing water that had been loud in the car was now deafening. Mixed with the sound was the rumble of stones being herded along the riverbed. She gripped the metal harder. If she fell, she'd be washed away before she could even cry out. Twisting her head, she looked behind her. There was no hope that way, just darkness. In the opposite direction was the rock the car was leaning against. Beyond that she could just make out what she thought might, perhaps, be trees.

She looked down at her brothers' upturned faces. "There's a big rock. I think we can climb onto it."

"Can you see the road?" asked Maurice.

"No."

"It must be there."

She held out her hand. "Give me the blanket."

For once, Maurice didn't argue with her. The blanket was heavy with water. She wrung it out on the edge of the door as well as she could, even as the rain soaked back into the wool.

Helping Tommy to climb was difficult. He didn't seem to understand what she wanted him to do. When he was finally out, he sat next to her on the door and stared blankly.

Maurice turned out to be even harder. He breathed in rapid gasps, making sucking sounds every time he shifted his injured leg. Twice he screamed and fell back. When at last he was up too, she pointed into the darkness.

"There. Do you see?"

"What?"

"We can go over those rocks, there. Come on."

Getting from the car onto the rock turned out to be no more difficult than stepping from a train onto the platform in the Underground. Maurice kept his arm around Katherine's shoulder. With Tommy following like a puppy they had saved from a sack, the children moved over the rocks in fits and starts, until they were standing on the bank. Shivering uncontrollably, they stared back at the car's headlight, their clothes clinging to their bodies. Rain plastered their hair across their heads. Their hands hung by their sides, water streaming from their fingertips onto the rocky ground.

"Father will wake up soon," Katherine said, quietly. "He'll follow us. And Mother too," she added, feeling guilty that she'd left her out, even for a few seconds. Maurice said nothing. He blinked the water off his eyelashes.

Katherine knew that headlights ran on a battery. If you accidentally left the door ajar, as their mother had done once, the small inside light stayed on and that was enough to *drain the battery*. Father had warned them about that at the start of the trip. So it stood to reason that the battery would eventually run out, leaving them in complete darkness. She looked behind her. All she could see was the slanting rain and the looming trees.

"We *have* to get out of the rain," she said.

Maurice didn't reply. He had slumped to the ground, his chin sagging on his chest.

"Maurice."

He glared up at her. "What?"

"We have to find somewhere out of the rain, or I think we're going to die."

TWO

Suzanne stood with her two grandsons in the doorway of her London house and watched as her son's car pulled up in the rain. Rising behind the roofs of the terraced houses on the other side of the road was the dome of the Imperial War Museum. Tim had gone to fetch the car, while the boys waited with her. Now, he was forced to double-park. The hazard lights flashed orange in the late-afternoon twilight. Inside the house, the phone began to ring.

The machine can get it, she thought.

Tim drove the boys up from Brighton to visit her every second Sunday. She looked forward to their afternoons. Sometimes they walked down the road to the Italian restaurant, or to the Greek place, which she was less fond of but her son preferred. If she was in the mood, which was about half the time, Suzanne would cook, usually a roast of lamb. Occasionally the boys' mother, Astrid, came with them, but more often than not it was just Tim and the boys. Suzanne didn't take Astrid's absences personally. Her daughter-in-law worked hard and no doubt welcomed a day to herself.

Today the rain had been on and off and they'd stayed home. After lunch she'd pulled the boys away from their iPad and all four of them had played Cluedo.

"Goodbye, Nana," said George. "Thank you for having us."

Dear George, always so formal. "You're welcome, dear. It was my pleasure."

"Bye," said Danny, and he hugged her quickly.

She watched them negotiate the flooded gutter between the parked cars. Danny took the front seat and immediately began checking his cell phone. George scrambled into the back. With the door still open he looked at her and smiled, teeth showing white against the dark of his skin.

Tim wound down the window and leant across Danny. "Bye, Mum," he called. "See you in two weeks. I'll phone you."

As the car pulled away, she heard the answering machine sound a single high note and the murmur of a woman's voice leaving a message.

Despite the rain, she stepped out onto the footpath to wave goodbye. This was something of a ritual, one she'd enacted with the boys ever since they were very young, although only George still took part. Turned in his seat, he waved frantically. Suzanne waved back more vigorously. In response George doubled his efforts until his hand became a blur. The car drew away and it became harder and harder for her to see him. At the end of the street, the brake lights flared and the car turned left. They were gone.

She stood for a moment, feeling the melancholy that always came over her at the end of their visits. Tim and Astrid had adopted the boys, who were biological brothers, from an orphanage in Ethiopia. Nobody knew exactly how or where their parents had died. Apparently there were no records. No relatives could afford to take on the boys, that was what Tim had been told. At the time Suzanne had harboured doubts—really, she supposed, primal fears—about the adoption, although of course she'd not said anything. Surely the children couldn't avoid being traumatised by their early experiences, although nobody seemed to be able to say exactly what those had been. Wouldn't interracial adoption raise myriad issues as the boys grew up? For Tim and Astrid, as well as for them. How could the whole arrangement not hopelessly complicate all their lives?

She'd met the boys for the first time fresh off the plane at Gatwick. Danny was less than two years old, barely walking. George was still a baby. They'd been so much blacker than she'd thought they would be. That sounded terrible, she knew, but their colour had thrown her off kilter for a long time. Every time she saw them, she was startled all over again. She'd found herself taking every opportunity to touch their skin, to secretly run her hands over their arms and legs as they dozed or sat next to her while she read to them, tales about paternal rabbits and conscientious trains. She traced the soft sacks of their bellies, their cheeks and shallow-buried bones. Their feet intrigued her the most. She often wrapped her hands around them, caressing with her thumbs the tops of their toes, at the line where the pink skin of their soles ended, as if she might be able to feel the exact place, a ridge, where the black began.

Now, twelve years later, the boys were perfectly well adjusted. They definitely weren't wounded hostages to their earlier lives. None of her fears had materialised. Sometimes, though, usually at odd moments, their colour would still catch her off guard. It had happened recently, at Tim's home, when Danny had emerged into the hallway dripping from the shower with only a towel held around his narrow hips. Or that day when she'd attended George's end-of-term presentation at school. He'd stood nervously at the front of the class holding his volcano diorama, wearing his white uniform shirt, his back to the whiteboard. And last summer, at the outdoor pool, when Danny had been poised above the water with his toes hanging off the end of the high diving board. Seen from below, her grandson had been like a beautiful black hole cut into the blue metal of the sky.

Back inside, she put the deadlock on and went into the kitchen. Tim made a point of calling her several times a week, but in all likelihood she wouldn't hear from the boys again until the next visit. A grandmother out of sight was a grandmother out of mind. Flicking the switch on the kettle, she took her favourite mug from the cupboard above her head and pushed the red flashing button on the answering machine.

"Hello. I'm not sure if I've got the right number, but I'm trying to contact someone: Suzanne Barnett. Her birth name was Suzanne Taylor. She was the sister of Julia Elizabeth Chamberlain. My name is Victoria Hall. I'm the attaché at the New Zealand High Commission here in London. I'm sorry to bother you on a weekend, but it's a matter of some urgency. If you would call me back I'd be grateful." The voice recited a number slowly and clearly.

The mug struck the edge of the kitchen counter, broke, fell to the tiles and shattered again. Suzanne made no effort to clear away the remains but stood straight and still among the shards. Occasionally she reached over to play the message again. She couldn't have told you how many times she listened to it. Enough to pick it clean of all the information it could give her.

Victoria Hall had that way of speaking used by New Zealanders who've been educated at expensive schools. It was also possible the woman had lived in England for a while and adapted. Only the occasional flat vowel—

thc first syllable in *Zealand* that echoed for a moment in the top of her nose—branded her as antipodean. Beyond that, it was hard to conclude much more than that Victoria Hall sounded youngish, competent, efficient.

Suzanne didn't call back immediately. Instead, she spent the next two hours tidying the house. The pieces of broken mug rattled from the dustpan into the rubbish bin. She put Cluedo back into its box, which went on top of the bookshelf. She moved through the rooms, seeking out anything askew, until it was dark outside. Rather than turn on any lights, she relied on the spilled glow from the streetlights coming through the windows.

Eventually, though, there was nothing left to do. Back in the kitchen, she dialled the number from memory. It rang five times before a man answered.

"Hi, Jeff speaking."

"Can I speak to Victoria Hall, please? She left a message."

"I'll just get her."

A girl's voice said something in the background.

The man said, "No, it's for Vic."

While she waited, Suzanne stared through the glass in the door into the night, where the cherry tree in the yard was almost formless among the shadows.

"Hello, Victoria speaking."

"Hello. My name is Suzanne Taylor. You left me a message."

"Oh, yes. Thank you for calling back. I may not have the right person, but as I said, I'm trying to track down the sister of Julia Chamberlain. Is that you, by any chance?"

Suzanne wanted to say, *No, I'm sorry. I've never heard of*

any Julia. What did you say her name was again? I haven't got a clue how to get hold of that woman. She'd say goodbye and hang up. Afterwards she would press hard on the phone's flashing button until all the life was squeezed out of it. That would be that.

"Yes, I'm Julia's sister."

"Oh, good. I'm relieved. The contact information we had for you was out of date."

"I use my maiden name, since my divorce. And I've moved a couple of times. What do you want, please?"

"I'm sorry, I don't mean to be rude, but this is quite a sensitive issue. I have to be sure that I have the right person. Would you mind if I asked you a few questions?"

"Go ahead."

It wasn't difficult for her to prove who she was. It felt strange reciting the names of her nephews and nieces. She realised that although she'd thought of them often over the years, it had been a long time since she'd said their names out loud.

"Now, can you tell me what this is about?"

"It's bad news, I'm afraid. About a week ago a PhD student in New Zealand who was researching a bird colony on the West Coast found some human remains. I'm sorry to have to tell you, but they've been identified as belonging to your nephew, Maurice Chamberlain."

"How?"

"I'm sorry? What do you mean?"

"How were they identified?"

"Dental records. The police had them on file as part of their missing-persons case. There's no doubt that it's your nephew. There was apparently also an engraved watch, his father's. It had the name John Chamberlain on the back ... Are you still there?"

"Yes."

"I'm very sorry to break the news to you like this."

"No, it's all right. It's a shock. I mean, after thirty-two years."

"Yes, of course, it must be."

"I'd given up."

"Of course."

"Were there any more bones? From other people, I mean."

"No. The police searched the whole area. There was nothing else."

There was little more Victoria Hall could tell her, except that the remains were found close to the shore of the Tasman Sea, at the bottom of a cliff.

William was right. "So, the car did crash into the ocean, after all."

"Actually, the police don't think so. According to the senior sergeant I spoke to, there are no roads anywhere near that spot. He suggested your nephew was most likely walking along the clifftop when he fell."

"Was he going to get help?"

"I don't know, I'm sorry."

"No, of course. I'm thinking out loud."

"The coroner's report will tell you more, but that might take a long time."

"Where was this place?"

"Let me check." The rustling of paper. "I know it's very isolated. Here it is. The place is about ten kilometres south of the nearest settlement, which is called Bruce Bay."

"I know Bruce Bay."

"Really?" She sounded doubtful, as though Suzanne must be mistaken.

"I made quite a few trips to the Coast over the years.

I've stayed at the lodge in Bruce Bay."

"I see. Well, you know more than me, then. I'd never even heard of it."

"Who found him?"

"I don't know his name, but I can find out, if you want me to. He was studying the gull colony."

Suzanne listened as Victoria Hall outlined what would happen next. The case would have to be investigated by a coroner in New Zealand. There would be a report, eventually—no, she couldn't say exactly how long that would take—and of course Suzanne would be the first to receive a copy.

* * *

Suzanne sat at her desk in the living room and opened a folder on her desktop. She'd had all the documents and photographs scanned. Not that the Chamberlains were a family who took many photographs. There were only a few dozen. Apart from a couple of nice candid shots of Maurice and Katherine, most of the photos of the children came from their schools.

There was Maurice. It was his last school photo at St Michael's, taken in late 1977, a few months before the family left for New Zealand, and now seemed very dated. He was the boy third from the right in the middle row, looking desperately serious. Suzanne tried to remember Maurice somewhere else, at Christmas dinner, or during that combined family holiday they took to Essex. It was all so long ago. The best she could come up with were memories of memories, incidents she'd revisited so many times it was impossible to wring anything new out of them.

The next folder she opened on the screen contained

scans of newspaper reports. For a while the Chamber-lains' disappearance had been big news, briefly in the UK papers but for much longer in New Zealand. Nearly all the articles used the same photo of the family, one she'd never liked. They were formally posed in a studio somewhere. Everyone had glossy, fixed expressions, as if they were on display at Madame Tussaud's. It had been taken three years before they disappeared. The children were too young: Maurice was eleven, Katherine nine, Tommy only four. Emma hadn't even been born.

It was almost midnight when she finally switched off the computer. She stood too quickly. Dizzy, she held onto the desk. When she closed her eyes she again saw the serious boy in the middle row. He was no longer wedged between his classmates but standing on the top of a high cliff with trees at his back. She saw the soft edge crumble beneath his feet. In her mind, he fell suddenly and without impediment. He fell with his arms flailing, stirring the misty air.

She opened her eyes before he hit the rocks. *Poor Maurice, what happened to you?* Without turning on any lights, she went upstairs to bed.

THREE

4 APRIL 1978

Maurice and Tommy huddled together beneath the wet blanket at the base of a tree only a few feet from the river. The car's headlight had faded to almost nothing. The water was like a train rumbling past.

Katherine appeared from the darkness. "Come with me."

Maurice looked up slowly. While his sister had been gone—he had no idea how long that had been—he'd sunk deep into himself. The rain and the cold and even the pain in his ankle, which had been like a living thing burrowing inside his leg, had all become pleasantly distant.

"What do you want?"

"Stand up. Come on."

"Leave me alone."

It was typical of Katherine to make a fuss. Under this tree really wasn't such a bad place to spend the night. It was fine; actually, better than fine. The root that had been digging into his side had gone away. Tommy had stopped making his annoying sounds. Maurice wasn't even cold anymore. In fact, the night was quite warm. It was what Father would call a *balmy evening*. He closed his eyes.

"Stand up, Mo!"

Maurice's chin jerked up from his chest. Why was Katherine shouting at him? Now she was pulling. She'd even had the nerve to snatch away his blanket. Rolling onto his side, he curled into a ball. She could have it. It didn't matter. She should just go away and leave him to sleep.

"Come on, Mo. You must. I've found somewhere dry."

"Don't touch me. I'm fine here."

"No, you've got to come with me."

With his sister tugging at his arm, he had no choice but to grudgingly get to his knees.

"Here, use this," said Katherine.

"What is it?"

"It's to help you walk."

He took the thing she was holding out, in the same way that he might take something given to him in a dream. It was a broken branch with a Y-shaped fork at one end. He stared at it blankly.

"Like this." She helped him to wedge the fork up under his arm.

He tested the branch and found that it could hold his weight. Katherine helped Tommy stand. Maurice followed his sister, moving in stumbles and staggers over the rocky ground, with the weak light at their backs. Each time he fell he would've been happy to curl up and sleep where he lay. Katherine, though, kept dragging him back to his feet. She wouldn't stop tugging and prodding at him. More than once she pinched him. If Father had been there, he wouldn't have let her get away with it. Maurice was going to tell him all about it later.

"We're here. This is it."

Maurice couldn't see what she was talking about. They were standing in front of a step in the land, at the very edge of the light. It was a long cross-section of gravel and roots and soil, like a wall, about eight feet high, marking the boundary between the riverbed and the forest, with trees growing along the top. Directly in front of them a large tree had been toppled, and had fallen backwards into another tree. A tangle of roots had been levered up in the bank.

"In there," she said, pointing at the roots.

"Where?"

"Look."

Katherine moved forward and vanished into the darkness. Maurice blinked in confusion. He hobbled closer on his improvised crutch. And then he could see it too, an almost-cave among the roots.

Katherine reappeared. "You go first."

Using his stick for support, he stepped over a small moat of flowing water and ducked beneath the roots. Suddenly the rain was no longer drumming against his head. The way ahead narrowed, forcing him to his knees. He couldn't manage his stick in the small space, so he left it behind. It hurt his leg too much to crawl on all fours—one painful attempt taught him that—so he lay on his stomach and levered himself onto his good side before beginning to pull himself forward with his hands. Thin roots or maybe spiderwebs brushed his head, but he was too tired and sore to care. When he touched a wall of dry earth and shingle he sat up tentatively. The ceiling was high enough that he could sit straight with his back against the wall. Beneath him he could feel dry leaves. The effort of dragging himself had made his leg throb.

"Maurice?"

Katherine's voice was right in his ear. "This is the end," he said.

There was shuffling and grunting in the darkness. A hand as cold as a beef steak touched him and he grabbed it. He realised that it must belong to Tommy. His brother's breath was sour in his face.

"Ahh! Careful—my leg!" Someone had pushed roughly against him.

"Sorry."

Katherine was spreading the blanket over him. He tugged at the edge, trying to get what was rightfully his.

* * *

Without the blanket, the children would merely have exchanged death in the open for dying in the ready-made grave Katherine had found. Before she'd clambered all the way inside their hole, she'd wrung the wool out again as best she could. Now she rearranged the blanket over their shoulders and backs. In the car, she and Maurice had bickered, much to their father's annoyance, over every inch of space. Now she welcomed the reassuring press of her brothers and the buried heat from their bodies. They were so close that each rippling shiver was contagious. The odour of earth and damp wool settled over them. She could also smell poo again. It was, she guessed, coming from Tommy. Occasionally, Maurice would sob or groan in pain. He moved often, breathing shallowly and quickly, rolling his weight from side to side, pulling thoughtlessly at the blanket.

Tommy hadn't spoken at all since the accident.

"Tommy?"

Nothing.

"Maurice?" she said.

He didn't reply either.

"In the morning someone will come and help us," she said, speaking to both of them and to no one. "Everything's going to be all right."

Outside, the car's battery finally died. As if in response, the rain surged and fell harder. Raindrops buffeted the highest leaves in the forest, trembling the broader leaves below, causing the serrated edges of the tree-ferns to shiver, twitching the plants on the forest floor, and finally sinking into the moss and loam. Rain on the rock face. Rain striking the surface of the flooding river. Rain on the boulders. Rain on battered metal.

* * *

At first, Katherine thought she was imagining the lights. They were glowing pinpricks, faint, almost bluish, clustered together among the earth and roots near the cave's entrance, close enough for her to see clearly, but not bright enough to illuminate anything beyond themselves.

"Maurice?"

He answered immediately. "What?"

She could tell even from one word that he was in a lot of pain. "There are lights. Do you see them?"

"Yes." And then another word.

"What?"

"They're fireflies," he repeated.

The only fireflies Katherine had ever seen had been flickering over a meadow in the south of France, near Nice, where Father had taken them all on holiday.

"They're not moving," she said.

"They're resting." He added, "Because of the rain."

"Maybe they have other things in this country. I mean, not fireflies."

She felt Maurice shift. There was the patter of shingle striking the ceiling and walls. The lights went out.

"Why did you do that?"

"They *are* fireflies," said Maurice.

Katherine lay for a long time staring into the darkness. The ground was uncomfortable and her ribs hurt when she breathed too deeply. She was glad when the lights began to blink on again. First one, so faint that for a time she doubted it was there at all, and then another as confirmation. A third drew a pointing line. She watched them come back one by one. She didn't tell Maurice. He might scare them away again with his stubborn, boyish stones. She watched the lights for a long time, until exhaustion dragged her back into that state that, on the first long night, pretended to be sleep.

FOUR

5 APRIL 1978

Even before the uncertain greying of the day, a bird in the tree canopy released four loud, clear notes towards the possibility of dawn. Katherine listened to the notes go up and down the scale, like her piano practice at home. The first bird was answered by another further away, and then another. Within minutes there was a noisy choir of overlapping singers.

She strained her ears, hoping to hear a familiar song from the back garden in Hornton Street or from Kensington Gardens, where she often walked with her parents and brothers on their Sunday morning outings. She recognised nothing. No blackbird. No thrush. Not a single blue tit. Not even a noisy rook like the ones that used to frighten her when she was small.

The solid darkness slowly became earth walls and a ceiling studded with shingle. Unbelievably, Tommy appeared to be sleeping deeply, as though he were in his bedroom at home, with its yellow wallpaper and warm quilt.

"Maurice?" whispered Katherine. And then fearfully, "Mo, wake up."

Reaching over Tommy, she touched the shadow that was Maurice's head.

He rolled toward her with a groan. "Don't."

"Is it your leg?"

"It really hurts."

"The rain has stopped. I want to go outside, so I can look."

"All right."

She shuffled around in the tight space and crawled towards the entrance. It hurt to move, especially her ribs but also her shoulder and knee. Dirt crumbled from the ceiling and landed in her hair, making her blink and spit. When she was able to straighten, she moved stiffly out into the open, stumbling on numb legs. She wished she had her glasses. Taking shallow breaths, she squinted so that the clearing came into focus.

She thought she'd led Tommy and Maurice a long way from the river but there it was, still very close. Low concrete-grey cloud touched the tops of the trees. Behind her, the forest grew right up to the edge of the earth wall. She picked her way over stones to the water, where she avoided looking at the car. The cliff over which they must have fallen formed the other bank of the river. It stretched for as far as she could see both up and downstream. Wet, black rock dotted with plants. Small waterfalls cascading down the face. There was no way to climb up.

When she stood still, Katherine was immediately surrounded by a swarm of small dark insects. She brushed at the air, then slapped the back of her wrist. She was revolted to see a mash of insect bodies, along with her own blood, smeared in a paste across her skin. She wiped it with her sleeve and scratched when it itched.

"Katherine. Katherine!"

Maurice was kneeling awkwardly in the mouth of the cave.

She walked back to him. "I'm here."

"Don't leave me behind. Help me."

She found the branch from the night before where

Maurice had dropped it. Even with his crutch, her brother struggled to walk. She let him put his arm over her shoulders, which made her ribs flare with pain. She couldn't take him far so lowered him onto a half-buried log, where he sat with his injured leg poking stiffly out in front. She watched him desperately looking around the clearing. His face was grey, with chalky blotches under his eyes. She could hear each breath scraping up his throat and rattling around in his mouth before finding its way through the slit made by his cracked lips. He began to slap as the insects found him.

"Would you like some water?"

He nodded. She walked back to the river but had nothing to carry water in so was forced to use her cupped hands. When she got back to Maurice he tilted back his head and she let the water that still remained in her palms drip into his mouth. His tongue was white when he licked his lips.

"I'm still thirsty."

"I'll get some more." This time she came back with even less water. "I'll help you down to the river."

Maurice shook his head. "No. My leg hurts too much."

"Where?"

"The bottom part. My ankle."

Her brother's trousers were so filthy that when she crouched to see, it was impossible to tell if she was looking at dirt or blood.

"Don't touch it!"

She had tried to raise the hem with her finger. "I need to look."

"No. Someone will come soon." He gazed at the top of the cliff, which was in the cloud.

"Let me look."

"Don't. They'll come soon, and then they'll take me to a doctor."

Maurice kept staring around him. It seemed to Katherine that he was expecting a bobby or an ambulance driver to emerge from the trees at any second. She plucked experimentally at his jeans.

"Stop it."

"You'll have to undo your belt."

"No."

"I've got to look at your leg! Please, Mo."

He shook his head vigorously, but then relented. "You can't touch it, though. You have to promise."

"All right."

"Do you promise?"

"Yes, really, I promise. It will be better if you get onto the ground."

Maurice edged carefully off the log until he was sitting with his back against the water-grey wood. He didn't look as she unlaced his remaining shoe. He helped her by unbuckling his belt and then, as a faintly embarrassing afterthought, unfastened the button and lowered the zip on his fly. He stared up at the clouds and his breath started coming in shallow gasps that puffed out his cheeks. With the tops of the jeans still only at his knees, he gasped.

"Wait."

Even though the morning was cold, there was sweat on his forehead and on the bridge of his nose. His hands were shaking. While she waited for him to be ready she brushed at the air and slapped her legs.

"All right," he said.

It was lucky, Katherine thought, that Maurice wasn't looking when she finally peeled away his jeans. From his foot almost to his knee was mottled shades of red, blue and purple, fading into yellow. His foot was so swollen that it was barely recognisable as a foot. The skin seemed too full, like an overripe plum that might split wetly if squeezed.

"Is it broken?" he asked.

"I can't tell."

Maurice looked down. Katherine heard him whimper. He only just managed to turn his head away before a gush of vomit came from his mouth, splattering onto the rocks next to her. The smell made her stomach lift and turn over and she had to move away. Hands on her knees, she coughed.

"Sorry," said Maurice quietly from behind her.

"It's all right."

When she felt ready to go back, she avoided looking at the sluggish pool on the ground. She breathed through her mouth.

"I'd be sick too if it were me," she said. "Anyway, I was, remember? I threw up last night, in the car."

"Did you?"

"Yes. Don't you remember?"

"Not really."

The river roared past, filling the silence between them.

At last Maurice spoke. "There's a first-aid box in the boot of the car."

Katherine felt silly that the idea hadn't occurred to her. Their father had brought the kit out when Tommy cut his finger on the day they'd left Wellington.

"I can try to get it," she said.

"Yes, you go," said Maurice, as though giving her permission.

"I'll check on Tommy first."

"All right."

At the mouth of their cave, she peered into the blackness. "Tommy," she called, but gently, in case she scared him. "Tommy, are you awake?"

There was a scuffling in the darkness beyond the roots, and her brother appeared, covered in dirt and blinking against the light.

"Are you all right?"

He didn't reply. She helped him stand and brushed at the dirt on his clothes, but he flinched away from her.

"There, that's much better," she lied.

Tommy was seven years old and big for his age. Father often said that he would grow up to be like Uncle Arthur, Father's older brother, a big, bearded man who taught at a university in Scotland and smoked a pipe. Katherine didn't like Uncle Arthur very much. He didn't smile and smelt of smoke. She didn't want Tommy to grow up to be like that.

"Tommy, what's the matter? Look at me."

His face was strangely expressionless and it made her uneasy. Adding to her worry was the way all the grey-green in her brother's right eye had been pushed to the edges, leaving it black. He squirmed as she held his shoulder.

"Stand still, I want to see. What's the matter? Look at me."

She found a patch of matted blood in his hair, above his right eye. Gently touching the spot made Tommy grunt. A lashing hand struck her face.

"Don't, Tommy, no!"

She was shocked to tears. Tommy had never hit her before, not once, not even when he was very small. He'd always been gentle. To stop him hitting her again she used both hands to hold him tightly. He struggled and began to make a terrible nasal groan that grew louder the longer she held him. The noise disturbed her so much that she let him go. Tommy immediately fell silent. He slipped past her and she watched as he moved to a puddle, seemingly chosen at random from the many among the rocks and hollows. Squatting on his heels, he stared into the water.

"There's something wrong with Tommy," Katherine said when she got back to Maurice. He was sitting with his trousers draped over his legs. Glassy eyed, he looked across at their brother.

"He looks fine."

"He won't talk. And there's blood on his head." She touched her hair to show where.

"At least he can walk."

"I think he hit his head in the crash."

"He'll be fine."

"How do you know?"

Instead of answering, Maurice slapped twice at his wrist. "What are they called, these insects?" asked Katherine, also slapping.

"I don't know."

"They were at the picnic place, the one by the river, on the first day, but there weren't as many."

"Itch-bugs."

"Who called them that?"

"It's what I call them."

As if to prove the truth of the name, Maurice scratched hard at his good leg. Katherine couldn't be bothered arguing. She fetched the blanket from inside the hole and Maurice arranged it over himself, covering as much bare skin as possible.

"I'm going to look at the car," said Katherine. "I'll try to find the first-aid box. Watch Tommy. I'm worried he'll go into the forest."

"All right."

But as soon as his sister walked away, Maurice drew the blanket up over his head, lay back, and closed his eyes.

* * *

The car had shifted during the night. Barged aside by the shoulder of the current, it had partially rolled onto its roof and moved into deeper water so that only three wheels showed. The boot was slightly open, although not far enough for Katherine to see inside. She moved out along the rock causeway to the end. It hadn't rained for hours and she thought the level of the river may have fallen slightly. She could no longer hear rocks rolling along the riverbed. With a bit of luck, she might be able to wade over to the car.

She took off her clothes so that she was only wearing her knickers and vest, folded them neatly and placed the small pile where it wouldn't slip into the water. After reconsidering, she put her shoes back on over bare feet before edging off the rock. The cold water gripped her legs and squeezed. By the time she felt the bottom, the water had come part of the way up her thigh. With one hand still on the rock, she hesitated. The current, stronger than she'd imagined, surged to her hip.

She let go and took a step. Teetering, arms outstretched, she felt ahead with her foot. One step. Two. Like an acrobat balancing on a wire. On only her third step, the riverbed dipped unexpectedly. The current almost pushed her off her feet. She leant into the water and somehow righted herself. She wasn't even halfway to the car.

I can't do it. I won't make it.
She turned back.

* * *

Katherine had dressed again when she saw her father's suitcase, as a navy blur a short distance downstream. Any further and she wouldn't have seen it without her glasses. With a cry of excitement she ran, afraid that it was about to drift away. When she reached it, however, she found the suitcase was wedged so firmly beneath an overhang of roots that it proved difficult for her to free. She could see her father's initials near the handle.

Half-carrying, half-dragging, she hauled the suitcase up the bank and over the rocks. Moving hurt her ribs, and it took a long time, with several stops to rest, before she finally got it back to Maurice.

"Look what I found."

Her brother's face appeared from beneath the blanket. "Where's the first-aid kit?"

"I couldn't find it."

She crouched and began to tug at the wet leather straps.

"Did you look in the boot?"

"Yes," she lied.

"Right in the back?"

"It must've floated away. But it's all right, we can make bandages for your leg with the clothes in here."

He made a disgusted sound in his throat. "It was a green box."

"I know. I didn't see it," she said loudly. And then, "Maybe Father put it in the car after he used it—under the front seat or something like that."

The second strap came free of the buckle and both

children leant forward to look as Katherine lifted the lid. Shirts and ties, a pair of shoes. Katherine was embarrassed to see several pairs of their father's white underpants.

"Everything's wet," said Maurice, slumping back.

"It'll dry in the sun. The clothes will keep us warm tonight."

"Tonight?" he asked, as though she was talking nonsense. "Someone's going to find us before then. There must be marks on the road up there, broken branches and," he struggled for the right word, "and signs. They only have to look over the edge and they'll see us."

He glanced up at the cliff again as if he could already see the concerned face of a truck driver or farmer, gazing down at them.

"But what if they don't find us today?" asked Katherine.

"They will," he said, annoyed. "Someone will come soon. They have to."

Maurice spoke with such conviction, but Katherine knew there was a chance he was wrong. She took pieces of her father's clothing out of the suitcase one at a time and laid them out to dry on the rocks. There were four shirts and three pairs of trousers, two woollen jumpers, one thin, the other thicker, and five pairs of black socks. It wasn't until the suitcase was almost empty that she uncovered the greatest find. Tucked into the corner and saved from the wet by its cellophane wrapping was an unopened packet of malt biscuits.

"Look," she said.

Katherine carefully tore open one end, keeping the hole as small as she could. The packet would solve the problem of bringing water up from the river. Having divided up the twelve biscuits, she placed the three piles carefully on a flat rock. She gave Maurice his share and watched as he scoffed two.

"Don't eat them all straight away. We should save some for later."

He glared at her resentfully but, even so, put his remaining biscuits next to him on the log. He reached into his pocket and took out five of the mint sweets that Mother had bought for them two days earlier.

"Where did you get those?"

"I saved mine. You can have one, if you like." He held them out and Katherine took two.

"I'll give one to Tommy," she said.

The puddle had lost its appeal. Tommy was now gazing, with the same enthralled focus he'd given the water, at some leaves on the end of a low branch. They were moving slightly in the wind.

"What is it, Tommy? What do you see?"

He didn't look at her, but made the grunting noise again when she touched his shoulder.

"Look, see what I've got you."

She had to wave a biscuit right in front of her brother's face before he turned away from the leaves. He snatched it from her, and ate even faster and with more crumbs than Maurice. She was glad that she'd only given him one. He would've eaten all four biscuits in a flash. The sweet disappeared just as quickly. With the food gone, Tommy wandered away.

Maurice had covered his face with the blanket again. Katherine sat on the log next to him and slowly ate two of her biscuits. They made her feel a little better. Because Maurice's so-called itch-bugs seemed less annoying when she was moving around, she began to rearrange her father's clothes on the rocks. Without planning to, she laid down his good navy trousers and then a shirt above that so that together they made a sort of empty scarecrow. The only pair of shoes that were in the suitcase, brown leather brogues, went below.

"Maurice," she said quietly.

He spoke from underneath the blanket. "What?"

"The car rolled over. It's on its back."

"Roof."

"Mo."

"What?" he said angrily.

"I think they died when the car fell."

"Yes!" He threw off the blanket. His face was twisted with anger, screwed tight, and darkened with dirt. "Of course they did! You're so stupid! They're both dead! They're dead!"

He rubbed hard at his eyes with his hands.

She thought he might try to hit her if she got too close. She moved away. Standing near the earth wall, facing the trees, she cried for a long time.

FIVE

21 JANUARY 2011

Nine weeks after the first phone call from Victoria Hall, Suzanne found herself standing in a hangar at a military airbase in Essex. Victoria had offered to drive her down from London. The traffic had been better than anticipated and they'd arrived in plenty of time. The plane, however, had been delayed.

Suzanne paced to keep warm, glad she'd worn her woollen coat. Victoria was on her mobile, speaking earnestly, trying to work out how long they could expect to wait. Nearby was a row of five chairs alongside a trestle table. The undertaker, who was Welsh, and his assistant were sitting next to each other, waiting without comment or complaint, bookends pressed together on an empty shelf.

Suzanne had received the police report a week ago. She was still grappling with the implications of what she'd read. There had been ten typed pages, along with half a dozen sometimes quite confronting photos, and several maps. Although the case was still being dealt with by the coroner, the police had concluded that in all likelihood Maurice had died from a fall onto the rocks where his remains were found. There had been multiple breaks in his right arm, and both legs. At least one of the fractures in his skull would have been fatal.

Just as Victoria had said in their first conversation, there was no possible way that Maurice was in a car. The highway was miles away through dense bush.

There wasn't as much as a farm track nearby. The most shocking revelation, however, was that Maurice was about seventeen or eighteen years old when he died.

He was alive for four years after they disappeared. Four years! How can that be true?

Maurice had broken his leg in a school football game, less than a year before the family moved away. The police in New Zealand had obtained the x-rays. Apparently it had been relatively straight-forward for a forensic pathologist to establish how old Maurice was when he died because teenagers' bones grew at predictable rates.

She had so many questions. Where had he been all that time? Had he been alone? Living with people? And, of course, had any of the other children been with him? Had Julia or John?

Victoria lowered her mobile and walked over. "The plane definitely landed half an hour ago. They should be arriving very soon."

"Good. Thank you."

"Are you sure you don't want to sit down?" She gestured toward the empty chairs.

"No, thanks. I'd rather keep the circulation going."

"Yes, it is cold."

The giant doors were partially open and Suzanne could see an expanse of runway and grass. At the other end of the hangar, three uniformed men moved around with purpose, too far away for her to hear anything but the edge of their occasional laughter.

It would have been simpler, and cheaper, if she'd arranged for Maurice's remains to be cremated in New Zealand before being transported. It seemed darkly comic to her that ashes could be carried as hand luggage. A partial skeleton, however, was a completely different matter. Bones raised bureaucratic flags. There were, apparently, issues of quarantine and protocol.

Victoria had explained all this to Suzanne when they met for the first time, three days after their initial phone conversation. Suzanne had opened the door to a woman in her late forties, with narrow eyes, thin lips, and dark shoulder-length hair. She was dressed professionally in blacks and greys.

Over a cup of tea, Victoria had told her that shipping Maurice's remains from New Zealand was going to cost Suzanne close to three thousand pounds.

"I'll have to dip into my savings."

"Before you do that, let me make some calls. Perhaps the High Commission can arrange something."

It had turned out that Victoria was able to negotiate through the Ministry of Foreign Affairs and Trade for Maurice's remains to be transported to London on a scheduled military flight. That had done away with most of the costs.

Victoria touched Suzanne's back lightly. "Here they come."

Suzanne heard the scrape of chairs behind her as the undertaker and his assistant got to their feet. Two men in uniform and wearing berets were coming through the hangar doors. One of them wheeled a white box the size of a small television set on a collapsible gurney.

"I thought it would be bigger."

"Come over here," said Victoria, holding her arm.

It seemed to take a long time for the gurney to be pushed from the doors to where Suzanne stood. When the men stopped not far from her, she saw that the second was carrying a long, thin package.

"Mrs Barnett?" asked the first man.

"Yes."

"We're sorry for your loss."

He wheeled the gurney so that it was in front of her and stepped back. The other man handed her the package. It wasn't as heavy as she'd expected. He stepped back so that he was exactly in line with his companion.

"Is there anything else we can do for you today, Mrs Barnett?" said the first soldier.

"No, I don't think so. Thank you very much for your help."

"No trouble at all." He nodded curtly. "Goodbye."

Suzanne thought they might salute her and was glad when they simply turned on their heels and walked back towards the hangar doors. As they departed, their duty completed, their bodies softened into more natural shapes.

Suzanne felt suddenly at a loss. She turned to the undertaker.

"We can take care of things from here, if you like," he said in his lilting accent.

"Yes, thank you."

"We'll take your nephew back to Sterling Street and make sure that he's looked after properly. Do you still want to view the remains tomorrow?"

"Yes. If that's all right."

"Of course. We'll be open from eight-thirty in the morning, but if you do want to come earlier ... ?"

"No. I won't."

"Perfect. So, we'll see you then."

He followed his assistant, who had begun to push the gurney away. One of the wheels squeaked faintly.

Suzanne could feel Victoria watching her, waiting to see what she would do.

"I'd like to open this now. Do you think that will be all right?"

"Yes. Of course."

Victoria produced a pair of scissors—typically, she had thought of everything—and Suzanne snipped at the cardboard package. The police had already told her what they were sending, but she wanted to see for herself. There turned out to be four discrete packages. The first, and largest, contained a piece of wood. It was less than two feet long and scored deeply from one side to the other with several dozen lines. The tips of Suzanne's fingers moved down the notches. The wood had silvered from being out in the sun and rain for so many years, but was not at all rotten.

"What do you think this is?"

"I'm not sure," said Victoria. "Possibly it's some type of calendar, to keep track of the days."

"Or the months."

"It's possible."

"I'm only guessing."

"A calendar would make sense."

The next package was much smaller. It held John Chamberlain's Rolex watch. Suzanne remembered it because it had been ridiculously expensive. John had made a point of letting drop how much it cost. Maybe it was still valuable as a collector's piece, although it no longer worked and the glass on the face was badly cracked. She laid it to one side. A leather dog collar appeared next. It was cracked and stiff. It was intriguing, but told her nothing. The fourth parcel held a roll of money. When she peeled off the new rubber band, the notes remained furled tightly in her hand.

"Do you know how much is here?" Suzanne asked.

"Nine hundred and fifty New Zealand dollars."

"What a mystery."

"Yes, it certainly is."

* * *

The next thing Suzanne knew, she was lying on the concrete looking up at the arched ceiling far above. Victoria's face appeared, hovering over her.

"Suzanne? Can you hear me? Are you all right?"

"Yes. I think so."

"No, don't sit up; stay there."

"I'm so sorry."

"Don't move. I'll get someone."

"No, don't, please. I get these dizzy spells sometimes. It's my blood pressure. I take pills but they don't always work. There's nothing you can do. I'll feel better in a few minutes."

"There must be a doctor somewhere here."

"Please, don't go. Stay with me."

As she had predicted, she soon felt well enough to stand. Victoria helped her to a chair. Apparently the men at the far end of the hanger hadn't even noticed what had happened. She was glad there wasn't a fuss.

"I feel much better, thank you."

She hated the look in the younger woman's eyes—the brewing together of sympathy and pity. There was a pinch of recrimination too. As if ill health were something that Suzanne could have avoided with enough forward planning. Victoria would find out eventually. Everyone got old—if they were lucky. She wished Victoria could have seen her on one of her trips to New Zealand. She was so fit back then, so able. She'd gone out in all sorts of weather, probing into the bush, exploring places without trails, climbing into gorges and over ridges, moving up riverbeds. Her legs had been so muscular from all the walking. Not the type of legs that would unexpectedly fold up under you as they had today, like a broken deckchair.

"I think I can walk now."

"Let me help. How's that?"

"Much better. Thank you."

"I'll pack these things up. Then we'll get you to the car."

"I really do feel fine."

She would put on a show, play the part of the perky old lady, the battler, the tough old bird with plenty of life left in her. Although she was fairly sure that wasn't true. More than just her blood pressure had gone haywire in the past few years. It didn't bother her. Nobody lived forever. She'd accepted years ago that Julia and her family were dead, and she'd been given so much longer than them, especially the children. They'd barely begun to live.

SIX

5 APRIL 1978

Maurice watched his sister carry stones across the clearing. She had the two vertical posts of her H. All she needed was the crossbar to link them. Such a stupid waste of time. The low clouds had blown away and sunlight had finally found the spot by the log where he lay. Not that the sun made him feel better. He was woolly-headed and too hot. His leg ached terribly. It was getting worse.

"Who do you think's going to see that?" he asked loudly.

"I told you, a plane."

He looked up at the patch of blue above them. "There aren't any planes."

"We came here on one," said Katherine. She put down another stone.

"That was a passenger plane. Even if one of those flew right over here, it would be too high up for anyone to see us. You need to go and find the road."

"You're supposed to stay in the same place if you get lost."

"That's not true."

"It is, so people can find you. I read it in a story."

"That was just a story."

"It makes sense."

Maurice jabbed his stick towards the cliff. "The road's just up there. I can't go because of my leg."

"I can't get up there."

"There's got to be a way. You just have to go further along the river and look."

"But —"

Maurice raised his voice. "What if there's an easy way out of here and we didn't see it because we sat here like stupid little kids? You could go down there." Again he pointed with his stick, downstream this time. Seeing that Katherine was already shaking her head, he said, "You don't have to go too far. And then you can come straight back."

Katherine squinted short-sightedly down the river. "No. I'll get lost."

"You won't if you stay close to the water."

"How far?"

"Until you see the road."

"What if I don't see it?"

He tried not to sound angry, but she was making things so complicated. "You will. Or you'll find a way to get across the river, then you'll be able to walk to the road. The road's close. It has to be."

"I can't." Katherine turned quickly and went back to work.

Maurice picked up a stone. In frustration he threw it as far as he could. It landed with a clatter among the trees.

* * *

Maurice had been nagging Katherine for most of the morning about going to find the road. He'd always been stubborn and never backed down, even after it had become clear to everyone else that he was wrong. Not that she was sure he was wrong this time. Maybe the road was close. It was possible she was silly not to go and look for it. The truth was that the forest scared her. She didn't want to be alone out there in the trees.

"Tommy, come here," she said. "Tommy. Will you help me?"

His mouth formed two round syllables. Not a real word, but at least it was an improvement on his ugly grunts. He wouldn't lift stones, though. When she put one in his hands he let it fall.

"Like this, see?"

It was hopeless. Soon he'd wandered away again. She watched him standing beneath a tree, chin on chest, staring down at the ground. She left him to it. She could probably get more done by herself anyway, but she kept an eye on him, afraid that he might wander down to the river and fall in or, even worse, go off into the forest. Then she'd have no choice except to look for him. Her brother didn't move, though, not an inch.

* * *

Poor broken Tommy. The dented boy.

He's focused on the puddle beneath the tree, his attention a narrow beam, unrefracted. Once hooked he's unable to look away. Oblivious to his damp clothes or the insects that are hanging around him in a cloud, he no longer feels their bites or the void in his stomach. Apart from the biscuits, he hasn't eaten in—how long has it been? He has no idea about time. Yesterday. Today. An hour ago. Ten minutes from now. All meaningless. For Tommy there is only the unfolding moment in which he is living.

Watershinewaterfaceflower ...

Why that particular puddle? After the downpour the night before, the clearing is dotted with waterlogged hollows and swales. The one he's chosen isn't particularly large. It's no deeper than his first knuckle, not that he touches it to find out. He's content just to gaze upon it. The surface is pewter, rippling slightly in the breeze and, now that the sun is out, there is the faintest reflection of the clouds. Occasionally, a raindrop that has collected on the branch above will hang for a moment before falling and hitting the surface. When the water dimples and leaps, Tommy's eyes go wide and he blinks quickly. It happens a dozen times. Each drop is a complete surprise.

The sun climbs in the sky. The rainwater dries on the branches and the drops fall less regularly. Eventually they stop. Tommy doesn't care. He doesn't remember that they ever fell. All there is, ever has been, and ever will be, is the water.

* * *

Maurice knew that no one would even be looking for them yet. His parents had said they were going to spend two weeks travelling before Father started his new job and they'd only been in the car for three days before this happened. So who was going to notice that they were gone? Aunt Suzanne wouldn't be worried if no letter or long-distance phone call came, possibly not for weeks or maybe even months. Poppa Chamberlain lived in a special hospital. He didn't even recognise Father, so he definitely wouldn't be raising the alarm. It wouldn't be until Father didn't turn up at his new work that anyone would think to ask where they were. Even then they wouldn't know where to look. He had heard Father tell a man that they were going to go "where their noses led them."

To stop himself from thinking about the pain in his leg, Maurice tried to make a fire. With two sticks and a small pile of dry leaves that he told Katherine to fetch from their cave, he attempted to rub a spark into life. All he succeeded in doing was giving himself blisters on his palms. Angrily he threw the sticks toward the river.

"It's not the right type of wood," he said loudly.

Later he dozed, slipping in and out of strange dreams that may only have been thoughts. It wasn't until the afternoon shadows moved across the river and reached where he lay that Katherine stopped work.

"The clothes and the blanket are dry," she said.

"So what?"

He wanted her to know he was still angry with her. She was wasting time with the stones when she should be looking for the road. He watched as she pulled Tommy away from whatever he was doing. Even though he fought and made strange sounds, eventually she had him wearing Father's sweater and a pair of trousers. She'd rolled up the cuffs, and a necktie worked as a belt. The sleeves hung past Tommy's hands.

"At least he'll be warm," said Katherine.

"I'm still thirsty."

Katherine brought him some water inside the biscuit packet, and handed out the remaining biscuits. He ate them, although he was feeling sick. Rather than wait until dark, they climbed into the hole while enough light still came through the entrance to see. His sister arranged the clothes they weren't wearing into a sort of bed. As the daylight faded he lay and listened to the sudden chorus of birds.

Father had told him that this was a country of birds. He'd produced an encyclopaedia from among the rows of books on the shelves in his study. There'd been a map of the two long islands with the other small island like a dot at the bottom of an exclamation mark.

"This is where we're going to be living," Father had explained. "These islands broke away from everywhere else long ago, millions of years, even before mammals evolved. That's why they have no native cats or dogs or horses or bears. Nothing like that."

"What about snakes?"

"No, only birds. It's a paradise for birds."

The encyclopaedia contained a painting of a giant bird with a long neck and powerful claws. It couldn't fly, though. Lying in the hole, Maurice couldn't remember its name, just that the bird had been much taller than the half-naked man with the tattooed face who was standing next to it holding a spear. A Māori. That was right. Father had told him and Katherine about them as well. Maurice had looked at the picture and thought that it was a silly place for the Māori man to stand, even if he did have a spear. The man looked very dirty and primitive. He must've been too silly to know any better.

That night, Maurice dreamt of claws and beaks. When sometime before dawn he groaned loudly and cried out, he felt someone touch his forehead.

"I think you have a fever," said his sister's voice.

He didn't reply, just rolled over so that his back was to her.

SEVEN

6 APRIL 1978

The next morning. Katherine stood beside Maurice on the bank of the river. He lay on a large rock next to the water. The low cloud had again been there to greet her when she crawled out of the ground. So had the itch-bugs. Her arms and legs were covered in small red lumps. The trick was not to scratch. That just made them worse. Tommy was still in their cave. Despite her coaxing, he had refused to leave.

She was worried about Maurice. His forehead was hot and clammy, and it had taken a long time for him to walk to the river. Sometimes he said things that made no sense.

"You need to go and find the road," he said, slapping and scratching. "We can't stay here. There's no more food. I'm hungry."

The mention of food made Katherine's stomach ache.

"You should go that way." He pointed in the direction the river was flowing. "You won't get lost if you stay close to the water."

"I could go the other way."

"No, that way's better."

"Why?"

"The road's closer that way."

"How do you know?"

Maurice scratched but didn't answer.

"How far would I have to go?"

"Until you see the road." He spoke as though it were

obvious. "Or if you find a way to get across the river. After that, you'll be able to walk to the road. A car will come."

"All right. I'll go, just to see."

"Good."

He handed her one of the precious sweets. Despite her hunger, she put it in her pocket for later. She set out, heading downstream.

* * *

Maurice waited for his sister to come back with help. He wasn't sure how long she'd been gone. His leg, stretched out in front of him, was aching and hot. At least it wasn't raining. Or it had been raining and had stopped. He wasn't sure about that either. His clothes were damp, so perhaps that was true about the rain. *Rain rain go away come again another day.* He giggled. Sometime during the morning his thoughts had turned slippery. Also, the river was too loud. The noise was inside his head and he wished there were a switch that would turn it off. He watched dispassionately as an itch-bug landed on the back of his wrist and began to drink. It felt as if it had nothing to do with him. It was like watching one of those television nature shows that Mother enjoyed. Eventually he crushed it with his thumb. Katherine had been gone for what felt like hours, but it was difficult to keep track of time. He thought about his father's watch, and glanced at the car, which was a short distance downstream from where he sat, but his mind shied away. He didn't want to think about the car or Father.

He took the last sweet out of his pocket and peeled off the waxed paper. The white cube had turned soft and it stuck to his fingertips. He bit off half with his front teeth and held the rest out to Tommy, who'd appeared sometime while he'd been lying on the rock and was now squatting, staring at a spot where the current made a small whirlpool.

"Here, Tommy! Here, look. This is for you."

He had to call out several times before his brother paid any attention. Suddenly eager, Tommy came over. He grabbed the sticky blob from Maurice's hand and pushed it into his mouth.

"Don't snatch. It's rude." Tommy ignored him. "Make it last. There's no more food until Katherine finds the road."

But his brother's mouth was already empty and he was walking away along the riverbank. Maurice watched curiously as Tommy stopped and turned towards the water and crouched.

"What are you looking at?"

There was no reply.

Well, that's fine. He can stay there like that if he wants.

He was thirsty again. Moving awkwardly, he eased down off his boulder, first onto one knee and then onto all fours and began to scoop water with one hand. A tiny dappled fish flicked away among the rocks. In his palm the water was the brown of brewed tea, but when he brought it to his cracked lips it was cold and refreshing and tasted strange but not bad. He drank as much as he could, then splashed some over his face.

He was about to try to get up again, when he saw the eel. It was lying in the shallow water off to his right, almost within touching distance. Its head was visible just below the surface, and behind it the long black body was a slow undulation. He'd seen eels before, during a family holiday. They'd gone boating in Essex with Uncle William and Aunt Suzanne and the cousins. Mother had refused to watch when the children fed the eels pieces of meat on the ends of long sticks. She said they were disgusting, like snakes. Later that day Father bought a jar of jellied eels. Of course Katherine had refused to even try it, but he'd eaten a little while Father watched. He'd said he liked the taste, although really he hadn't at all.

He watched as the eel let the current carry it a few feet downstream. Perhaps if he caught this eel he'd be able to dry it on the rocks in the sun. Fishermen did that sometimes, dried fish. He'd read about it. Slowly, slowly, Maurice reached for his stick. One hard whack on the head might kill it. The eel flickered and vanished into deep water.

Maurice stood painfully and scanned the water. Good, there were more. There. And over there, swimming in the shadow close to the cliff, was an even bigger one. Amazingly, it was almost as thick as his arm and just as long. And two more, closer to him but down deeper. They were hard to see in the stained water. He realised that they were all heading in the same direction.

"No!"

Tears blurring his eyes, teeth gritted against the pain in his leg, Maurice got himself to the end of the big rocks. This was as close to the car as he could be without going into the water. Just as he thought, the eels were gathering at the car. The water was thick with them. They writhed and twisted in ecstatic knots. When they rolled over on the surface their bellies showed white.

"Get away from there! Get away!"

In desperation he shouted the worst word he could think of. He'd never said it out loud before. It was a word reserved for boys who went to other schools. But even that didn't work. Only hitting the water with the stick had any effect. Then the bed of eels shuddered and broke, but less than a minute later they were back. He hit the surface again and again. Every time the results were less obvious. It wasn't long before the eels were ignoring him completely.

"Get away! Stop! Leave him alone!" His voice was hoarse. He was sobbing, and snot and tears ran freely over his lips. Looking back, he saw Tommy watching him gravely. "Tommy!" His brother's eyes rolled. "Listen, I need stones. Stones, Tommy!"

He performed an awkward charade of picking up stones. "Get some stones! Put them in your pockets!"

Instead of doing what he was told, Tommy wandered aimlessly toward the sleeping place. Maurice was forced to make his way painfully to the bank. He needed more stones than he could fit in his pockets, so he picked his way back to the hole, where he found one of his father's shirts. He tied the sleeves together and began to carefully fill it with stones.

By the time he got back to the river, there were even more eels than before around the car. After selecting a stone the size of his fist from the pile near his feet, he tested the weight. He took careful aim and threw it as hard as he could. It smacked the water almost where he had intended. The eels vanished. After that, whenever there was any sign of movement, he threw another stone.

* * *

The stone in his hand was the last. His pockets were also empty. He could get more, but his leg was worse than ever and he was so light-headed that he had to sit down. He barely had the strength to throw. If he were brave, he'd get into the water. He would wade out to the car, splash and shout. That would stop them. But he knew he could never do it. He would've been afraid of the eels even if his leg hadn't been bad.

A shadow fell over the river as clouds, dark as oil-smoke, appeared. He heard the first drops of rain striking the treetops, and the surface of the water twitched and jumped. A large black head appeared in the middle of the deep pool. It was by far the biggest eel that he'd seen, so big that he reeled back on the rock with a cry and the stone in his hand bounced and rolled into the water.

He tried to reason away what he was seeing. It must be a floating branch that just looked like an eel in the dim light. But as it came slowly closer he could see its body moving from side to side. It was as thick as a grown man's leg and as long as his father was tall. The head was as big as his. Never taking its black eyes off him, the eel swam closer.

Maurice was sure that it was weighing him up. When it was almost at the bank, it stopped. He waited for it to rise out of the water and seize him. Swinging away, it moved with the current. Maurice breathed again. The eel had seen that he was just a skinny boy with a badly hurt leg that throbbed. A boy who was too afraid to protect his father. Full of shame, he watched a smaller eel join the first, and then others, until there were half a dozen swimming together. The biggest eel—*the King Eel*—was escorted back to the car, where he knew it would feed.

EIGHT

6 APRIL 1978

It was impossible for Katherine to say how far she had walked. The riverbank was a jumble of boulders, mostly small but occasionally as big as a car, and the trees jostled one another right up to the edge of the water. She had to pick her way carefully. Even so, walking beside the water was not unpleasant. The sun was shining, and moving seemed to keep the itch-bugs away. She was terribly hungry, though. She tried not to think about sandwiches and pies or the steak-and-chip dinner from two nights ago. When the craving for food got too much, she filled her stomach with brownish water scooped up in her hands.

At times, however, she had no choice except to go into the forest. Even a few steps back among the trees there was no direct sunlight. The mossy trunks were sometimes so close together that she had to turn her shoulders to push between them. Everything was damp. Above her, tattered flags of lichen hung limply. Ferns grew in the forks and hollows where water collected. She often paused to decide, if not the best way to move forward, then simply a way.

It was among the trees that her imagination began to play tricks. Shapes in the bark turned into faces and back again. There was movement that, when she looked closer, wasn't anything at all. Father had told them that there were no bears or lions or any dangerous animals in their new home. *No crocodiles either*, he'd said when

Tommy had asked. *You're thinking of Australia. And no snakes.* Even so, Katherine picked up a smooth stone and cupped it in her hand, ready to throw.

She finally stopped at a place that overlooked rapids. The water was loud as it pushed through the narrowing in the rocks below her. She'd still seen no sign of Maurice's road. She put her sweet in her mouth, and as it melted against her tongue, moved the warm goo around. She pressed it up into her palate until it formed a ball. The sugar trickled down the back of her throat.

The sweet was almost finished when the clouds rolled over and fat drops fell—nothing and then a deluge. She stood with her back to the trunk of a large tree and watched the rain. Even sheltered by the branches, she was soaked within seconds. She looked down the river, but the rain was veiling everything. When she got back, Maurice would tell her there was an easy river crossing around that next bend. He'd be sure that it was only a short walk from there to the road. She would've found it if she hadn't been such a girl. Such a little sister.

But Maurice wasn't here, was he? She was the one who was tired and hungry. Her clothes were wet through again, not her brother's. Turning her back on the river ahead, she began to retrace her steps.

* * *

Katherine thought she must almost be back to the clearing, but it was impossible to know for sure. The rain was still falling and she walked next to the river with her head down, thinking about what she'd say to Maurice. He'd ask her awkward questions. Her brother always needed details. Did she walk quickly or slowly? Where did she try to cross the river? Did she rest?

You should've gone further—Katherine could almost hear him saying it, now, over the sounds of the river and the rain—*just a little further. Then you would've found the road.*

Her answers formed as muttered protests and emphatic movements of her head, small sighs and clicks of her tongue. She'd walked as fast as she could. Yes, she'd gone a long way. Miles and miles, probably. No, there was definitely no sign of the road. Of course she was sure.

She stopped walking. It was the colour that had caught her eye. Red, among all the greens and browns. It was difficult to make out what it was, without her glasses. Just something red, slowly turning like a broken compass needle, in the calm water behind some rocks. She moved closer until she recognised baby Emma's bed. The gift from Aunt Suzanne. It was upside down and almost completely submerged. Oblivious to the rain, she sat and stared at the slowly turning bed. She'd seen their father in the car. She knew he was dead, although she didn't know how to feel about that yet. She still clung, however, to the idea that Mother had gone to get help, and had taken Emma.

With the water up to the tops of her thighs, she managed on the third attempt to hook the bed with her outstretched finger. It was difficult to drag it against the current into the shallow water. When she got it close to the bank, she hesitated before rolling it over. The baby's eyes were half open. The skin on her face was mottled blue and white. She didn't look like something that had ever been alive. Death had made Katherine's little sister unconvincing. Like a badly painted doll.

Katherine stood and cried for a long time.

The rain had eased when she began to gather rocks.

Although her ribs were sore, she soon created a rough pyramid. The idea of taking Emma out of the bed was too terrible, so she left her sister as she'd found her. She was sure that at least some of the rocks were pressing down on the body, but it couldn't be helped. Anyway, the grave wasn't going to be permanent. In a day or two she'd lead the people who came to rescue them back here. After that Emma would get a proper coffin, made of shiny wood, with silver handles. There'd be a church as well, with coloured glass and organ music instead of the sound of the river.

For now, she was simply protecting her sister, although from what exactly she wasn't sure. The biting clouds of black insects, certainly, although they didn't seem interested in the small grey shape. From the coming darkness, yes. And although part of her came close to accepting Father's belief that there were no wild creatures in these forests, she didn't really believe it. So the rocks would keep them away as well.

The final rock, which she placed on the top of the pile, was dark green veined with lighter shades, and felt like a lump of melted glass. She was glad that she'd found it and put it aside. It seemed fitting. She should say something. "Our Father," she began tentatively, "who art in heaven." She'd learnt that at the church close to school. On the last Wednesday of each term, all the students in her year walked there in straight rows. The minister who took the services was very old and his hair stood up as though he'd pushed a fork into a power socket (as Mary Lambert had once said, before everyone melted into fits of giggles). Katherine wished he was here to say the right words for Emma. Some of the girls she knew went to church every Sunday with their families, so they also would've known some good words to say.

Katherine's parents, though, had never taken her to church, not even at Christmas.

She began again. "Our Father who art in heaven, hallowed be thy name. Thy kingdom come. Thy will be done on earth as it is in heaven."

Something moved in the corner of her eye. She stopped and looked into the trees on the far bank. There was nothing there. For a moment she'd thought she'd seen a man standing among the trunks. Except he wasn't a man, not exactly. He had the head of a bird with a hooked beak. Of course there was nothing there. She'd just imagined it.

She wouldn't pray after all. Those words seemed more likely to be heard by God when you said them in London. They were words for when you were safely sitting between your friends, with everyone in their brown striped blazers and their hair tied back in ribbons, navy blue or black. In the end, she simply told Emma that she would be safe here for a while. She'd be back for her very soon. All her baby sister had to do was wait.

* * *

Katherine was exhausted by the time she finally got back to the clearing. She crawled, dripping, into the hole where Maurice and Tommy were already curled. Maurice looked up at her. His face was very pale in the near-darkness, and close.

"Did you find the road?"

"No."

"How far did you go?"

"A long way."

Surprisingly, he didn't ask her any more questions. He lay back and closed his eyes, and she could hear the strange rasp of his breathing. Even before she touched his forehead she felt the heat off his skin. There was nothing she could do except curl up next to him. She didn't say anything about Emma. And nothing about the bird-headed man she thought she'd seen while she was building the grave, and again among the trees during the journey back.

Maurice said nothing to her about the eels, though all that night they swam in and out of his fevered dreams.

NINE

The dogs appeared just before noon. The first one to bound from the treeline was a squat, muscular bitch of no particular breed. It ran into the open just a few feet from where Katherine was standing. She froze. The dog skidded to a halt, confused by the unexpected smells and the sight of strangers. It barked loudly several times and ran in a tight circle before darting back the way it had come.

Maurice raised his head. He'd been lying near the entrance to the hole all morning, not speaking beyond gushes of mostly angry words. Katherine had gathered some of the tall springy fern, and after clearing away rocks and larger stones had made a bed for him. She'd covered him with the blanket as protection from the itch-bugs and fetched him water in the biscuit packet.

Ignoring Tommy's grunts and thrashing, Katherine pulled him across to where Maurice lay. Their mother had often warned them about the danger of dogs. Even dogs on a leash could bite. Well-groomed dogs, dogs with wagging tails, small, deceptively comical dogs— none of them could be trusted. Just what the right way to deal with a dog was, Mother had never said. It was just best to stay away from them altogether. And if a shiny-coated collie in Hyde Park was dangerous, there was no knowing what this creature with its foam-flecked jowls and mud-caked legs was capable of.

Two more dogs materialised from the forest. Katherine

watched as they came together, milled, sniffed one another, circled, sniffed the air, sniffed the ground. They all had mottled brown fur, blocky heads and thickly muscled shoulders. She lost track of which one had appeared first as they wheeled in and out, turning, twisting, and looping back until they seemed to form a single creature. And then it was running up to them. It was everywhere. Pressing with its three black noses, jumping up with its six front legs to bark meaty breath into her face. White teeth, too many to count, surrounded by pink and black shellfish-gums. Drool flicked across her cheek, but she was too afraid to wipe it away.

"Leave us alone! Go away!"

Her voice only seemed to inspire more frantic jumping, more excited barking. She waited for the inevitable biting. Instead, bored with the unresponsive children, the creature dropped to the ground and moved towards the river, turning, as it ran, back into three dogs.

Katherine didn't notice the man step silently out of the trees close to her. Even when she turned and saw him, she thought he wasn't real. Compared to other adults she knew—her parents, her teachers, her neighbours in London, even homeless people she'd seen on the street—he seemed improbable. He was wearing black shorts and a faded orange rugby jersey. On the top of his head his hair was a wispy grey-white cloud, yet above his ears it transformed into hundreds of matted ginger strands, each as thick as her little finger. They hung thickly, twisting over and under each other down to well past his armpits, curtaining his solid shoulders and chest. His cheeks and throat were hidden behind a grey beard, which he had shortened and shaped at his chin. His thick moustache was stained yellow. His forehead, which was creased in consternation, and his nose were brown with sun and dirt.

"Who the hell are you lot?"

Katherine didn't know where to begin.

"Well?"

"We've been in an accident."

She pointed to the river and the car. The man grunted his surprise. He looked up at the cliff and, frowning harder, back at the three children. He took in the drying clothes and the lines of stones on the ground.

"How long've ya been out here?" The eyes staring at her were pale blue.

"Last night," said Katherine, struggling to remember exactly. "And two nights before that. The car crashed in the dark."

"Where're ya parents?"

"Our father's still in the car."

The man walked across to Maurice. He had a rifle slung over his shoulder, which he slipped off along with a muddy backpack. Crouching down, he laid a large hand on Maurice's forehead.

"How long's he been like this?"

"Since last night."

Katherine watched as he left his pack but took his rifle and strode to the river, where he stopped at the water's edge and laid the rifle on a rock. Rather than use the rock causeway, the man waded into the water and headed straight for the car. If he felt the cold he gave no sign. The wave that pushed into his thighs barely wet his shorts.

By the time Katherine reached the bank, the man had worked his way around to the front of the car. She watched him grasp the axle and search for a footing. The three dogs were lined up close to her, watching intently. One of them whined as the man hauled himself up onto the car and moved forward on his knees. As he leant to look in through the driver's window his dreadlocks fell forward over his face.

Katherine let herself hope. The man would come back and say that Father was only badly injured. The man would be able to help get him out of the car. Soon Father would be safely on the bank.

The man lay on his stomach and edged forward so that she could no longer see his head. After a while he pushed himself up. There was something in his hand. When he got back to the shore, water oozed from the top of his boots. He was holding Father's wallet and his watch. As she watched, he began flicking through the wallet and held up a driver's licence.

"Is this ya father?"

"Yes."

"And your mum was in the front seat? Is that right?"

"Yes."

The man glanced downstream.

"What about Father?" said Katherine.

"What about him? He's dead."

He spoke with no more feeling than if he'd said *"Oh, he's resting"* or *"He'll be along soon."* Katherine nodded once and looked at the ground. She started to sob.

"Have you lot eaten anything?"

Snot ran from her nose and her words bubbled when she spoke. "Just some biscuits."

Back at Maurice's bed, the man opened his pack and took out some strips of dried meat. There was an apple, which he cut into pieces with the hunting knife on his belt. Katherine ate quickly while he examined Maurice's leg. When he touched the ankle, her brother cried out from inside his fever.

"His leg's broken," said the man. "I can put it in a

splint. That'll have to do in the meantime. Are you hurt?"

"My ribs."

He crouched in front of her. "Where?"

"Here, when I breathe deeply."

A thick finger prodded her side and she gasped.

"Maybe just cracked, I reckon. You'll have to wait for them to come right." He gestured to Tommy, who was staring blankly. "What's wrong with him?"

"He hit his head."

When the man went over to Tommy, he shied away.

"Bloody hell, keep still."

Katherine watched with alarm as, with one hand, he seized Tommy under the jaw. Tommy thrashed and grunted, but the man easily held him. He brushed, not ungently, at the patch of blood-stiff hair.

"Jesus fuckin' Christ! Keep still!"

"Don't hurt him!" said Katherine.

When Tommy was released he moved away, his indignation already fading.

"He's got a dent there the size of an eggcup."

"He hasn't said anything since the accident. He used to talk all the time."

"Where do you lot live?"

"England. London. We've only been here a few days."

"You mean here in Westland?"

"No, in this country. We came in a plane to Wellington City. Then our father hired a car."

"You got rellies living here?"

"What?"

"Relatives, people who know where you've got to, who'll be out looking for you?"

"I don't think so. Father's new job isn't supposed to start for weeks."

The man stood in front of her, tall and solid as a tree. She noticed he didn't pay any attention to the itch-bugs. Impatient to be moving on, the dogs circled nearby.

"You pack everything up, all the clothes and shit."

"Are you going to take us to the road?"

"Nah. I'll take ya back with me." He gestured into the trees.

"Where?"

"To the farm where I live."

"But the road's just up there."

He glared. "Ya arguing with me?"

"No."

He pointed at Tommy. "Will ya little brother follow you if you walk?"

"I don't know. I think so."

"I'll go slow."

"What about Maurice?"

"I'll have to carry him."

After breaking Maurice's crutch over his knee, the man used the two halves and some rope from his pack that he cut into four pieces with the hunting knife to make a splint. He paid no attention to Maurice's screams as he tied it in place.

"You're hurting him," said Katherine.

"It needs to be tight."

When he was finished with Maurice, the man came and inspected the clothes Katherine had laid out on the rocks. Most he put back into the suitcase, but a few things he pushed down into his pack. He closed the lid of the suitcase, buckled it tightly, and tossed it as far back into the forest as he could.

"Why did you do that?" asked Katherine.

"It's too heavy to carry."

He walked around the clearing, kicking with his

boots at the stone letters. What had taken Katherine half a day to write took him only a minute to make illegible.

"Right, let's get going."

He bent down, easily scooped Maurice up and draped him over his shoulders. Maurice groaned. He lay across the top of the pack, head on one side, leg poking stiffly out on the other. Shrugging Maurice into a slightly better position, the man began to walk.

"Come on, Tommy. Come with me."

Katherine was relieved when Tommy began to follow her. Thrilled to be on their way again, the dogs ran ahead, their tails stirring the air.

* * *

They made a strange caravan. The man led the way through the forest, with Maurice riding the swell of his stride. The latest clouds to roll over had brought a premature dusk, into which rain was sieved through the thick canopy. They moved along streams and half-tracks formed by deer and wild pigs.

Maurice floated above the ground in a fever dream. He imagined he was swimming. The man's dreadlocks turned to strands of seaweed in which he'd become tangled and was drowning. He struggled weakly to free himself. He could smell stale cigarette smoke mixed with a sharper old-sock reek, and baked beans cooking. There was the musky odour of dogs. His injured leg brushed against a tree and he cried out.

"Don't yell in my fuckin' ear!' said a loud voice. Later the same voice told him to "stop whingeing like a little girl."

To Katherine, every fern, hollow, mossy trunk, and

dim clearing they came to was the same as the last. Most of the time she was just trying to keep Tommy moving with a mixture of prodding words and motherly praise. When they came to fallen trees, or tangles of vine, she had to lead him around or, awkwardly, under. Once, the man got so far ahead that she lost sight of him. Grabbing her brother firmly by the wrist, and despite his loud protests, she rushed through the trees, calling for the man to wait.

"Next time, stay closer," was all he said when they caught up.

She was grateful when he stopped to let them rest. She watched him lift Maurice off his shoulders and lay him down on the ground. The man yanked up the bottom of his shorts before a heavy stream arced through the air. She looked away, but not before she'd glimpsed steam rising from the mulch and a length of dark flesh. Shocked and embarrassed, she stared into the trees. For a long time she could hear the man's pee splashing on the ground. When the sound finally stopped she dared to look. One of the dogs was sniffing at the spot.

"Get away," said the man, and he half-heartedly kicked at the animal with his boot. He wiped his hand on his shorts. "At this rate we won't make it back before dark," he said bitterly.

He took some rope from his pack. "Stand still," he said to Tommy.

"What are you doing?" asked Katherine.

"I don't want to have to spend the night out here."

Tommy stared down at his shoes as the man looped the rope around the boy's back and chest below the armpits, deftly tying a complicated knot. The other end went through the man's belt. There was about five feet of rope between them.

"I'll go slow, but ya betta keep up, okay?"

With Maurice back on his shoulders, the man set off. The rope tightened and Tommy stumbled forward. He hadn't taken three steps before he tripped.

"Stop!" said Katherine.

The man swore. Tommy lay on the ground, looking confused.

A wet leaf was stuck across his cheek like a postage stamp.

"Don't just stand there, girl. Help him. I swear, if he falls over again I'm not gunna stop. I'll drag him all the way back to the farm if I have to."

There were tears in Katherine's eyes. "Come on, Tommy. Stand up."

Tommy got back to his feet. The man set off again. After that, the only things that seemed real to Katherine were the next step, Tommy, and the demands of the rope. Much later, she'd be angry with herself for not paying more attention to the route they took. All she remembered were a few landmarks. There had been a cliff face with dark and light grey stone stacked in stripes. At another place, they unexpectedly left the trees and came out into a wide riverbed. For a while they followed the shingle upstream through bushes with black, brittle, twisting seedpods. After that, or possibly before, there was a noisy waterfall, where they all drank using their hands. Each place they came to seemed brought into existence by their arrival. After they'd passed, that part of the forest faded from the world.

No, she'd never be able to find her way back, not if she had a hundred years.

TEN

5 FEBRUARY 2011

On the morning of Maurice's funeral, Suzanne woke early. She had a shower and put on the clothes she'd already laid out on the chair next to her bed. In truth, it was her nephew's second funeral. The first one had been in November of 1978. Although officially a memorial service, it was a funeral in everything but name. Hundreds of people had turned out, including a lot of children who'd known Katherine and Maurice and dear little Tommy from their schools. A tragedy brings out the crowds; there'd been standing room only.

Both her sons, Cameron and Tim, had offered to pick her up, but she'd decided she would rather walk. St Mary's was only twenty minutes from her house, even for an old ambler like her. She walked there almost every Sunday anyway, to attend the morning service. Only a storm or snow ever forced her to call a taxi. Her friends at church joked that she was like the postman—somehow she always got through.

Out on the street, the day wasn't warm, but the sun was out. There were more people around than usual. A neighbour who knew her, at least to nod and say hello to, was clearly interested to see her all dressed up on a Saturday. The fat Scotsman who worked in the corner shop was standing outside as she passed. His face was tilted to the sun.

"Good morning, love," he said loudly.

"Good morning."

Tim was waiting for her outside the church on Kennington Park Road. St Mary's, Newington wasn't a big church, which was part of what she liked about it. Suzanne was led inside on her son's arm. The stained-glass windows coloured the sunlight from the south. At the end of the aisle, in front of the altar, was the small coffin containing Maurice's remains. The funeral director had placed a photograph on top, next to a bouquet of white lilies.

It wasn't a bad turnout, considering the circumstances. Her family were already seated in the first row. Apart from them, there was a smattering of maybe two dozen people, dressed in coats, sitting alone or in pairs. The undertaker and his assistant stood at the rear. Everyone seemed to have spread themselves out, possibly to make the church look fuller than it was, or, more likely because they were, on the whole, strangers to each other. Cameron had let people know about the funeral on the internet. Apparently a few of Maurice's former classmates had written back saying they would attend. As she walked down the aisle, Suzanne thought she could pick them: late forty-somethings, mostly sitting alone, looking slightly surprised that this was how their weekend had turned out.

And there in the third row was William. Unsurprisingly, her ex-husband had married again, but his new wife wasn't with him today. Suzanne hadn't seen William since Cameron's birthday. She was pleased to see that he looked well. It took her a moment to realise the man next to him was John's brother. It had been, she guessed, at least fifteen years since she'd seen Arthur. She vaguely recalled that he was using his retirement from the university to work on a book, something he'd once described to her as *definitive*, to do with Vikings.

Arthur had shrunk, possibly by design, but more likely, at his age, her age as well actually, as a result of poor health. He still had a beard, but it was a brittle white. The little hair left on his head was combed over in long strands.

Someone should tell him that he looks ridiculous. Cut it off and be done with it.

Everyone was turning to look at her. It made her feel like the Queen on a walkabout. Danny and George were with their mother in the front row. She smiled to show them that she wasn't upset. Strange to think that they were orphans and yet this was their first funeral.

When she reached the coffin, she let go of Tim's arm. She had seen the bones laid out at the funeral home. They were already in the coffin, on burgundy silk. The smallest bones, the delicate machinery of the hands and feet, were gone. The police report mentioned "predation of the remains by rats and large birds." The skull was there, thank goodness, cracked and mottled and water-stained but accounted for. Without that, this would have been a farce. All the larger arm and leg bones had also been found, and the majority of the vertebrae. Maurice had become a stick figure, a child's drawing of a person.

Viewing the bones had left her dissatisfied. She could've been looking at a display in the National History Museum, thirty thousand years old rather than thirty.

"Let's sit down, Mum," said Tim.

She moved into the front row. Cameron and his partner both stood as she passed. Cam gave her a long hug, and Benoît, resolutely French, placed two solemn kisses on her cheeks.

"How are you feeling?" asked Cam, quietly.

"A bit strange, but I'm fine."

"Good."

As she sat between her two boys, the organ music swelled and faded, and the Reverend Gadwall appeared, wearing his white surplice and stole over a black cassock. He welcomed everyone and made some remarks. When everyone stood to sing "Abide with Me," which she had chosen herself, Suzanne found it impossible to focus on the music. Her thoughts darted from place to place and wouldn't stay where she wanted them to.

* * *

Julia and her family had been missing for almost three weeks by the time the alarm was finally raised. Suzanne's first inkling that anything was wrong had come when William answered the phone one evening. He'd listened with that slight frown that he always got when the unexpected happened, anything that might interfere with the planned trajectory of his day.

"It's for you," he said, and passed her the receiver.

She wiped her hands on a tea towel. "Who is it?"

"Someone in New Zealand, from John's new work."

"Has something happened?"

"He won't say. You'd better talk to him."

The caller had been one of the executives at BP Headquarters in Wellington. He didn't want to alarm her, he was sure everything was fine, but John hadn't appeared for work on the day he was supposed to start. No one was answering the phone at the house the Chamberlains had rented. When the office sent someone around, despite the family having left a lot of their luggage there, it didn't look as if they'd actually moved in. Could Suzanne cast any light on the situation?

"I'm sorry. I'm afraid not."

"Are you sure? Anything would be helpful."

"No, sorry. I haven't had any contact at all with them since we said goodbye. That was the day before they left here. All I know is that they were flying to New Zealand, going through Singapore. Julia said something about showing the children some of the country; a holiday before they started at their new school."

"All right, I see. Do you know what route they planned to take?"

"They didn't say. I don't think they knew, themselves. It was a general plan."

"Is there anything else you can think of that might explain where they are?"

"Really, no. I'm sorry I can't be more helpful."

"Not at all. As I say, I'm sure there's no real problem. It's most likely just some confusion about dates. It's easily done."

She could hear behind the man's corporate optimism that he had doubts. Of course nothing was wrong, not officially. No one had made a mistake. There was certainly no liability. He gave her his work phone number and told her that she could call collect if she heard from John and Julia. He would let her know the second the Chamberlains appeared.

William also reassured her that the whole thing would turn out to be a simple misunderstanding. A secretary had probably incorrectly jotted down the date John was supposed to report for work.

"The most likely explanation nearly always turns out to be correct," he said.

"Yes, I suppose so."

When Suzanne didn't hear anything for two days, she took it as a good sign. Several times she thought about calling back the man from John's work, Townsend was his name, although she didn't want to seem alarmist, or to make a fuss. Once, she found herself standing in the hall by the telephone with his number in her hand before she remembered that the hours in New Zealand were topsy-turvy and so it was no good calling in the middle of the day. They lived their lives while she was sleeping.

The New Zealand police rang the next day. This time she answered the phone. The officer identified himself as Senior Sergeant Gordon Davis, from Christchurch. The Chamberlain family was officially missing. A search operation had begun on the West Coast.

"Of which island?"

"The South Island. The West Coast is actually the name of the province. The last confirmed sighting of your sister's family was at Fox Glacier. It's a small tourist town. We're pretty sure they ate dinner in the restaurant there. The waitress recognised their photo."

"Is it possible they're just staying somewhere, I don't know, in a rental house?"

"It's possible, of course, but we think it's very unlikely, after this long."

"Then, what *do* you think has happened?"

"We're keeping an open mind."

"Yes, but you must have a theory."

"In all honesty, Mrs Barnett, the most likely reason your sister and her family have gone missing is a car accident."

There was a faint crackling on the line. "I see. But, I mean, wouldn't someone have found the car by now?"

"The West Coast is rugged terrain, Mrs Barnett. You'd really have to see it to understand. There are mountains and rivers and bush, what you'd call forest, and a lot of coastline as well. There's places where a car could go off the road and not be found, not for a fair while, anyway."

After she had put down the receiver, Suzanne stood in the hall with her forehead against the wall and her eyes closed. She could still hear the crackling of the line in her ears. That was the first time she imagined Julia and the children in the twisted wreckage of a car. She hadn't yet seen the West Coast, of course. The wreck she pictured was sitting in an isolated field, next to a hedgerow, somewhere that, in retrospect, was so hopelessly English it was ridiculous.

It took her three days to make the arrangements, all of it done on adrenaline. She had to take time off from the small law firm where she was a legal secretary. Cameron, who was sixteen, and Tim, fourteen, were left in the care of William's mother. To say that the boys weren't thrilled was an understatement. "Any port in a storm" was what she told them; "even Agnes." They didn't kick up a fuss. They knew what had happened, and saw how fraught she was.

It was two more days, door to door, before she and William stepped off the plane in New Zealand. Arthur had taken leave from his university and joined them the day after they flew into Christchurch. The Chamberlains' disappearance had been in the headlines in New Zealand, on television and in the newspapers, but interest was already waning by the time they touched down. Their arrival, however, created a fresh flurry among the media. William spoke at length to several reporters in the hotel lobby only hours after they got off the plane. Although it was her sister that was missing, she'd preferred to leave the talking to her husband. That evening she watched him on the television news looking suitably grim, his widow's peak and thinning hair obvious under the bright lights.

Everything felt unreal. Suddenly it was autumn instead of spring. She was surrounded by strange accents, eating snatched meals and walking along wide streets, between wooden buildings. The jet lag didn't help. It was far worse than she'd expected; either she was wide awake at four in the morning or weary to her marrow over lunch.

The police assigned a liaison officer to the family. He was a huge young man with the scar of a corrected hare lip. There wasn't much he could tell them. The Chamberlains had spent one night in what was supposed to become their new house, an expensive rental in a nice Wellington suburb. The next day John had gone to a bank and changed three hundred pounds sterling into New Zealand dollars. That same day he'd hired a car: a late-model blue Ford Fairmont sedan.

Two days later, the family had travelled by ferry from Wellington to the top of the South Island, to a town called Picton. They'd made no advance bookings. A seaman on the ferry had remembered them. They'd had a flat tyre and he'd helped them change it. On the car-rental papers John had written that the intended route for their journey was "the circumnavigation of the South Island." Suzanne thought it typical of Julia's husband to use a six-syllable word on a rental agreement. The police had made a televised plea for information, which had led to the waitress in Fox Glacier.

In their own rental car, Suzanne, William, and Arthur travelled from Christchurch over the alps to the small West Coast town of Hokitika, where the police were basing the search effort. Although the town was on the sea, like everywhere on the West Coast it was also close to the mountains, which ran the length of the South

Island like a spine. William joked that you could shoot a cannon down the main street of Hokitika during rush hour and not hit anyone.

"And even if you did, they'd be grateful."

The joke was old and Suzanne had heard him make it before. It was true, though, that the town had the feel of a set from a Western. Even so, it had a rugged beauty that she liked. The sea was grey and the waves charged the shingle beach with intent. Shattered driftwood marked high tide. The locals soon found out who the strangers were. People would stop her on the street to give her cakes, biscuits, or greaseproof-paper packages of frozen whitebait, the tiny, thin, silvery fish the locals netted at the mouths of the rivers.

It was clear the police assumed that this was what they called a *recovery operation*. That's what William and Arthur talked about as well. They believed that John and Julia's car had gone off the road and everyone had been killed. Otherwise, where were the survivors?

"You have to be realistic," William told her, that first night. He was in the bathroom of their motel, laying out the contents of his toilet bag on the shelf while she stood in the doorway.

"I'm just talking about the possibility that they're still alive," she said.

"You shouldn't. It will only get your hopes up."

ELEVEN

22 MAY 1978

As the car slowed, Suzanne peered from the passenger-side window. They were somewhere north of the tiny town of Haast, heading south toward the pass, and approaching another single-lane bridge. Considering this was the main highway, there were a lot of places where cars had to pull over and give way. Each bridge had a sign with the name of the river or stream it crossed, sometimes in Māori, like Paringa or Moeraki, although just as often Coopers or Sullivans. Occasionally, they came across a name that was almost comically prosaic, such as Muddy Water.

"Harris Creek," she read. "Stop here."

William pulled the car to the left so that two tyres were on the verge but didn't switch off the engine. Suzanne had the map open on her knees. It was a detailed topographical map she'd bought from a hunting and fishing store in Christchurch, the same type used by mountain climbers and serious hikers. Hers was carefully annotated in red ballpoint. She had also been logging the details of their search in a notebook that was on the floor at her feet.

"I think we looked here before," said William. "A couple of weeks ago, when we first arrived."

"No," said Suzanne.

She wondered how he thought he could tell. The highway, the bridges, the bush, it all looked the same.

"Are you sure? This all looks very familiar."

"We definitely haven't stopped here."

"I've been writing it down," she said. She jabbed a finger at the map, more emphatically than she had intended, her voice too loud. She would have to be careful. There was nothing to be gained from getting into another argument. Part of the problem was that she was too hot, stifling. William liked the car to be what he called *warm*. She rolled down the window a few inches and cold air flowed in over the lip of the glass. And, of course, emotions were frayed. It was their second-to-last day in New Zealand and they'd made no progress toward finding Julia and her family. Before dawn the next day, they'd have to begin the drive back to Christchurch. The flight for the first leg to London left in the evening.

Arthur was sitting behind her, breathing slowly and heavily in the small space. As usual he stank of the pipe smoke that had infused all his clothes, probably even his skin. Suzanne believed that the pipe was an affectation, a prop for his job at the university, to go along with his beard and woollen jackets, the pockets of which rattled with pipe-related paraphernalia. She glanced into the rear-view mirror and saw him scratch his throat where the black beard thinned untidily.

"Where are we?" he asked, leaning forward.

William half-turned. "Harris Creek."

"Right," said Arthur, as if that meant something to him.

"Suzanne doesn't think we've looked here before."

"We haven't," she said.

"All right, well, of course, if you're sure. We should get out and have a look, but this will have to be the last one. It's getting late."

The autumn air was cold enough that Suzanne could

see her breath. The West Coast had air you could roll around in your mouth. You could probably pass judgement on it in the same way that some of William's friends talked about wine. Air and ocean and mountains and trees. Nothing had prepared her for the trees. On the plane, she'd read a guide to New Zealand that had described the West Coast as containing sub-tropical rainforest. She'd thought of Kew Gardens; the manicured palms, arranged by species, staggered at aesthetically pleasing heights. Her first hour on the Coast had shown her what a joke that idea was. The forest here was vast and tangled. Trees, ferns, creepers, and moss grew next to, on, over and through each other. It frightened her.

Arthur was standing by the car, fiddling with his pipe. William was looking over the side of the bank of the river, and Suzanne joined him. The water was a constant roar, as though they were standing above a high-pressure pump.

"See anything?" she asked.

Hand to ear. "What?"

"Anything?"

William shook his head emphatically. She stepped closer to the low rail. The gorge wasn't wide but was cut deep by the soft blade of the water and was full of rocks. William reached for her, but must have thought better of it because he let his hand hang for a moment in the air between them before it returned to his side. She pretended not to notice and pointed downstream.

"You can't see past that outcrop."

"There's nothing there."

"I just want to be sure."

She began to pick her way down over the rocks towards the water. William said something behind her, but she pretended she hadn't heard. She'd lost track of how many rocky ravines next to bridges she'd peered into in the past two weeks, always thinking that she might see the crumpled shell of a blue Ford. William and Arthur both favoured the idea that the crash had happened next to the ocean. They believed the tide had pulled the Chamberlains' car out into deep water. Though it was true there were numerous places where the highway curved above the Tasman Sea, most had a low wooden fence on the edge of the road, painted white and red. Neither William nor Arthur could explain to her why the police hadn't found any broken barriers.

John would have been driving. In truth, she'd never warmed to Julia's husband. He'd always struck her as habitually privileged, with no idea that life had handed him roses on the day he was born. Instead, he thought he'd earnt everything. After Julia and John were married and he became a rising star among the young executives at the oil company, he was even more convinced that his opinions were the right ones, his tastes the best. Of course, she'd never said anything, but she believed John was in many ways bad for Julia. Her sister had graduated with a degree in fine art, specialising in portraiture. She'd had two small shows at a gallery in Soho but had given it all away. Suzanne was sure that John had pressured her to focus on the children and the house. When she was with John, her sister seemed quieter, less vibrant. It was hard to imagine the married Julia arguing religion in the kitchen with their mother. That Julia wouldn't break one of the good plates before calling Jesus a *proto-fascist* and storming out to stay with a friend for three days.

Close to the water the rocks were black with spray.

Suzanne was wearing old trainers, and the rubber soles were worn almost smooth. She made her way slowly, often with one hand on a rock. The air was cold. The current could easily have shunted a car who-knows how far. The torrent echoed and re-echoed off the rocks, folding into itself over and over so that the noise seemed like something to be moved through. She had to go further. To be sure. What was the point, otherwise?

They could be close, just around that bend.

* * *

"Where have you been?" William was standing by the car, arms folded.

"I went further downstream."

"You've been gone for over half an hour. It's getting dark."

"Then why didn't you come and look for me?"

"I was just about to. There was no point in us all getting lost."

Arthur hung back awkwardly. A car flew past and the children in the back seat turned to stare at the people arguing out in the middle of nowhere.

"How much longer were you going to wait?" asked Suzanne.

"Come on, let's get going."

They both got into the car.

"I didn't find anything, by the way."

"That's exactly what I thought."

William made a sharp U-turn. They began the long, silent journey back to town.

* * *

That evening in their motel, Suzanne carefully folded and packed the map. She also had newspaper articles, police reports, and copies of the missing-person flyers she'd had printed showing photographs of Julia and her family, and, of course, her notebook.

"It's our last night. Why don't we go out to a restaurant for dinner?" said William.

He was making an effort so she agreed. When they asked Arthur to join them he tactfully declined. The restaurant was part of a hotel. They'd eaten there before. Cheap and cheerful summed it up. She ordered the whitebait fritter and William wanted steak. They shared a bottle of sauvignon blanc from the top of the South Island, which William pronounced "surprisingly good."

"I'll be glad to be home," he said, putting down his glass. "I'm sick to the stomach of this place."

"It will be good to see the boys. I miss them."

He reached across the table to put his hand on top of hers. "Nobody can say we didn't try."

"Yes. I suppose."

Suzanne almost told him her plan, but she knew there would be another argument, maybe even a full-blown scene. She was going to come back to New Zealand. There was no question about that. The best time would be during the southern-hemisphere summer, probably as early as November, if she could arrange things. Next time, she would have proper hiking boots, not just old trainers. Other equipment as well: a lightweight backpack, a compass, binoculars—everything she needed. And the skills to use them. As soon as they got back to England, she would make enquiries about hiking clubs, outdoor survival courses. Perhaps she'd join Search and Rescue as a volunteer, if that was possible. She wasn't sure of the details. Whatever relevant skills were on offer, she would learn them. She would sign up with the damned Girl Guides if she thought it might help. She was done with tentatively poking her head into the trees on the edge of the road and gazing over the sides of bridges.

William would have a dozen reasons why returning to New Zealand was a folly. Some of them were probably true. But Julia and the children were family. She owed it to them to keep looking.

William took back his hand. "You look serious. What are you thinking about?"

"Nothing, really. Just how much I'm going to miss these whitebait fritters when we're back in England."

TWELVE

7 APRIL 1978

Lifting her head, Katherine squinted the land ahead into focus. The man had brought them to the foot of a valley. A sign nailed to a tree was painted with drip-tailed words, *Trespassers Will Be Shot*. She could make out long green grass marked with what she thought might be fence posts. The flat land was maybe a mile wide and stretched away from her into the blue-green blur of the distance. Half a dozen huge trees grew alone, dotted about in the open. On both sides of the valley, forested hills rose steeply. There was no sign of a house or even a road.

"Welcome to paradise," said the man.

Katherine couldn't tell if he was trying to be funny. Maybe paradise was the name of the valley.

"We're almost there," he said. "The light'll be gone soon. We'd better hurry up."

He led them along a squelching path between tall flax and clumps of reeds. They passed a small lake of black water that held reflections of the clouds, and she saw a blue and black bird the size of a chicken, standing on long red legs in the shallows. Using one foot, it lifted something before pecking at it with its red beak. Beyond the swamp they followed a river that ran down the north side of the valley. She had no idea if it was the same river the car had fallen into. She saw two deep, clear pools before the man angled away from the water across the trackless grass and they passed beneath one of the isolated trees. The trunk rose straight to the first branches far above the ground. It would take at least ten children with their hands linked to circle the trunk.

The house they eventually came to was marked off from the land around it by posts, three strands of wire, and a gate. She moved close to the fence and half closed her eyes so that she could see better. A wide veranda ran down two sides. To her, the rusted and patched iron roof, and curling, blistered paint, made the house seem abandoned. In places the weatherboards had rotted to sawdust. Three grey concrete steps led up to a couch next to the front door.

The man lifted the latch and pushed the gate, which did not swing by itself, aside. The three dogs wheeled excitedly around, sending chickens and a few ducks running, wings beating. The man cursed and the dogs fell back. He crossed to a chopping block, where he shrugged Maurice off. Her brother lay dead-eyed and openmouthed among the chips and shards of wood. The man unwound the rope from around his waist and let it fall. Tommy didn't seem to realise he was free. He stood with his chin touching his chest, taking fast, shallow breaths.

The man called toward the house. "Hey, Martha?" A pause. "Woman, you in there?"

The woman who came onto the veranda was dressed in trousers and a long woollen cardigan that covered her broad hips and large sagging breasts. Woollen socks bunched at her ankles. Her hair was cut short and jagged. It was dyed such a dark shade of purple that at first Katherine thought it was black.

"Who've you got there?"

"I found this lot in the bush. Their parents' car went

off the road into the K'mata, down past the gorge."

The woman looked back along the valley, as if she expected to see more strangers trailing across her paddocks.

"Nah, their olds snuffed it in the crash," said the man.

Katherine's eyes blurred and her face flushed.

"They died," she said. "It was an accident."

The man ignored her, but the woman's eyes moved to Katherine's face.

"My brothers are hurt. Can you help us, please?"

"Hold your horses, girl." The woman looked back at the man. "When was this?"

"They reckon they'd been out there three nights."

"Three?"

"Yeah."

"That right, girl? You been out in the bush for three nights?"

"Yes. We found a hole."

The woman pursed her lips and looked down the valley again. Slipping her feet into black wellingtons, she came slowly down the steps. Katherine could tell that there was something wrong with her. The woman chose her footing too carefully, grimacing and shifting her weight as if her feet were sore. When she got close, Katherine saw that her knuckles were red and swollen and some of the fingers were twisted. There were tattoos like ugly rings. On the loose, pale skin below the woman's throat was a jumble of black lines and curves, the edges of larger pictures. Katherine had never seen a woman with tattoos before.

"What's your name, dear?"

"Katherine."

"Hello, Katherine. I'm Martha. You sound posh. What's that accent, English?"

"Yes. We live in London. Used to, I mean. We've just come here, to this country."

"On holiday, eh?"

"No. Father got a new job in Wellington. We were going to live here. There."

The woman nodded sagely, as if she already knew all about Hornton Street and Father's job.

"And these are your brothers, I suppose."

"Yes. That's Maurice, his leg's hurt. And Tommy."

Tommy was standing exactly where he had stopped. He was staring into space with his mouth open. The rope hung from his waist.

"What's wrong with him?" said Martha.

"He hit his head in the car crash. Can you help us, please?"

The woman clapped her hands loudly and grinned.

"Well, what are we waiting for? We'd better get you lot inside."

Without comment, the man picked Maurice up again. Katherine thought it was a bad sign that her brother no longer protested at being handled like a sack of coal. Stopping only to prise off his boots, the man went into the house. Tommy followed blindly, keeping the same distance between himself and the man as if the rope were still connecting them.

Martha flapped her twisted hands. "Come on, girl. It's almost dark. Don't worry, everything's going to be all right, eh."

In the end, Katherine went gratefully. These people weren't like anyone she'd ever met before, but they were adults, so they'd know what to do. The important thing was that she and Tommy and Maurice weren't lost anymore. They'd been found. They were safe.

* * *

A gulleting hallway ran from one end of the house to the other, with rooms on either side. Furniture of all types and sizes had been stored along the walls; one piece stacked upon another, another upon that, in places right up to the high ceiling. Some piles had settled into the solidity of rock formations. Others were spindly-legged and looked as if a gentle draught might send them tumbling.

Katherine followed Martha along the narrow space between the piles and through the first door on the left into a large room. It was muggy from the open fire and hazed with cigarette smoke. Tall bay windows looked out over the veranda. A kerosene lamp, several candles, and the flames in the fireplace provided the only light. Every inch of space on the oak dresser, and the table, even the floor, was home to something or other.

"Over here," said the woman. "Put him on the couch."

Maurice groaned as the man placed him on a grey-and-white quilt of possum skins. The woman put her palm on Maurice's forehead. Again Katherine saw how raw and swollen her knuckles were and how her fingers bent at strange angles.

"He's got a fever."

Tommy was standing by the door, swaying. He flinched when the woman touched him. "So's this one, although not so bad."

"Can you call a doctor?" asked Katherine.

"Don't worry, love. I'm a healer, and a good one at that. Isn't that right, Peters?"

The man grunted, but whether in agreement Katherine wasn't sure. He seemed too big for the cluttered space and fidgeted as if eager to leave. The woman helped Tommy to a spot in front of the fire, where the light was better. She tried to check his head. He grunted and pulled away.

"Can't you ring someone?"

"Did you see any telephone poles or wires out there? This is the wop-wops, girl."

"I don't know what that means."

"The boondocks. The arse end of nowhere. There's no phone here, no electricity. Hasn't been for years. Now, watch your brothers for a sec. I'll be right back."

The two adults left the room. Katherine went to the window, where she could see them standing in the shadows by the gate. It was clear that Martha was doing most of the talking. After a while Peters turned and strode in the opposite direction to the way they'd come.

When Martha came back, Tommy was lying in front of the fire, already asleep. Katherine was trying to get Maurice to drink some warm water she'd found sitting on the table. On the mug she was holding was printed *World's Best Dad*.

"Good girl," said Martha. "You're doing well."

"Can you help him?"

"Let's have a look."

Martha used scissors to cut off Maurice's trousers. He groaned and moved his head from side to side. When she pulled the material aside, she clicked her tongue loudly and murmured to herself.

"Mr Peters said it was broken."

"Mr Peters doesn't know his arse from his elbow, not about healing. Your brother's leg might be broken or maybe the tendons are just ripped. It's hard to say, with all this swelling. Either way, the real problem's that the wound's infected."

"Is he going to be all right?"

"I'll clean it up. Then I'll give him something to get the fever down. Come with me."

Katherine followed Martha to a large, warm kitchen at the back of the house. There was a bench and a sink but no taps. She saw cupboards and shelves, and bins below the bench. Bunches of drying herbs and leaves hung from the ceiling. The heat came from a wood stove, on which pots were simmering. The smell of meat made Katherine's mouth water and she had to swallow several times.

"You must be starving. Do you want some kai?"

"I don't know what that is, either."

"It means food, in Māori. Do you want a feed? I've got heaps."

"Yes, please."

"Your little brother can have some when he wakes up."

Katherine was served a stew of thick-cut carrots, potatoes, and dark, stringy meat. While she ate, she watched Martha select several jars. The shelves, floor to ceiling, held jars full of what looked to her like leaves and twigs and withered mushrooms. There were no labels, but Martha was unerring in her choices. She filled a pot with water from a jug and put it on the stove. A little bit of many things were pinched in.

"This is medicine for your brother."

Katherine was dubious. "Is it the same as the doctor would use?"

An indignant look. "Better than that, eh. This is the real McCoy. The stuff our ancestors used for thousands of years."

"Do you mean the Māoris?"

"Them as well."

"Are you a Māori?"

Martha grunted. "Do I look Māori to you?"

"I don't know," she admitted.

"Nah. My people were Irish and English. My mother reckoned there might've been a bit of Polish in us as well." She pointed at the stove. "You don't have to be a bloody Māori to know about this stuff."

Soon a bitter smell cut through the aroma of the stew. Martha let the pot boil for a few minutes before pouring some of the liquid through a tea strainer into a cup. While that cooled, she crushed boiled bark with a pestle and wrapped the hot pulp in grey muslin.

Katherine followed her back to the living room and watched carefully as Martha wrapped the bundle around Maurice's ankle. He groaned and twisted, speaking nonsense, as she tied it in place with twine.

"This'll draw out the infection. Help me sit him up."

Katherine held Maurice's head up while, sip by sip, the medicine was poured into his mouth. He felt hot and his hair was oily. Only when the cup was empty was Maurice allowed to lie down again.

"Good," said Martha. "That'll start to take away his fever."

"What is it?"

"A secret." Twice she tapped the side of her nose with a finger stained yellow. Then, unable to restrain herself: "Mānuka leaves for the fever, and kōwhai and kawakawa for the wound. There's good medicine in the bush, if you know the right places to look."

* * *

That night Katherine woke in the dark. She was curled on the floor next to the couch, her head on an embroidered pillow. The fire had died down. She must've been asleep for a while, because the candle was a stub rather than a pale finger. She sat up.

"Maurice?" she said quietly.

He turned his head towards her, and a creaking noise pushed through his cracked lips.

"Don't worry, girlie. He's no worse." Martha was standing in the shadows by the fire, Tommy curled on the rug near her feet. "I've been getting him to drink the tonic every hour, and as much water as he'll take. I've changed the poultice as well."

"Thank you."

"You were sleeping like the dead. How are your ribs?"

"Still sore."

"They'll hurt for a while, but don't worry, they'll come right."

Martha took a piece of wood from the pile, dropped it onto the embers, and jabbed at the fire with a steel poker. The flames jumped, and light spilled across the room. Martha had taken off her cardigan to reveal a singlet. Katherine tried not to stare at the tattoos.

Martha nodded down at Tommy. "I waited till this one was out of it, then put some salve on his head. That should stop any infection."

"Will he be all right?"

Martha plucked at her bra where the straps had grooved the pale dough of her shoulders. "I think so. Do you want a drink?"

"Yes, please."

Martha poured water from a plastic container on the table. "Here you are."

"Thank you very much."

"You've got good manners. I like that."

"Thank you."

Up close, Katherine could see the tattoos clearly. They

seemed badly drawn; a jumble. There was a wilting flower and a crouching angel with a sword. Also a skull with a dripping candle sitting on top, next to what might have been a rabbit or perhaps a fox. A bee rested on the bone that ran from her left shoulder to her throat. But it was Martha's other shoulder that held Katherine's attention. It was covered by a large spider outlined in heavy black. The head and fat body and the tops of its legs were, as far as Katherine could tell by candlelight, shaded orange. The spider was moving down a web into the already cluttered space above Martha's heavy breasts. Katherine couldn't imagine why anyone would want pictures like that on their skin.

"I lost my parents when I was young, as well. I still remember it hurt."

Katherine nodded.

"I don't remember them much," said Martha.

"There was my little sister too."

"When was this, in the crash?"

"Yes. She was only a baby."

"I didn't know that. Peters didn't say."

Martha reached out a hand and stroked Katherine's hair with her twisted fingers. Katherine wanted to move away but knew that would be rude. At the same time, if she closed her eyes it was possible to imagine it was her mother touching her hair. Not that her mother ever really did that, not with her hand. Sometimes, though, she did use the tortoise-shell brush before bed.

"Who looked after you when your parents died?" she asked, opening her eyes.

"My old nana, for a bit, till she got too crook. That was when I was ten. How old are you?"

"Twelve."

"Almost the same age, then. After that it was foster

places. They weren't too good, eh." Her face screwed up, as if she had eaten something sour. "There were some bad buggers at some of them places." The hair stroking grew harder before it abruptly stopped. "Then I got old enough to go out on my own."

"Do you have any children?"

"Two girls. I had them young, so they're grown up. They live up north. I don't see them."

Worried that the stroking would start again, Katherine got up and crossed the room to check on Tommy. He was still sleeping deeply. A patch of his hair looked sticky from the ointment Martha had rubbed on.

"Will he really be all right?"

The tattoos shifted and twitched alarmingly in the firelight when Martha shrugged. "Hard to say."

"Tomorrow, can we get a doctor?"

Martha's face hardened. "I've already told you, it's too far to go. Anyway, I'm as good as any doctor. Don't you think I know what I'm doing?"

"I didn't mean that."

"Do you think I'm an idiot?"

"No, I don't. Sorry."

Martha went to the door. "Do you want me to help your brothers or don't you?"

"Yes."

"'Cause if you don't ..."

"I do. I'm very sorry. Please."

But the strange woman's mood was blowing cold. Martha left the room and Katherine could hear her in the kitchen roughly opening and closing cupboards, rattling pot lids, walking with heavy steps on the bare boards. Katherine had been going to ask exactly how far it was to the nearest town, and how soon would it be before someone set out to fetch help. If Martha had to stay to look after her brothers, couldn't the man, Peters, go by himself to get a doctor? A door slammed. Now was obviously not the time. She put her questions back in her pocket.

PART II

THIRTEEN

EARLY SUMMER, 1981

The baby was awake and cooing into Kate's ear as she walked along the trail that ran in and out of the trees on the far bank of the river. He was held snugly by a bolt of berry-dyed cloth that crossed between her breasts before cinching at her waist. His hands were bundled at his side. If she left them free, he'd make a game of pulling her hair or he'd twist her ear. Even if she used her scolding voice—something she could never bring herself to do with any real fire—it wouldn't be long before his hands would be weeding her scalp or she'd feel a finger hook into the corner of her mouth.

When she reached Castle Pool the trees were thrumming with cicada song. Kate unwrapped the baby and placed him on the ground in the shade. He stretched out both hands, reaching for her face, and she played the finger-dancing game, making him laugh. His face was dimpled and round and his wrists were cuffed with rolls of fat. Martha said it wouldn't be long before he could move around by himself, "and then he'll be into everything. You'll wish he was still a wee baby."

"Wait here," said Kate over the sound of the insects. "I've got important things to do, eh."

The shrine she'd come to tend was above the pool, far enough from the water that it couldn't be washed away by the spring floods. She'd made it using a large flat stone, which she'd laid over a gap between two natural pillars of rock. Inside was a small, bronze bowl, a candle, which had turned the stone above it black with soot, and a clay statue.

She had five shrines around the valley, all roughly the same as this one. Each was guarded by a statue. All seven of the giant kahikatea trees also had their own clay guardians, although only two trees had shrines. She'd sculpted dozens of figures out of the clay from the bank up the valley near the burnt tree. Only some, however, got to stand watch. The rest she biffed away. It was difficult, even for her, to say why one was chosen over another. Some just came away from her hands more alive than others.

She cleared away the remains of the last offering from inside the bowl, before relighting the candle. It took her less than a minute to catch a cicada. Only at the last instant did it sense her. A second later it was vibrating its leadlight wings inside her cupped hands. The feeling didn't bother her. Cicadas didn't bite or sting. She brought her palms together until she felt the insect's body crack. When she carefully opened her hands, it was slowly revolving on its side.

She was an expert at catching insects of all kinds: cicadas, crickets, wild bees, even the large, hard-shelled wetas that she found inside decaying logs, although they *did* bite, hard, and scratch with their legs. She would also catch butterflies, or bland moths if nothing else could be found. Even the shiny green blowflies, so tricky to catch, were sometimes acceptable. Now and then a mouse would still be alive in one of the traps at the house and she would put it in her pocket and bring it to the nearest shrine. Insects, though, were easier.

From her pocket she pulled a scribble of white cotton. She knotted one end around the cicada. The cotton had to be attached where the body segments joined but couldn't be drawn together too tightly or the insect would be cut in two. It was no good tying it anywhere else. A leg would inevitably break. When that happened, even a half-crushed insect would buzz-spin itself out of the bowl and onto the ground, where it was bloody useless. As she worked, Kate was never totally unaware of the baby.

Even when she wasn't looking in his direction she was listening to his burbles. More than likely she'd come back to find his chin chocolatey with dirt. Martha said eating dirt was good for his guts. She also reckoned that it rooted him firmly in the valley. That could only be a good thing.

Kate carried the cicada across to the shrine and placed it in the bowl, then tied the end of the cotton to a stick wedged into place. Worried that the insect had died, she prodded it with her finger. It vibrated defiantly. Bowing her head, she named out loud all the people she wished to be safe. Tommy was the one she feared for the most so she mentioned him twice. Poor Tommy. Last winter she'd found him one morning in the hay barn feverish and almost strangled by hacking coughs. She'd carried him to the house and into her bed. Tommy didn't like being inside but had been too weak to escape. She'd forced him to drink a warm infusion she made from boiled kūmarahou leaves that was good for clearing the lungs, along with as much chicken-and-onion broth as he'd take. It was almost a week before his cough faded. One afternoon she came back to her room to find that he'd slipped back outside.

She said the names of Maurice and Martha. She even mentioned Peters. Thinking that the last name spoken might be the first remembered, she added the name of the baby. She didn't want the spirits to come for any of them, but least of all for him. His life had only just started. She'd rather they took her than her son. To seal the contract, she sang a short snatch of a song.

Now she could relax. She carried the baby to near the edge of the pool, where he lay on the grass and watched as she pulled off her clothes. Naked, she waded across the river and clambered up half a dozen natural steps in the rock to a small ledge, above the deepest part. Below her the water was clear. The stones on the river-bed appeared to shift in the current. She was about to jump when she heard the kingfisher. Eventually her weak eyes found it, sitting on a branch in the shadow on the far bank. It was a dab of turquoise against the green leaves, with a priestly white collar. She watched the kingfisher for a long time, neither of them moving. Even the baby, for whom stillness was unnatural, lay quietly below her on the riverbank. The breeze had died away. Leaves hung limply in the heat. The idea occurred to her that the whole world was waiting for the bird. It was possible that, without the kingfisher's consent, nothing at all could ever move on.

It's a type of key. It has to be wound.

No sooner had the idea come than the kingfisher *was* and then *wasn't*. She glimpsed a gas-flame flash of iridescent blue as it passed through the sunlight. The suggestion of a splash, barely audible above the long vibration of the cicadas and the burble of the down-stream rapids. A moment later, the colours that were the bird reappeared on the same branch, with movement that may have been a flopping cockabully in its beak.

"Look, do you see?" she called, and pointed out the bird to the baby.

Kingfishers didn't often come to the valley. To see one

was a very good sign. To see one successful in its hunt was even better. She took its presence as a promise of good things to come in the days ahead.

"Hey," she called, "are you watching?"

The baby's face turned towards her.

"One, two, three!"

Jumping out as far she could to avoid the rocks, she entered the water feet-first in a dress of silver bubbles. She surfaced, gasping with the cold, laughing, skin tight. Even in summer the river was freezing. Using her arms and legs in the same way that Bess and the other dogs swam, head high, she headed for the bank. When she reached the shingle, she moved on her belly like an alligator, with only her eyes above the surface. She waited until the baby wasn't looking, before rushing from the water to scoop him up, pretending to eat him. His eyes widened and then he laughed. The cold of her wet skin briefly confused him. He squirmed as she sat on the bank in the sunlight with him in her arms. As she put him to her breast, she felt him drink from somewhere deep inside her.

FOURTEEN

SECOND WEEK IN APRIL, 1978

There was no thermometer to gauge how high Maurice's temperature climbed during the children's first days in the valley. Martha nursed him, day and night, without complaint. She dripped her homemade medicines into his mouth, swapped his soaked sheets for fresh, bathed the boy's pigeon chest with a damp flannel. When sweat pooled in the hollow of his stomach she wiped it away. The poultice on his ankle regularly needed changing.

Sometime during the long second night Maurice stopped swallowing. From the kitchen cupboards Martha dug out a large plastic syringe with a rubber bulb on the top. It had been used, she told Katherine, for feeding orphaned lambs. Katherine watched anxiously as Martha pushed the tip between Maurice's cheek and teeth, then massaged his throat until he swallowed.

"It's no good just sitting there; you might as well give us a hand around the place," said Martha, the following morning. "There's heaps to do."

Katherine thought she was going to help look after her brother. Instead, she learnt the right way to feed scraps and milk to the pigs. She was shown how to gather eggs from the henhouse. She was surprised to discover that ducks also laid eggs that could be eaten, although they hid theirs and they had to be searched for, in bushes away from the yard. The washing of clothes and sheets was done in a shed at the back of the house. Everything was boiled over a fire in what looked like a giant metal helmet, before being squeezed between rollers that had to be turned by hand.

The job that scared her most was chopping wood for the fires—the one in the living room and the kitchen stove—both of which were almost permanently burning. The woodshed was full of large pieces of dry wood. The axe was heavy and Peters kept it very sharp. Hitting a piece of wood hard in the right place to make it split into pieces was difficult. Sometimes the wood refused to balance on the chopping block and she was forced to hold it with her left hand and bring down the axe with the other. She could only pull her hand away at the last second.

Preparing food took more time than anything else. Every day, about an hour before dark, Peters came from wherever he'd been working, left his boots on the veranda and joined them for dinner. He expected a meal to be waiting. Vegetables needed to be picked or dug from the garden. The dirt had to be washed off. With no taps in the house, water had to be carried in buckets from the rain barrel or, if that was low, all the way from the river. Potatoes, she was told, didn't peel themselves. Or mash themselves, either. The ears of corn she got from the storeroom needed husking. Flour had to be transformed into bread. Chickens' feathers clung stubbornly to their headless bodies. There was always something that needed doing. Her days were full.

At first, Katherine found Martha unnerving. It wasn't just the tattoos. She seemed incapable of silence, although she required very little in the way of reply. If Martha wasn't talking to her, or to the fever-dumb Maurice, she was muttering to herself. She would also sing or hum, snatches of different tunes Katherine didn't know.

While Maurice was sick, Martha slept in the arm-chair in the living room and Katherine on a kapok mattress on the floor. Even while sleeping, Martha was never entirely quiet or still. Like the old farmhouse, she was full of unexpected creaks and groans and puffs of air. She was forever snorting awake, before hauling herself out of the chair to feed the fire with a fresh log or to jab life into the flames. She would endlessly shuttle backwards and forwards to the kitchen, where there was always tea or medicine brewing or meat cooking slowly. Even when Martha sat for any length of time, she wasn't still. Despite her crooked fingers, jerseys and scarves and gloves grew from the tips of her steel knitting needles.

Also, there was the way Martha was always making jokes about terrible things: losing fingers beneath the axe; cutting your throat with the kitchen knife; getting kicked by a horse; falling into the bonfire; a chicken dashing away from the chopping block with blood pumping from the stump of its neck. Horror and tragedy made Martha laugh like a drain. One day, she teased Katherine that if Peters didn't manage to hunt meat for the table that evening, they would have to fatten up one of her brothers.

Martha used potty words, as Katherine's father had called them, all the time. Shit, crap, bum, arsehole, fanny, cock, and wanker—useless wanker, most often, which could apply equally to Peters or the faulty tin opener. At first, Katherine's mind reeled back, as if the woman were whipping her with language. It wasn't until much later that she realised Martha used son-ofawhore (about a broody hen), little arse-biter (a leaking pipe), and fuckin' hell (an all-purpose invocation that could be attached to both good and bad things) with no real thought. The words were just decoration, like the tattoos on Martha's body.

On the fourth morning, a bird flew through the open front door and fluttered around the living room, twittering. Katherine wasn't concerned; she liked birds. When Martha saw it, though, she began to wail. Katherine quickly opened all the windows and the bird soon flew outside again. Martha was inconsolable.

"It was a bloody fantail," she said. "A fantail in the house means someone's going to die."

Katherine glanced uneasily at Maurice. "It's gone now. I've closed all the windows."

Martha stared at the ceiling, as though the bird might have magically returned. "Maybe. We'll just have to hope there's no harm done."

* * *

Apart from helping care for Maurice, and all her jobs around the farm, Katherine also had to look after Tommy. At night, her little brother sought out the lights and the warmth of the house. He slept on the floor in front of the fire on a pile of blankets. During the day, though, he preferred to be outside. Most often she found him at the back of the house, by the rain barrel, slack-jawed, staring into the water. That became the first place she looked. If she tried to draw him away, he would make his noises and thrash. His ugly gurning made her want to cry. It was easier to leave him where he was.

It was only on the third day that Martha was able to get a close look at Tommy's head in the daylight. Katherine watched her brush at the matted hair. Martha whistled through the wide gap between her front teeth.

"What's the matter?"

"Your brother's noggin took a hell of a knock."

"It was when the car fell off the cliff."

"It wasn't the fall that got him, it was the landing."

The dusty joke was lost on Katherine.

"Is he going to be all right?"

Martha wasn't going to upset the girl by saying straight out that her brother was Humpty Dumpty. Before the boy flinched away, she'd felt the bone shift and turn spongy beneath the thin bandage of skin.

"Don't worry, girlie. I reckon he's gunna be fine."

* * *

By the morning of the fifth day, Maurice's temperature had dropped. His leg was still badly swollen, but the skin was no longer a poisonous red. He was sleeping less fitfully. Apparently the fantail had been wrong.

Martha woke Katherine just after dawn. She handed her a pair of boys' trousers and an old jumper that smelt of cigarette smoke. When Katherine pulled it on, the hem hung to below her knees.

"It's too big."

"It'll keep you warm, won't it? Come on, girlie-girl."

"Where are we going?"

"You'll find out."

Katherine looked over at Maurice asleep on the couch.

"He'll be fine for a bit," said Martha.

Most of the valley was in shadow and the air was cold, although there was no frost on the long grass. The sky was a pale blue glare that made Katherine screw up her eyes. Martha stood on the veranda and rolled a cigarette using tobacco she took from a leather pouch in her pocket. Katherine watched her lick the edge of the paper.

"Put on those gumboots there. They should fit you."

Katherine obeyed, but even wearing the thick woollen socks Martha had given her, her heels still lifted with each step. Martha handed her a metal bucket.

"Here. You'll need this."

"What for?"

Martha lit her cigarette with a match. "Wait and see."

Martha led the way down the steps and out the gate, smoke trailing back over her shoulder. The wet grass soaked the legs of Katherine's trousers above the top of her boots. They had to pass the graveyard. The graves made her nervous. Half a dozen wooden markers sat alone in the open, close to being lost in the long grass. The names carved on the wood had almost been erased by the rain and the lichen.

"Are the people buried there your relatives?"

"Nah. Just the lot who used to own this place."

It was a short walk to a paddock where two cows lifted their heads. Katherine watched the animals nervously as she followed Martha over a stile. Mounds of wet, green dung steamed in the cold air. Martha pointed at a three-legged stool next to the stile.

"Grab that, girlie."

As they approached the cows, Katherine hung back.

"That dark one's pregnant," said Martha. "You know what that means, don't you?"

"She's going to have a baby." She demonstrated her knowledge by adding, "A calf."

"And do you know how it got in there?"

Katherine felt her cheeks flush.

"Ha!"

Martha's laugh was a series of hoots that turned into a cough that bent her at the waist. When the fit eventually passed, Martha spat into the grass. She ran her nose along the back of her sleeve and pulled in more smoke from her cigarette.

"I don't suppose you've milked a cow before?"

"No."

"It's not that hard once you've got the hang of it. I'll show you. Give me that."

Taking the stool from Katherine, Martha sat and put the metal bucket under the cow. Her swollen fingers managed to wrap around a teat. "Come on, girlie. You can't milk a cow from over there."

Katherine edged forward.

"Jesus Christ, she's not gunna bite. Now, watch. You hold it up here, at the top. See?"

"Yes."

"You've got to be pretty firm, but you don't want to hurt her, 'cause this old bitch will try and give you a kick if you do."

Katherine looked nervously at the cow's bony legs and pointed hooves.

"You watching?"

"Yes."

"Pull down like this."

A long squirt of milk rattled the bottom of the bucket. "See that?"

"Yes."

"White gold. That's good stuff. It'll fatten a skinny wee thing like you up in no time." Another white jet into the bucket. "See what I'm doing?"

"I think so."

"Now you have a go, eh."

"I don't think I can."

"You'll be fine. Come on."

Katherine reluctantly traded places. Her head was almost touching the side of the cow, which rose and fell with each breath. She could hear strange noises coming from inside the animal and its smell filled her mouth and nose. Uneasily, she reached forward and wrapped her hand around a teat. Hard and yet soft. The cow shifted and Katherine pulled away her hand.

"Go on," said Martha. "We haven't got all bloody day."

The first time, she managed only a few drops of milk. They dripped pathetically into the bucket. She could feel Martha watching her. Gripping slightly harder, she drew down as Martha had showed her. She was rewarded with a hard gush.

"I did it!"

Martha beamed and patted Katherine's shoulder.

"Good work. Keep going, there's still a lot left in there."

The milk came in fits and starts. Her hand was aching by the time Martha told her to stop.

"I reckon that's not bad for a first go."

Katherine carried the half-full bucket back proudly, making sure none of the precious milk spilt onto the ground. At the house, Martha led her to the kitchen and showed her how to use a funnel to pour some into glass bottles.

"We'll drink some of that. We'll use the rest to make butter and cheese. What's left over you can take to the pigs."

That evening, Martha took her to milk the cow again. This time she managed more milk, and in less time. The following morning, they were back. By then, Katherine was confident enough to rest her forehead against the cow's side and allow the ebb and flow of breath to gently rock her. Martha peered into the bucket.

"You're a bit of a natural, I reckon."

Katherine smiled. "Thank you."

"From now on this can be your job."

"Every day?"

"Twice a day, morning and night. I'm busy looking after your brothers, so it's fair enough you help out, isn't it?"

"Yes," said Katherine and meant it.

FIFTEEN

THIRD WEEK IN APRIL, 1978

"Jesus, look at him," said Peters's voice. "Useless little bastard."

Katherine put the bucket of water from the rain barrel on the grass by the side of the house. Peters and Martha were sitting on the veranda and couldn't see her. Peters had come for dinner, as he did nearly every evening, but they hadn't yet eaten. Afterwards, the adults would drink and smoke while they played card games and maybe draughts or backgammon, which she was learning, in the living room, by the fire.

Martha's voice. "The accident scrambled his brains."

"No shit."

She left the bucket and moved closer to the corner of the house. They were talking about Tommy. From the veranda, Martha and Peters would be able to see her brother in the orchard. He'd been there all day. He was staring at the leaves from the poplar trees, which had gathered in a yellow and orange drift against the side of the woodshed. The wind blowing down the valley from the mountains made the leaves quiver and shift. When occasionally there was a gust, the top leaves lifted, and some swirled into the air, a few rising up the wall of the shed, almost as high as the roof, before settling back onto the pile.

"What's he even looking at?" said Peters.

"Who knows? Nothing."

"I tried getting him to carry some firewood this

morning, just kindling. He didn't even understand what I was saying, then had a spaz when I touched him."

"He's not right."

"If he was a dog, I'd put a bullet between his eyes."

Katherine stiffened. Peters didn't like Tommy. He didn't like anything that didn't work properly. Tommy was like a baby now. He even wet his pants—and worse. Just last evening he'd left a puddle in the middle of the hallway. Peters had shouted and made threats. It had become her job to take Tommy down the path to the outside toilet—what Martha called the dunny, the long-drop, or sometimes the crapper—whenever she thought he needed to go. Her only clue was the way her brother fiddled with the front of his trousers. She was also responsible for changing him when he didn't get to the toilet in time.

"Fucking disgusting." That's what Peters said the first night Tommy ate at the table. The next evening her brother had his food by the fire, but even that had been too much for Peters. Now it was her job to bring Tommy his dinner on a metal plate, out on the veranda. She had to shut the dogs out of the yard or tie them up. They'd cheerfully steal every last bit of food if they could, before licking Tommy's face clean for dessert.

"Reckon a bullet would be doing him a favour," said Peters.

Martha laughed as though he'd made a joke.

"Poor little bugger's not doing any harm," she said mildly. Peters grunted.

When Katherine eventually came around the corner of the house carrying the bucket, Peters was standing, looking towards the orchard. He was smoking one of his cigarettes that smelt like old socks. His favourite dog, Bess, was lying at his feet. Martha was on the couch, rubbing the swollen knuckles of one hand with the thumb of the other. Grasping a whole finger in her palm, she slowly pulled, milking temporary relief out of the joints.

"You got those potatoes on the stove yet, girlie?"

"Yes."

"Well, better get on with the rest of it."

Katherine could feel them watching her as she walked up the steps and across the veranda. As she went through the front door she heard Peters say, "Fuckin' useless." Glancing back, she saw that he was still looking at the orchard. He reached down and scratched Bess behind one ear. Even from inside the house she could hear the thump of the dog's tail on the wood.

* * *

That evening Katherine stood on the top step, with the candlelight coming through the window behind her. She was waiting for her eyes to adjust to the dark. She could hear Peters and Martha in the living room playing a last drunken hand of cards. Soon Peters would take his dogs and walk away to wherever it was he lived.

Sometime during the evening the wind that had been moving Tommy's pile of leaves had swung to the north and grown stronger. As she started along the track to the toilet it flicked the tops of the trees and rattled the loose iron on the roof of the house. Martha had given her a torch, but the batteries were almost dead. The beam on the ground in front of her feet was barely stronger than the moonlight. As she passed the coop, the chickens raised soft rustlings and bubbling clucks. The old horse that she had never seen ridden stood perfectly still beyond the fence.

Martha had let her drink two large glasses of beer as they played cards. She hadn't liked the taste very much, it was too bitter, but she did like the light-headed, careless feeling it gave her. Despite everything that had happened, she felt almost happy. Now, however, she badly needed to pee.

The toilet was on the last flat land before the treed slope. As she approached it, the trees moved together, back and forth, in the wind. Martha had warned her never to go up there. The ground was riddled with old mineshafts and hidden sinkholes. Martha had painted a vivid a picture of the broken bones and lingering death anyone stupid enough to wander among those trees could expect. Even so, Katherine had been curious. She'd ventured up the slope a few days earlier. She wanted to be sure that Martha wasn't hiding something. She hadn't gone far before her foot slipped knee-deep into a hole. She'd heard water flowing beneath her as she waited to break through the surface. It had been enough to scare her.

The toilet was a narrow shadow in the darkness. The door rattled as she opened it. When Martha had first shown her where to go, Katherine had been disgusted, although she hadn't said anything. There wasn't even a lid, just a circular hole cut into the middle of a low bench. The air stank, and on that sunny day the hole had its own droning voice. She'd made the mistake of looking down into the lumpy swamp. Now, she couldn't bring herself to pull down her pants and sit. Not in the dark.

She closed the door and moved closer to the trees. The wind was loud through the branches as she carefully placed the torch on the ground, pulled her trousers down around her ankles, and squatted. The grass tickled. Her pee hissed embarrassingly.

She was almost finished when something in the trees close to her made a loud sound.

More-pork. More-pork. More-pork.

Unseen, the owl took to the air, swooping past her head. She raised her arms to protect herself and felt the downbeat of its wings against her face before she fell back. A moment later a small animal screamed.

That was when she saw him again. He was standing very still at the edge of the trees, staring across at her with yellow eyes. He was naked. His skin was the pale of the moonlight. She thought she could see the shadow of his wings arching above his bare shoulders.

Crying out, she yanked at her clothes. She ran blind. The torch had been left behind. She stumbled and almost fell. And then a few steps later she did fall and her knee hit something solid. She jumped up and ran on, not daring a glimpse back. She knew without looking that he was right behind her. She could feel his breath on her neck. She could hear him clearly. He was saying her name in the sloughing voice of the wind. *There!* The lights of the house. She'd been running in the wrong direction. She veered to her left. She had to get back as fast as she could. Before it was too late.

Martha and Peters looked up from their cards as Katherine rushed into the living room.

"What's the matter?" asked Martha, alarmed.

"Is Maurice all right?"

"Same as when you left."

"Tommy?"

"He's fine. Why, what happened?"

Katherine looked around the room. Nothing seemed to have changed. Tommy was asleep by the fire. Ignoring Martha's and Peters's stares, she sat on the edge of the couch and forced her breathing to slow. Maurice's face was thin and his eyes sunken, but he was still alive. She'd been sure she was going to find him dead. She looked to the big windows, expecting those yellow eyes to be staring in at her. All she saw, though, was the distorted reflection of the room in glass so old it had thickened near the bottom of the pane. The spirit had not come for her brothers, after all. Not tonight, anyway.

Martha was still looking at her strangely. "You look scared out of your wits."

"It was just the dark. It frightened me."

"You sure you're all right, girlie?"

"Yes, I'm fine now," she said. "Thank you."

SIXTEEN

MAY 1978

Katherine carried the bucket of body-warm milk into the kitchen. Her ribs were almost healed now, just as Martha had said would happen. Using the funnel, she carefully poured some milk into two bottles, before putting them into the meat safe on the shaded side of the house. A couple of pots were simmering on the woodstove. Taking the lid off one, she stirred the liquid with a wooden spoon. It was medicine for Maurice. He was still weak and needed to drink a tablespoonful mixed with a glass of warm water, at least twice a day.

It seemed there was almost nothing Martha couldn't cure with herbs, dried bark, roots, mushrooms, or flowers. She was teaching Katherine all about them, where to find them and at what time of year, how to store them. Some were boiled for hours. One thick scab of bark had to be softened over a whole three days before it could be used in a poultice. Many plants were crushed into a paste with a pestle and mortar. Some were boiled into tea. Others had to be inhaled with steam. Very few could be applied in their raw state to an ache or wound.

Martha told Katherine that what she was teaching her was secret knowledge. It was only passed on from one woman to another. Martha said that Katherine had a gift for healing. Apparently most people didn't. Even with the gift, it wasn't easy. The names were especially hard. They were full of jagged syllables that sat uncomfortably in her mouth. Martha teased her about being too posh to speak properly. She said her cheeks were full of marbles. As she did her work around the farm, Katherine practised, reciting the names to the chickens and the pigs. "Harakeke, kawakawa, rātā, kōwhai, kahikatea."

She found Martha on her knees in the living room rebuilding the fire. Morning sunlight was coming through the crystal hanging in the window, the light splashing across the wooden floor, dyeing the boards red and yellow.

"Good morning," said Katherine.

"Morning, girlie. Milking go all right? You get much?"

"About the same as yesterday."

"Good-oh."

Katherine watched Martha get painfully to her feet. She'd never said what was wrong with her, beyond "a touch of arthritis." She was always stiffer and slower in the morning. That was when she tended to growl and snap. Today, though, she seemed to be in a good mood.

"Porridge is on the stove."

"I saw, thank you. How's Maurice today?"

"See for yourself. He's awake. Why don't you take him some breakfast, eh?"

Maurice had shifted into his own bedroom. Like every other part of the farmhouse, it was cluttered with old furniture and dusty knickknacks. Katherine found him propped up on his pillows.

"How are you feeling today?"

"My leg still hurts."

She handed him the bowl of porridge. He began to eat, which she took as another sign he was improving.

"I'll get you some more mānuka tea. It helps with pain."

"It doesn't really help that much."

"You do look better, though."

Maurice turned his face to the window. Although it had rained hard for the last few days, blue sky was visible near the top of the glass.

"Where are your real clothes?" he asked.

She was wearing stained work trousers and the woollen shirt that Martha had altered to fit her. Martha had said that she didn't know who had worn the clothes originally, just that they'd been left behind by the people who owned the farm before her. The shirt itched, but Katherine wore it over a singlet, which meant it wasn't so bad. The important thing, now that each day was colder than the last, was that the clothes were warm.

When she didn't answer his question, Maurice put his bowl on the bedspread. "Have you asked them yet?"

"Martha says you're still too sick to go anywhere."

"I should be in a proper hospital with a real doctor."

She glanced at the open door. "Shhh. You'll make her mad again."

Martha had yelled at Maurice yesterday. She'd called him bad names.

"I don't care," he said, but lowered his voice. "They should've gone and got help when we first arrived."

"It's too far."

"The town can't be that far away."

"It's miles and miles. There are no roads."

He lay back on the pillows and again looked out the window. "I just want to go home."

"They saved us, Mo. We would've died if Peters hadn't found us."

"There must be a road. Someone could drive a car or a tractor here. They could take us away."

"There isn't any road, just tracks that go nowhere. You'll see when your leg's better."

"That doesn't make sense. You can't build a whole house like this without a road." He pointed at the furniture stacked against the far wall. "How did *that* get here? What about the wardrobe? That's really heavy. And *that* and *that* and *that*?" His finger jabbed.

"Maybe there used to be a road."

"No," said Maurice stubbornly. "There is a road. You just haven't seen it."

"You're probably right," she said, not because she believed it but because she wanted him to stay calm. If he started to yell again, Martha would come to see what all the fuss was about. Then there would be trouble. "You'll probably find the road when you're better."

She took his almost empty plate and rearranged the pillows so that he could lie flat. "Ask them when we can leave," said Maurice, gazing up at her.

"All right."

"Will you ask today?"

"Yes."

"Promise?"

"All right, yes. I promise."

Carrying the bowl, Katherine went to the door. When she looked back Maurice's eyes were already closed. Even when he was almost asleep, her brother still looked angry.

* * *

Katherine waited until dinner that evening to ask Maurice's question. Of course, she also wanted to know when they would be able to leave the farm. Maurice's recovery, though, had given her faith that Martha, and to a lesser extent Peters, had the children's best interests at heart.

Katherine and Martha brought the plates and steaming pots in from the kitchen and placed them on the table. That night's meal was duck meat from a bird Peters had shot down at the lake. There was pumpkin and potato mash with gravy, steamed carrots and boiled cabbage. Peters stubbed out his cigarette in the ashtray, and everyone began serving themselves.

Katherine had already given Tommy his food out on the veranda. When he was finished, he'd drift inside, drawn to the fire. She'd wipe his face and hands. Most evenings he was asleep in front of the hearth before the meal was over.

She waited until everyone was eating.

"Now that Maurice is better, I wondered if someone could go, I mean, you said they would, to get help?" She tried to speak casually.

Peters didn't look at her. He blew loudly on his food so that the edges of his moustache fluttered. Martha glanced at her sideways.

"I already told you, girlie. The nearest town's a long way away."

"How far is it?"

"Too far for us to go right now. We've got a lot on here. Like I told ya, there's no proper tracks through the bush. It's hard going. Isn't that right, mate?"

Peter's confirmed with a grunt.

"What's the town called?" asked Katherine, carefully.

"Nothing," said Martha. "It's too small to have a name."

"I thought even small places had names."

"Are you calling us liars?" said Peters loudly.

"Relax," said Martha. "She's not calling anybody anything. Are you, girlie?"

Katherine shook her head.

Martha held her fork awkwardly in her twisted fingers

as she gestured. "Maybe where you come from every group of houses close together has a name. Things are different here. Lots of places have never been called nothing. Do you understand?"

Katherine stared down at her food. "Yes."

"Good. Now eat your dinner, eh. Before it gets cold."

Peters and Martha ate and drank gin, and Martha talked about the goat that had broken free again that morning and, later, about rats coming out of the bush. They were stealing the pigs' food and would need to be trapped before they got into the walls of the house. After a while, however, she circled back around to Katherine's question.

"Anyway, we can't go anywhere at the moment 'cause of the rain. The rivers are all flooded."

It was true that in the last few days it had rained so hard that Katherine had watched the water flowing off the roof in sheets.

"The problem is, we're getting into winter," Martha continued. "Most winters it's at least a couple of months before we can leave the farm." She saw Katherine's expression. "Sorry, girlie. That's just the way it is around here. This place's always cut off in winter."

Peters was following the conversation closely. "Yeah, that's true, it always is. A couple of months, that sounds about right."

"It was bad luck you kids turned up here when you did. It would've been different in summer. But don't worry," said Martha, still watching Katherine's face, "as soon as spring comes, Peters will be happy to show you the way out."

"Sure," said Peters.

"Do you promise?" asked Katherine.

Martha's smile showed teeth stained with tobacco

and coffee. "'Course. I might even come with you my-self. I could do with a change of scene."

Months.

Katherine couldn't believe it. Although she tried not to, she began to cry.

Martha tutted. "Don't be like that. It's not so bad here, is it?"

"But people must be looking for us. They'll be wor-ried." Martha's puzzlement was poorly acted. "Who's that then, eh? Who do you think's going to be looking for you lot?"

"The people where Father was going to work," she said, remembering what Maurice had said back at the clearing.

"Nah," said Peters. "They'll just figure your old man changed his mind. It happens all the time. People get cold feet about a new job and don't show up. I've done it myself."

"Father wouldn't do that. We came all the way from England."

"We're just saying what people *might* think," said Martha. "And I don't reckon your relatives in England are going to kick up a fuss. I mean, of course they'll be expecting a postcard or two while you're away, right? But do you really reckon they're going to get all worked up just because they don't hear from you for a while?"

"I don't know."

"Nah, they won't, trust me. They're certainly not going to fly all the way to the other side of the world."

"One of my uncles or aunts will ring someone."

"Who're they gunna ring?" asked Peters.

"The rescue people."

Peters grinned. Martha shook her head rucfully and chuckled.

"The *rescue people*," she echoed, mocking. "I don't mean to be rude, love, but you're talking like a little kid."

Katherine, confused, didn't know what to say.

Martha pointed her fork at Peters. "We're the ones who found you. We took you in. Isn't that right?"

"Yes," said Katherine softly.

"So I reckon that makes us the rescue people. Right?"

Katherine nodded.

"I nursed your brother, didn't I?"

"Yes."

"He would've died if I hadn't."

"I think so."

"He would've."

"Yes. Thank you."

"You have to grow up, girlie. What you and your brother need to realise is that your parents are dead. They're gone. That means Peters and me are the only people you've got to look after you. Do you understand?"

"Yes."

Satisfied, Martha nodded. "Good girl."

For a while the only sounds were the cutlery scraping on the plates and Peters slurping gin from his glass. When one of the cows bellowed loudly, like a deep horn in the distance, all three glanced at the window for a moment before turning back to their food. Eventually Martha spoke.

"Don't get me wrong. You and your brothers aren't prisoners. You don't have to stay here. You'll be able to leave when spring comes, if that's what you want. We'll be happy to show you the way."

SEVENTEEN

WINTER, 1978

As soon as Maurice was well enough, Martha made a show of presenting him with a pair of crutches. Stamped on the wood in faded letters were the words *Property of Greymouth Hospital.*

"Where's that?" he asked.

"Dunno," said Martha. "They were just lying around in the back room. Someone must've broken their leg years ago. Lucky for you, eh?"

Maurice practised with the crutches, first in his room and then, as he became more confident, up and down the hallway, between the stacks of furniture. His ankle was still swollen and the skin patterned in yellow and blue. He avoided looking at it. After three days, he moved outside, where his *place, swing, land, place, swing, land* scattered the chickens and left rows of pockmarks in the yard. Martha sat on the veranda, knitting and watching his progress. She wore a thick jumper against the cold. When Maurice started to use only one crutch, she pronounced him capable of helping out around the place.

He was given warm clothes and gumboots and put to work pruning the low branches in the orchard. When that was finished, he weeded in the garden. Later, there were winter vegetables to plant. Because of his leg, he was awkward and slow. In a day, he got through less than half the work of his sister.

In the evenings he now sat at the table opposite

Katherine. He seldom spoke unless asked a direct question. One night, he poked with a fork at the food on his plate.

"What type of fish is this?" he asked.

"What's the matter, don't you like it?" asked Martha.

"No, it's nice," said Katherine quickly. "I just don't think we've had it before."

"It's tuna," said Peters.

Katherine nodded. "Oh, we've had tuna. It comes in tins."

Martha shook her head. "Nah, that's different. Peters catches these in the river and smokes them. Tuna is a Māori word. It means eel."

Maurice didn't even have time to turn his head before he was throwing up onto the table. Twisting in his seat, he vomited again, this time onto the floor. Peters swore loudly. He jumped to his feet, knocking over his chair. Martha snatched up her plate. Katherine looked away from the mess and tried not to breathe. There was nothing to do except wait until Maurice reached the bottom of his stomach.

"Jesus, boy," said Martha. "You should've said if you were feeling crook."

Peters walked over and lifted the sash-window to let in fresh air.

"Don't just sit there, ya moron. Get this mess cleaned up. We're not your bloody servants."

Maurice wiped his sleeve across the back of his mouth and glared.

"I'll get some water," said Katherine quickly.

Martha and Peters took their food to the kitchen, while Katherine and Maurice, who was pale and shaking, used old rags to wipe up the mess.

"I'm going to bed," said Maurice, when they were

done. He wouldn't meet her eye. "Goodnight," said Katherine.

He didn't reply.

* * *

The next day was windy and overcast, and spots of rain flicked the grass. Peters turned up at the house just before noon, the dogs swirling around his feet. He didn't bother coming through the gate. Martha was waiting on the veranda. She'd already sent the girl down to the river with a plastic container to get water.

"Is he ready?" asked Peters.

"All set," said Martha. She called to Maurice, who hobbled on his crutch over from the coop where he'd been told to gather eggs.

"We decided it's better if you live up at Peters's place for a while," said Martha. "He's got some work you can help with."

"What type of work?"

"This and that. You'll see."

"I want to stay here with Katherine and Tommy."

"Nah, this'll be easier," said Martha, scratching her head. "Don't look so sour, you'll still eat dinner down here most days."

"But I don't want to go."

"Stop bloody arguing!" Peters's nostrils flared. "You're going, one way or the other, you little ponce."

It was clear to Maurice that everything had been planned. He watched as Martha fetched, from the veranda, a rucksack of clothes. From the pocket of her apron appeared a package of damp muslin, containing several thick cuts of salted ham.

"This'll tide you over till dinner tonight."

"Let's get going," said Peters.

Maurice reluctantly pulled the rucksack onto his back. He put the food into the pocket of the stained and patched jacket he'd been given and followed Peters along a track that led up the valley. He was soon exhausted. This was the most exercise he'd done since his accident. His leg was aching badly by the time they stopped outside a shearing shed next to the broken railings of a disused sorting yard. He'd imagined that Peters lived in a smaller version of Martha's house, so it was a surprise when Peters pointed out an old bus in a paddock beyond the shearing shed. The bus's axles rested up on cinder blocks. Grass and weeds grew almost up to the windows, which were blacked out with cardboard. The chimney pipe of a wood burner broke crookedly through the roof.

"The farmer who used to own this place had the bus cut up and carried in over the hills, piece by piece."

"Why?"

"It's true," said Peters.

His shadow fell over Maurice, who froze and stared at the ground.

"I just wondered why."

Peters sniffed. "He was a mad old cunt, that's why."

During the years Maurice lived with Peters, he'd hear several versions of how the bus came to be in the valley. Not that storytelling was a big part of Peters's nature. Most of the time he kept his words to the essential. When he'd been smoking his foul-smelling cigarettes, which was most days, he was even quieter. But alcohol never failed to loosen Peters's tongue. It was while he was drunk that he first contradicted himself. Rather than being cut into pieces, he claimed the bus was carried into the valley whole by thirty men. They hoisted it, he said, his words slurring and head lolling, onto their shoulders to cross the rivers. They sang as they dragged it over the hills with ropes. On another occasion, Peters told Maurice that the bus was rafted in from the sea. That, apparently, was back in the days when the river flowed much deeper and straighter than it did now.

Maurice's favourite story, because it was the one that made Peters seem the most foolish, was when he drunkenly claimed that the bus had appeared after a hurricane battered the valley.

"There it was the next morning," he had said.

They had been playing cards after dinner at the farmhouse. Maurice joined in only because they made him. He often played badly on purpose, making mistakes that disrupted the game or cut it short. It was sometime during the first summer, and the evenings were long so the games went on for hours.

"That's right," said Martha, nodding half-lidded encouragement over her glass. She was as drunk as Peters.

"Like Dorothy's house," said Katherine, laying down a card.

Peters blinked slowly. "Who?"

"Dorothy, in *The Wizard of Oz*. It's a film."

Peters looked for signs of mockery. "I've only been to the flicks a few times, when I was a kid. Liked it, though."

"What did you see?" asked Maurice cautiously. He was always looking for new information he might be able to use.

"Something or other, don't remember." Peters stood. "That's enough for tonight, eh. Come on, boy. Let's get going."

"We haven't finished this hand," said Katherine.

"Nah," said Peters mildly. "Fuck off to bed now."

That conversation, however, was in the future. The first time Maurice saw the bus, the only explanation he was given for how it came to be in a valley with no roads was that it had once been cut into pieces.

The dogs waited by the door of the shearing shed as Peters led Maurice inside. It was dim, and the air was colder than outside and smelt of greasy fleeces. Wooden steps led up to a raised floor with half a dozen cubicles with swinging doors, where he supposed the shearers used to shear the sheep. Peters pointed out some hay bales stacked in the corner that were defined by a pile of grey woollen blankets and a pillow.

"That's where you'll be sleeping."

"I can't sleep there. It's not even a real bed."

One moment, he was standing; the next, he found himself on the floor. The back of his head was suddenly hot. One of his ears buzzed loudly as he watched his crutch slide across the wood and hit the wall.

Gripping Maurice's shoulders hard enough that there were finger-shaped bruises there the next day, Peters jerked him back to his feet. He started to shake Maurice as he yelled into his face. Maurice's head whiplashed on top of his spine in time with Peters's words.

"I said. This. Is. Where. You. Sleep! Okay? You understand, shithead?" His eyes were showing white. His dreadlocks danced. "Do you?"

"Yes."

"What?"

"Yes. Please. Don't."

The shaking stopped. Peters's contorted face remained close, though; his nose almost pressed against Maurice's. He was forced to breathe in the man's ash-and-meat breath.

"I don't want to hear you fuckin' whingeing again. You'll do what you're told, okay?"

"Yes."

Maurice was released. He fell onto his backside on the floor.

"You'd better hear me, you posh little shit."

"Yes."

"Better."

Muttering, Peters stamped down the steps and across to the door, which was dragged shut. When Maurice was sure he was alone, he crawled to where his crutch lay. Getting to his feet made him feel dizzy, so he sat on the edge of the hay bales. The back of his head was stinging and his left ear rang. He wiped the tears and snot on the sleeve of his jacket. Blood was leaking from his mouth.

One of the dogs, Bess, had stayed behind. She was standing by the door, watching him. "Come on, girl." She came closer, tail moving tentatively, and climbed the steps. Sniffing his fingers, she pushed her head into his hip. He knew what she wanted. Taking the sandwich from his pocket, he tore off some ham and offered it to her. She turned her muzzle sideways as she ate it from his palm.

After the food was gone, she lay on the floor at his feet. Maurice was grateful when she let him stroke her warm fur.

EIGHTEEN

WINTER, 1978

There were many rules for Maurice to follow, although they were never spelt out directly. They existed, however; as real as if Peters had painted them on the side of the shearing shed in white letters a foot high. Do all your jobs and do them well. Don't ask questions—unless it is about the best way to do a job. Don't complain. Never talk back. Talking about the time before the crash—what Maurice thought of as his *London life*—always earned him a punishment; anything from a clip around the back of the head to a kick from a heavy boot.

Real insolence got him locked in the tool shed. It was about ten feet square, with windowless walls of corrugated iron and a concrete floor. How long he remained in there seemed to depend less on his crime and more on Peters's mood. During that first winter Maurice often spent the night on the pile of sacks beneath the workbench, among the smell of two-stroke petrol and motor oil and the sharp chemical odour that rose off the calcified sack of superphosphate fertiliser in the corner.

He began to speak less and less, even to his sister. During dinners at Martha's house, he said please and thank you. The corners of his mouth lifted when he heard what passed for a joke. If asked, he answered, although only with a few words. However, to give an unforced opinion about the log jam near the top of the river, or the beehives, or the garden, about Peters's horse, Bess or the other dogs, the cows, the pigs, the horses, the goat, the rotten weatherboards on the house, any of it, would be to admit that he was part of what went on in the valley. He wasn't. He never would be. He'd work to avoid punishment. Beyond that he would give them nothing.

He became Peters's water carrier. Also his collector of firewood. He was groom for his big, docile horse. His butcher of chickens, ducks, and rabbits, and killer of less useful animals. Possums he caught with the serrated jaws of gin traps that he set himself. He killed them, as they hissed in anger, with blows from an old axe handle. He trapped rats by the dozen. Whenever Martha needed an extra hand in her garden or the orchard, he was on call.

The job that took up most of Maurice's time, though, was cultivating a large crop of marijuana. Peters was deadly serious about all aspects of growing what he called dope. He'd built a secret propagating room in the shearing shed. There was a false wall, and a hidden door. Inside were hundreds of tiny seeds on trays lined with damp sacking. The room was kept warm with lagged pipes connected to a wetback stove. It was Maurice's responsibility to keep the fire going. At night he could hear the groans and clicks from the pipes. Peters conducted random inspections to make sure that the thermometer on the wall hadn't dropped. He made it clear there'd be hell to pay if he ever found the mercury below twenty-six degrees.

One morning, Maurice woke to discover that nearly all of the seeds had uncurled overnight. A miniature forest of leafless shoots stood free of their husks. Peters declared himself happy with the success rate.

"What are they?" asked Maurice.

"It's a type of tobacco."

That same morning, he helped Peters to put together the framing for a tunnel house. The metal pieces had all been hidden beneath the bus, next to rolls of plastic. Maurice saw straight away how the frame screwed together, like giant Meccano.

For three days they worked together on the north side of the shearing shed, where the tunnel house would be in the sun for most of the day. Peters said the work had to be done quickly. It wouldn't be long before the plants were big enough to be transferred, with tender fingers, into containers filled with a potting mix of Peters's own creation. There were close to a thousand seedlings.

* * *

Maurice's first attempt to escape was a bad joke. After his anger and humiliation had faded a little, he was able to admit that. He'd only been living with Peters for three days. It was early afternoon and he was gathering firewood near the river when he realised Peters was nowhere to be seen. Until then the big man had been constantly supervising him.

Dropping the sticks he had under his arm, he set off downriver. He had no food except for the last of some oat biscuits Martha had given him the day before. Predictably, or so he realised later, he planned to follow the river back to where the car had crashed. Despite what his sister had said, the road couldn't be far from there. The only reason she hadn't found it was because she was a girl and too frightened to look properly. Now that he could walk again, even with a crutch, he didn't have to depend on her. He wouldn't turn back before he found the road.

He was tired even before he came to the swamp and the small lake, so he had a short rest and then carried on downriver. It became obvious that walking along the riverbed was going to be impossible. The ground was too uneven. Falling and injuring his leg again was only a footstep away. There was also the danger that he'd wedge the crutch between rocks and snap it. Several times he came close to disaster. He had no choice except to move into the trees.

He wasn't too concerned when he realised he could no longer see, or even hear, the water. He was sure that he was still heading west, toward the coast. Walking, however, was slow. The trees grew close together and the ground was boggy. He had to rest often. The air was cold and damp. When he stopped to eat, he found his biscuit had been ground back into oats in his pocket. His only meal on the run was crumbs pinched from his palm.

Peters used the dogs to sniff him out. Bess was the loudest. Maurice recognised her hollow barks, although it was impossible for him to tell what direction they were coming from. One moment, the barking was far away, muffled by the lichen on the tree trunks and the thick moss on the ground, the next, the sound was ricocheting around him. Here, and then over there. Panicking, he began to move as quickly as he could.

When the dogs were almost upon him, he dropped his crutch and squirmed into a hollow beneath a fallen log. He lay among the soaking-wet ferns, trying to breathe quietly, and waiting for the dogs to pass.

Bess found him first. She didn't even pause before she was burrowing in beside him, trying to lick his face. The other two arrived. They all nosed and pranced, tails snapping the fern leaves.

"Get out of there, ya idiot."

Peters's voice rumbled overhead. He was standing on top of the log, looking down. "Hurry up, Slowpoke."

Maurice crawled slowly out and the dogs came with him. He waited for the blow, but it didn't come. Peters pointed.

"Go on. Start walking."

Maurice was surprised and ashamed when, within half an hour, they were back at the valley. He'd been walking through the trees in twisted knots. Peters didn't say a word. They passed the farmhouse, but there was no sign of Katherine or Martha. Peters unlocked the tool shed and shoved Maurice inside. He heard the padlock snib. A few minutes later there was scrabbling, and he saw a wet nose and the white patch on Bess's muzzle in the narrow gap under the door. He stroked her and was rewarded with a lick.

"It's okay, girl. It's not your fault."

Sniffing him out in the trees had been a game for the dogs.

For what remained of that day, and nearly all of the next, he stayed locked up. He was given no food or water. Resigned to spending a second night on the pile of sacks, he was surprised when, near evening, Peters opened the door.

"Get out here."

Tucking his crutch under his arm, Maurice came out slowly. He looked for signs that Peters was drunk. That would make any punishment twice as bad. The big man was holding a tin plate of mutton stew which filled Maurice's mouth with saliva. He could smell the heavy gravy.

"Where'd ya think ya were going?"

He kept his eyes on the ground. "Home."

"Orphans don't have a home. I should know."

"I'm not an orphan."

"Course you bloody are, ya moron. You're a kid with no parents. That means you're an orphan. A crippled fuckin' little orphan."

Maurice screwed up his face against the tears. Peters stood watching him and shaking his head, before he handed Maurice the plate.

"Well, what do ya say?"

"Thank you."

"What?"

He said it again, louder.

"And are ya gunna run away again?"

"No," he lied.

Peters eyeballed him sceptically. "You'd better bloody not. There'll be a lot worse for you next time. Do ya understand?"

"Yes."

"Now finish that up and piss off to bed. You've wasted enough of my time today. We've got heaps of work to do in the morning."

For the rest of winter and into the first spring and summer Maurice did as he was told. He worked hard and without complaint, until even Peters seemed satisfied. His thoughts, though, were his own. While he tended to the seedlings, while he screwed together the tunnel house, while he planted, weeded, lifted, trapped, killed, and hauled, he waited for his leg to heal and thought about the future. There was no tool shed where Peters could lock up Maurice's plans to return home.

NINETEEN

SPRING, 1978

After a week of undeniably warm days, Katherine found the courage to again ask Martha when she and her brothers could finally leave the valley. They were in the kitchen, preparing the evening meal.

"Once you've cleared your debt."

"What debt?"

Martha raised an incredulous eyebrow. "There's all the food you've eaten, for a start."

Katherine looked at the half-peeled potato in her hand. It had never occurred to her that food was something they had to pay for.

"Plus there's the medicine I used to save your brother's life. That would cost a lot in the city." Martha was carefully building her hand, card by card. "Also, you can't expect to sleep in someone's house without paying board. Your parents must've told you that?"

"I don't think we ever stayed with anyone."

Martha tut-tutted and shook her head sadly. "They should've taught you this stuff. I know you and your brother do a few things to help out around the place. That's good. I've taken that into account. The problem, though, is Tommy. He doesn't do a thing except eat my food. Do you see how it is?"

"I suppose."

"It's not right to let a debt build up like you kids have. You'll need to pay it off before you leave."

"But we don't have any money."

Martha pretended to think. "I reckon we could do some sort of a deal. I could let you work off what you owe."

"We already work."

"You'll need to do some more. It won't take long until we're even-stevens."

"How long?"

"I suppose it depends on how hard you work. Do you think you could do that?"

"Yes."

"Good girl."

"And then you'll show us the way to town?"

"Too right. I'll take you there myself in a parade with bells and whistles and a painted elephant leading the way." Martha broke into a grinning jig.

Despite her concern, Katherine laughed. "How will we know when we've paid you back?"

"Don't worry, girlie. I'll work it all out properly. Do we have a deal?"

Katherine looked at Martha's outstretched hand. She had no idea of how many weeks they'd been at the farm, just that it was a long time. Did it really matter if they stayed a little while more?

"We'll have to leave before next winter, otherwise we'll be stuck again."

"Of course, there's no worries about that."

"All right."

They shook hands.

* * *

"That's not fair!" said Maurice.

Leaning heavily on his crutch, he kicked at the ground with his good leg and a spray of dirt and stones flew into the river. Katherine watched her brother nervously. She'd been putting off telling him about the money they owed.

"She gave me this." She reached into the flax bag, which, with Martha's help, she'd woven herself.

Maurice took the piece of wood his sister was holding out. It was smooth and as long as his forearm and reminded him of the blade of a cricket bat, but narrower. Deep grooves were cut across the surface. Katherine watched as Maurice ran his finger in and out of the cuts.

"What is it?" he asked.

"Martha said it's to show what we owe. Peters made it."

Maurice turned the wood over. "How does it work?"

"She said each cut means ten dollars. That's our half to keep, so we know."

Maurice counted thirty-six cuts. "That's not true. We don't owe them anything. All we've done since we got here is work."

"We owe them for food and for staying in the house."

"I don't even sleep in a house."

"And for medicine and clothes. Martha's worked it all out properly."

Maurice shook the stick at her. "It's a lie," he said. "Anyway, Peters took Father's wallet, I saw him. There was money in there."

She'd heard this from him several times before. "It might not've been that much."

"There were notes. A lot. And he took Father's watch as well."

"The money here is strange."

"Why are you always on their side?"

"I'm not."

"Yes, you are!"

"Stop shouting."

She looked around. They weren't supposed to meet secretly like this. Voices could sometimes carry for long distances in the valley.

"If you help people, you shouldn't expect them to pay," said Maurice. "It's not ..." he searched for the right word before finding an expression of their father's, "it's not civilised."

Drawing back his arm, he threw the stick out into the river. It landed in the current and was quickly carried downstream.

"Now they'll be angry," said Katherine. She squinted, keeping her eyes on the blur that was the stick as it floated towards the bend.

"I don't care."

"Anyway, it doesn't matter—they still have the other half."

We don't owe them anything. When my leg's stronger, I'm going to run away again." .

"You don't know where to go."

"It doesn't matter. I'll walk until I find someone to help us."

"Who?"

Maurice had already started to walk away from her. He spoke over his shoulder. "Anyone except those two. I hate them."

When Katherine was sure he was gone, she walked downstream. It took her a long time to spot the notched stick floating among the reeds on the far bank. The water was shallow and she waded across to retrieve it. From that day on, she kept the stick in her room, where her brother wouldn't see it. It didn't matter what he said. She'd pay Martha back what they owed. Every dollar. That's what their parents would have wanted.

TWENTY

1978–79

The days and months were never called by their names. There were no calendars in the house. Nothing was ever crossed off or marked down as pending. Not once did the children ever hear Peters or Martha say, *Today's Monday, so we'll ...* Or, *It's Friday. Why don't we ...* Even Sunday, which back in Hornton Street had meant church bells in the morning, Father home all day, and a roast for lunch, here in the valley was just another working day. There was no Guy Fawkes or Easter. Not even Christmas Day. The years folded into each other unnoticed.

The most important thing was for the children to get through the work that had to be done before it got dark. Today and tomorrow, that's all there was. And the four seasons.

Martha was in charge of the vegetable garden—it was almost a quarter of an acre, close to the farmhouse—and the orchard. Early spring meant planting: beans, beetroot, broccoli, carrots, lettuce, peas, spring onions, corn. There were seemingly endless rows of potatoes, which they ate prepared in various ways almost every day. Later in spring it was the turn of cucumbers, courgettes, capsicums.

Summer was for weeding and thinning out. If the rain did not come for more than a few days, the garden needed watering by hand. Then Maurice would be sent down from Peters's place to help. He and Katherine would ferry buckets to and from the river. They poured water gently along the rows. Summer was also when the plums softened and went dark and had to be picked before the birds ate them.

Autumn was by far the busiest season. Not only did most of the vegetables have to be harvested but nearly everything in the orchard needed to be picked. There were three varieties of apples, also pears, early and late, and a windbreak of soapy feijoas. Leave it too long and the fruit would rot on the ground. Without proper care, the vegetables would go to seed. Martha hated it when food was wasted.

Harvesting, though, was only the beginning. A lot of the fruit and vegetables had to be placed in barrels or bagged and stored in the dry, windowless shed out the back of Martha's house that served as a root cellar. The rest was bottled or transformed into chutney, pickles, or preserves. Through the alchemy of sugar and heat, fruit became jam and was put into glass jars, of which Martha seemed to have an endless supply. That first full autumn on the farm, Katherine spent long days surrounded by the tropical fug of fruit steam. From morning until late at night the house exhaled sweet, diabetic breath.

* * *

Katherine was back in the clearing where she'd buried her baby sister. It was very important she check that Emma's body was still beneath the pile of stones. The stones, though, were much larger and heavier than she remembered. The final one was almost impossible to move. It was shiny green. But that didn't make sense, did it? That was the last stone she'd put on top of the pile, so it should've been the first one she took away. When she lifted it, the stone felt hot in her hands. That was when the bird-headed spirit spoke to her from the trees.

Katherine opened her eyes to the black of her room.

"You in there?"

The voice came again. It was Peters. It took her a few seconds to realise he was calling from outside the house.

"Woman, you there?" He sounded drunk.

With no clock it was impossible to say how long she'd been asleep. Peters called out twice more, sounding increasingly irritated, before Martha's padding footsteps passed Katherine's bedroom. The front door creaked.

"Where the hell else would I be?"

Martha sounded amused more than angry. And also a little drunk herself, as she was most nights. Katherine sat up in bed.

"Can I come in, or what?" said Peters.

"What do you want?"

"I brought you some venison." He paused as if thinking. "And a jug of the new grog."

"Man, you only left here a couple of hours ago."

"Yeah, I know. So?"

"Get that out of my face!"

Katherine guessed that he'd shone his torch into Martha's eyes.

She could imagine Peters swaying in the shadows beyond the gate. As well as drinking, he'd probably been smoking his stinky cigarettes, weed or dope. They made him sleepy and strange. Martha sometimes smoked it as well, although it mostly just made her laugh too much and go to bed early.

"Better bring it in, then."

The veranda creaked and Katherine heard the double thud of Peters's boots. As he passed her bedroom, light showed beneath the door, and she heard his heavy breathing. Martha began talking about the meat. Her voice rambled into the kitchen and almost immediately came back into the hall before fading. Katherine guessed they'd gone into the living room.

She lay down again, closed her eyes and tried to sleep, but knowing Peters was still in the house made her uneasy. He'd never gone away after dinner and come back again, not that she knew of, anyway. She slipped out of bed. Her socks made no sound on the floorboards in the hallway. The living-room door was open a crack, just far enough that she could see inside.

It was hard for her to be sure what was happening. The only light came from a guttering candle on the table. Peters was standing in front of the couch with his back to her. His bush shirt was still on but, strangely, his trousers had fallen to his ankles. She could see his pale bottom—what Martha would've called his *arse* or his *big hairy arse*. It was a split thing. Like the boulder near the first bend in the river, or the hoof of a cow or a pig.

It wasn't the first time she'd seen Peters without his clothes. Once when he was swimming she'd stood in the bushes and watched. It was a hot day and he was floating, rolling slowly in the current from his front to back and over again. She'd come to the pool intending to swim. Luckily, she'd seen Peters before he saw her. His dreadlocks lay across the surface, and matted hair made a pelt of his chest and shoulders. Nested between his legs she could half see the dark eel of his penis and remembered how he'd peed on the ground on the day he'd found them. She'd left quickly, before he could realise she was spying.

His bottom was moving. It was going up and down. No, towards her and away. Peters wasn't silent, as he'd been when he was floating in the river. The noises he was making were similar to Tommy's new voice, grunting and urgent.

She almost cried out when Martha lifted her head from the deep shadow of the couch. Martha's face was turned towards the door but her eyes were closed. Her knees were up on either side of Peters's hips. Katherine could just make out the spiderweb tattoo stretched over one knee. She didn't understand why Martha wasn't yelling at Peters to get off her. Martha's hands were free. Nothing was stopping her from scratching at his face. Peters's noises had grown louder, and he was moving faster. The candle guttered and the light waned and then flowed back. That was when she saw the wink of a pale eye watching her. Confused, and frightened, she stepped back into the hall.

Later, as she lay in bed in the dark, she thought about what she'd seen, trying to work it out. She fell asleep still unsure. In the morning she told herself that it had been a dream.

* * *

Maurice had learnt many lessons from his first attempt to escape. It was no good leaving in winter. Even in spring, a pleasant day could be followed by a cold night or a southerly storm. He needed to get away in summer. Only then were the days and nights consistently warm. His leg also had to be stronger. His ankle still hurt if he put much weight on it. He was beginning to suspect it would always be sore. In the evenings, he sat on the edge of his hay-bale bed and repeatedly lifted the leg off the ground. Five lifts and then he rested. Five more.

Next time, he'd take proper food, not just a silly biscuit. He'd make sure to wade along the rivers and streams he came to. That would stop the dogs following his scent. He'd seen it done in a film about escaped prisoners during the war. The hardest thing was knowing which was the best way to go. The mountains to the east would be too hard to cross. South wasn't a good idea, either. His sister had told him that the ridge behind the house was full of dangerous mineshafts. He remembered Father saying that the West Coast was a coal-mining area, so that made sense. Katherine said that she'd almost fallen into one.

Probably he'd go north into the next valley, maybe even the one beyond that. From there he'd walk to the coast. The seashore would be his road home.

Meanwhile, Peters found plenty for him to do. Most days they worked side by side. He would've preferred it if Peters was a constant ogre. Instead, there were many confusing kindnesses drip-fed into the days, which muddied the waters of Maurice's hatred. The dogs were one example. Although Peters was gruff with Bess and the other two, Maurice saw that he didn't strike them unless it was earnt, and even then, he only hit them hard enough to show who was boss. He often saw Peters scratching behind the dogs' ears. If they rolled onto their backs, he took the time to rub their bellies. Although the dogs usually slept in the kennels at the back of their runs, once, on a midwinter night, Maurice had seen, through the open door of the bus, Peters with all three dogs piled around him on the bed.

When Bess had her chest ripped open by a large boar so badly that the air sucked audibly through the flaps of the wound, Peters had carried her out of the bush.

His eyesight didn't allow him to thread the needle, so Maurice did it and he'd held the trembling dog still as Peters sewed the wound. All the time, Peters had talked to Bess, telling her everything would be all right. For days he'd regularly cleaned the wound with one of Martha's potions to stop infection.

The beehives were another source of confusion. Peters showed them to Maurice for the first time the day after his sister gave him the stupid notched stick and he'd thrown it into the river. The hives were in a paddock close to the top of the valley. Even before he got close, he could hear their massed thrum. When he came to the edge of the clearing, he stopped. There were thousands of bees on the wing, catching the late-morning sunshine. Peters was standing by the tallest hive, four stacked boxes, as bees flew all around him. His only protection was his dangling dreadlocks. Lifting away a heavy stone, Peters took off the hive's metal top and put it on the grass.

"What are ya doing, Slowpoke? Come over here."

"They'll sting me."

"Bullshit," Peters said mildly. "They don't sting unless ya do something stupid. Get over here."

Reluctantly, Maurice moved closer. Peters had two hives that he'd built himself. He called them Blue Hive and Yellow Hive, although the paint on the stacked boxes was sun-bleached to a uniform white. Maurice watched, interested despite himself, as Peters stuffed a handful of dry grass into an old coffee pot. After taking a matchbox from his pocket, Peters lit the grass. The smoke was directed into the top of the open hive.

"This helps keep 'em calm, although honey bees aren't normally aggro, not if you've got a good queen."

Peters put down the smoker and slowly drew out a

frame. It was thick with honeycomb and crawling with bees. He held it out to Maurice, who drew away.

"Here. Hold this. Go on, take it."

"I can't."

"Don't be a girl. Nothing's going to happen."

Maurice copied how Peters held the frame at the top, watching nervously as the bees crawled close to his fingers.

"There, ya see?"

Peters slowly trawled a finger through the waggling mass. Maurice saw how the bees moved aside or clambered onto and over the finger. None bothered taking flight.

"They're good as. D'ya see?"

"Yes."

"Nearly all this lot are foragers. They're the ones who fly off and get the nectar and pollen from the bush. When they're younger they build all the honeycomb, see, this stuff here. They clean it as well, and make the honey. There's no such thing as a lazy bloody bee, everyone works."

His blue eyes studied Maurice. "Do ya know what I mean?"

"Yes."

"Let's see if we can spot the queen. She's bigger than the rest."

Peters removed the two top boxes from the hive, placing them carefully on the grass. He took the frame from Maurice and gently slotted it back into place.

"There's only one queen in each hive. She's too big to get through this mesh. That's how we keep her in this bottom box."

"Why?"

"Otherwise she'd lay eggs in the frames in the top

boxes. When the larvae hatch out they'd eat most of the honey. There she is. Do ya see her?"

"Yes."

Maurice leant in. The queen was at least three times bigger than the workers. The other bees moved around and over her.

"See what she's doing?"

"Trying to hide, so we can't see her."

"Nah, dickhead. She doesn't give a stuff that we're looking. She's laying eggs."

Maurice looked on as the queen bee again lowered her long abdomen into a honeycomb chamber. Only her head and wings showed. Peters was a good teacher. He kept things simple and allowed Maurice to handle the different parts of the hive. It wasn't long before Maurice's fear had almost disappeared.

"See this one, what's different about him?" asked Peters.

"Bigger?"

"Yeah. And?"

"The eyes are larger, and blacker."

"Right, so he's a drone."

Peters pinched out a bee from the rest. He held its wings between his finger and thumb. It struggled, legs waving, but made no sound.

"Drones are always male but don't have stingers, so ya can do whatever ya want with them. There's only a few of them in each hive, compared to workers. They don't gather food, or clean. They don't make wax, or guard the entrance. Take a guess what they do."

"I don't know."

"It's their job to fuck the new queen when she's ready." He winked. "Not a bad life, eh?"

Maurice was embarrassed and looked away. Peters

laughed. He tossed the bee into the air. Maurice watched until he lost sight of it among all the other flashing specks. Although he always rebelled against his life in the valley, and never stopped thinking of it as temporary, from that day on, the bees were his secret love.

* * *

Tommy wakes with the sun. He finds himself in the hay barn. The three walls of corrugated iron stop a foot short of the roof. He's curled on a blanket covered with dog hair, among bales of hay. Instinct and muscle memory lead him outside, where he stands blinking and rubbing at his heavily gummed eyes. In front of him, the valley is still in shadow.

Many things might decide which way he'll go from here. If he sees a rabbit he will sometimes follow it, at least until he spooks it below ground. Red-beaked gulls, which often fly in from the coast to feed on the open grassland, might draw him on. Today, though, as happens most mornings at this time of year, it is the sunlight reflecting off the snow on the tops of the mountains that makes him head east.

Tommy's feet are bare. The soles are callused and black. He can walk over jagged shingle or sticks without noticing. He's wearing the heavy jersey his sister gave him—not that he remembers where it came from. The wool is stained with food and dirt and barbed with grass seed. His trousers are a ragged tatter. He comes to what was, forty years ago, a macrocarpa hedge, but is now a line of interwoven trees. At the end of the row, he stops and rocks contentedly. The crotch of his trousers darkens and a pleasant warmth flows down the inside of his leg. A small depression in the dust holds the liquid for a few seconds before it drains away.

He is only a few steps into the paddock beyond the trees when he falls under the spell of a daisy. Who knows why he notices that particular flower? It's one among thousands.

An hour passes before one of Peters's bees lands on the flower. The bee's body is dark and bristled. Its hinged legs twitch as it shuttles over the petals. Tommy grunts. He doesn't like insects, except sometimes butterflies on the wing, which he will follow. He tries to grab the bee and is stung. Yelping, he stumbles backward. The pain sends him on his way with a badly swollen finger.

When he arrives at the river his finger is still throbbing. He quickly forgets it, though, as his eyes dart over the water, by now in the sunlight. The surface sparkles and glints. There are red-and-black dragonflies, and the reeds downstream flick in the current. He has arrived at the deep hole that Katherine calls Castle Pool. He doesn't remember that sometimes on hot days he has met his sister swimming here. There are rocks on the far bank from which she jumps. The splash startles him every time.

Directly in front of him is a weir formed by a rock shelf at the downstream edge of the pool. A small trip, and the water tumbles into a sudden shallowing and rolls forward once before flowing away loudly over the shingle. For Tommy, it's an endlessly repeating wonder. For the rest of the day, he squats there, arms wrapped around his knees. His eyes don't shift. Apart from his slow breathing, he's still.

Watershinewaterfaceflower ...

It's late afternoon when the shadow of the ridge

moves across the pool. Tommy sighs and looks around. As stiff as an old man, he unbends. His stomach surprises him by groaning loudly. His eyes stretch wide and he stares down. There, again, like a blocked drain. Lifting the hem of his stained jersey, he tries to see where the noise is coming from, curling forward into himself, but when the mystery is not repeated, he loses interest. Suddenly desperately thirsty, he lies on the bank. Laps and sucks. Some water ends up in his nose and he splutters indignantly. He jumps up, edging away from the treachery.

He's hungry. If there was food in his hand, he'd put it into his mouth. He'd chew and swallow. Food that's already in your hand requires no planning. It needs no mental image of the journey across the fields to the house, where Katherine is at this moment cooking dinner. Later she will come looking for him. He begins to walk, retracing the path he took that morning. That's the direction in which the sunlight is retreating in a broad crescent. Most days the light leads him back to the barn.

TWENTY-ONE

22 FEBRUARY 1980

Suzanne poured herself a second glass of wine before spreading her papers over the kitchen table. William still wasn't home from the office, and his dinner was slowly withering under silver foil in the oven. It was unusual for her to bring work home, but she'd only been back from her third trip to New Zealand for a week and there was a lot to catch up on. One of the two partners at the firm where she was the sole legal secretary had unexpectedly resigned, for health reasons, shortly before she left. They had been very understanding, but the timing hadn't exactly been ideal.

The house was quiet as she worked. Tim had helped her with the dishes but had then biked down the road to watch a video at a friend's house. Cameron was living in Wales, tutoring at a small boarding school outside Cardiff as part of his gap year. Although he'd only bothered calling home twice, she gathered he was enjoying himself.

She worked for an hour and a half before putting away her papers. After pouring herself another wine, she went through to what used to be the spare room but was now an office. Theoretically she shared it with William. In practice, however, it had become more and more her space. Pinned to the wall was a large map of West Coast, New Zealand. It was annotated in her cramped writing and orbited by tacked-on photographs and handwritten notes. She sat at her desk, stared at it, and sipped her wine.

William had done his best to talk her out of going back a third time. When he'd told her he was definitely not coming with her, not under any circumstances, she had felt what? Shocked? Abandoned? Betrayed? Perhaps a mixture of all three. The Germans probably had a very long word for the feeling of a wife whose husband does not support her in an important decision. Before that, though, he'd tried to change her mind.

"We've been twice. Don't you think that's enough?"

"Obviously not."

"I mean, what good will a third trip do?"

"Who knows, it's possible I might discover something new."

"Such as?"

"I don't know, something might turn up."

That particular conversation had happened in the kitchen. It had recently been remodelled, more William's idea than hers. As she listened to him talk, she washed a lettuce that she'd grown herself in the small vegetable garden she'd started at the back of the house. William had poured two glasses of wine but left them sitting on the new counter next to the bottle as they faced each other over the black marble, the cold water from the long, silver neck of the new tap running over the leaves in her hand.

"I don't see how this trip will help," he said. "I'm sorry, but I really don't. And Arthur obviously doesn't either."

"He couldn't get leave from the university this time."

"So he said."

"Yes, I know your theory."

"Arthur's just being realistic. The chances of you or any of the family actually discovering something after more than two years are next to nothing."

"I can't give up. Not yet, anyway."

William shook his head and sighed deeply. She found herself irritated by his theatricality. Did he think he was trying to persuade a child?

"I'm not saying give up hope, of course not, but it's time to leave it to other people."

She turned off the tap. "I don't want to give up. I need to keep searching."

"Look, you've got to be logical about this. It's not as if you're popping over to France for three weeks every year, although even that would be a major disruption."

"I know."

"The police file is still open. Can't you just wait to see what happens?"

"No, I can't. Julia's my sister. Her children are part of my family. Our family."

"You're not going to achieve anything by going back." He sounded bitter. "We've been up and down that bloody highway between Hokitika and whatever it's called, Haast, who knows how many times?"

In fact, she did know. It was all there in her notes, but she wasn't going to bait him by naming a figure. She let him talk while she stood silently on the other side of the counter, the lettuce in her hand dripping onto the benchtop. William was one of those people who made mental lists. If he could think of three reasons for, say, going on holiday with friends, or upgrading the kitchen, but four reasons against, well then, he just wouldn't do it. This particular list was headed up "Reasons Why Suzanne Shouldn't Return to New Zealand." It included the disruption to the boys' routine, to her career, and the inconvenience to him personally. The expense had come up in different guises several times. Plus, there was the emotional toll William believed going to New

Zealand took on her. He claimed that she "wasn't the same" afterwards.

She'd nodded and made small sounds acknowledging the truth of his arguments. They were true, at least partially. Not that it made any difference. Nothing William could've said would have changed her mind.

The next day, she'd used her lunch break to drive to a travel agent in Bournemouth. She had the inheritance from her mother, plus the money she'd saved over the years in her own bank account. You didn't work for lawyers who carried out as much divorce work as her firm did and not stay financially independent. She'd seen too many women who'd given up careers and raised children, only to be left practically destitute when their marriages failed.

That had clearly been the turning point for William. He began spending more and more time at work. When the day had come for her to leave, he hadn't driven her up to Gatwick. He hadn't picked her up, either, when she'd come back last week. She'd arrived home to find he was sleeping in Cameron's old room. A stranger observing them now might think they were boarders who, forced together by nothing more binding than circumstance, were sharing the same house. It would come as a surprise to discover they'd been married for nineteen years this December and shared two wonderful sons.

Last Sunday, the day after she got back, she was pottering in the garage, still jet-lagged, when Tim had asked if there was anything he could do around the house.

"I just thought it might help, you know, with things being, I suppose, a bit weird between you and Dad."

Beautiful, wavy-haired Tim.

She could've hugged him, but she knew he'd be embarrassed. Instead, she tousled his hair.

"Don't worry, your father and I will work things out."

"He doesn't like you going back there."

"I know, but it's something I have to do."

"He was in a bad mood the whole time you were away."

"I'm sorry. That can't have been easy."

"It wasn't *too* bad. I got to eat a lot of takeaways."

"Great, that's another thing for me to feel guilty about."

"I hung out with Simon a lot. His mum didn't mind me going over there."

"Simon whose older sister is Ginny?"

"Yeah, I guess."

Tim grinned like a pirate duke and she'd realised how much he'd changed in the past few years. His face was so angular. And when had he grown so tall? She was suddenly sad. To think he was almost to the other side of the bridge from boyhood to the rest of his life. In another year he'd finish school. He'd probably opt to go to university in another city; in fact, he'd already talked, although only vaguely, about Edinburgh. There would be other girls after Ginny Woods. Ones who were more flattered by his interest. After Tim left, it would be just her and William.

She took her almost-empty glass and walked slowly through the house, picking things up, inspecting them, running her hand over the often dusty surfaces. She found it impossible to remember when they'd purchased most of them, or why. On the wall in the hallway hung three watercolours; landscapes. One by one she stared into them. Despite passing them several times every day for years, she never really saw them.

William still wasn't home. She thought about another

glass of wine, but decided against it. Later, in her night-gown, teeth brushed, she opened the top drawer of her bedside cabinet and took out her Bible. It was a King James edition, a gift from her mother on Suzanne's thirteenth birthday. The Bible had been a longer-term companion even than William, whom she hadn't met until her first year at UCL. Julia had also been given a King James on the same birthday. By then Suzanne had been seventeen and already looking forward to leaving Ringwood—predictable, rustic, totally stifling Ring-wood.

"I'd rather have roller skates." That's what her little sister had said as she'd come into the bedroom they'd shared.

She'd watched, shocked, as Julia threw the Bible into a bottom drawer, shoving it shut with her foot. Suzanne would never have dared treat a Bible like that. It felt dangerous, somehow, and not only because it seemed to go against God. Even at seventeen she'd understood that it was their mother that her sister was really dis-carding. As far as she knew, Julia never so much as looked at a Bible again. Nor, despite their mother's shouts and threats and final cold retreat, did her sister ever go back to church.

Brave, brave Julia.

She, on the other hand, still belonged to the local parish church, St Luke's. Since Julia and the children had disappeared, she'd been attending every Sunday. The reverend Lewis had been counselling her. He'd advised her to follow her intuition. Also to listen for the voice of Jesus, to be open to His presence in her life.

"The right path is rarely the easiest," he said.

Sitting up in bed, she deliberately let the Bible fall open in her lap. Doing this always felt as if she were inviting God to step to the forefront of her day. A small intervention. It opened at the book of Jonah. Yes, she could see that. Like Jonah, she was on a journey—one that took her to foreign places. And although not totally alone as Jonah must have been, she was lonely. She lowered her head and began to pray.

She was almost asleep when William's car pulled into the drive. The garage door rattled up. The heels of his shoes sounded on the new tiles in the kitchen. She heard him swear. His meal was probably ruined. After that, there was only silence. She imagined William picking from his plate any food that was salvageable. She could almost hear him adding the ruined meal to the list of things he held against her.

TWENTY-TWO

LATE SPRING AND SUMMER, 1979

Maurice had been called down to the house to help Katherine deal with an invasion of large, brown slugs. He was on his knees in the vegetable garden, between two rows of lettuces.

"Katherine."

She turned and looked down the row. As she worked she'd been worrying about Tommy. She hadn't seen him since yesterday. He'd need a good feed and cleaning up. "What?"

"Have you had your birthday yet?"

"I don't know. I must've."

"And what about Christmas? We've missed that too."

Fingers glistening with slime, she shook a slug into her bucket.

"I could bake you a cake, if you want. I know how. I don't think Martha would mind, eh."

"I don't want a stupid cake. And don't talk like that."

"Like what?"

"You sound like them. And sometimes you swear. Father said only stupid people need to use words like that."

Katherine picked another slug from the lettuce and didn't reply. Maurice stood. Balancing without his crutch, he deliberately nudged his bucket with his foot so that it tipped onto its side.

"We don't even know how old we are," he said, watching the slugs move toward the rim.

"I'm thirteen. I must be, by now."

"But you don't know, not for sure."

Katherine also stood up. She wiped her hands on her trousers. "I feel older."

"That's stupid," said Maurice.

He stared at her so angrily that she felt uneasy. "It's not."

"Sometimes I think you don't even want to go home."

"Of course I do."

So that she didn't have to look at him, she carried on pinching slugs from the leaves. The slugs had appeared almost overnight. They were so large she could hear them land in the bottom of the bucket with a soft plop.

When Maurice finally spoke again he didn't sound so angry.

"Peters sometimes goes out in the morning and gets back with supplies before it's dark. They try to hide it, but I've seen. It happens more than you know."

She didn't bother denying it. Things—packaged food, mostly; flour and sugar, cooking oil, matches and other stuff they couldn't grow or make themselves—trickled into the valley. Martha removed all the boxes and labels, but she'd noticed.

"I think there's a place they store things," she said. "A shed or something in the bush."

"No. The town's closer than they say."

"I don't think so."

"Why are you always making excuses for them?"

"I'm not."

"You are."

There was silence. Two more slugs fell into Katherine's bucket.

"Anyway, it doesn't matter," she said. "We still owe them money. Until we pay it back, we can't leave." She had her half of the notched stick in her room. Lately, though, Martha had mentioned it less and less.

Maurice was suddenly shouting. "They're liars. I told you, we don't owe them anything!"

He snatched up his crutch from the dirt. She was sure that if he'd been standing closer, he would've hit her.

"It's only going to get worse," he yelled. "Don't you see?"

He limped away. She saw how the soft soil made it difficult for him to use his crutch. It wasn't until he was beyond the stick teepees where the beans grew that he could move quickly.

* * *

Maurice shook the weed so that the soil fell from the roots, before he lobbed it underhand toward the trees. They hadn't visited this plot for almost a month. Give or take, there were a hundred marijuana plants inside a mesh fence that kept away the possums and deer. The plants had grown quickly, but so had the weeds. Peters said it would be another two weeks before they'd cut down the plants and take them back to the shearing shed to be hung and dried.

"Does the river have a name?" Maurice spoke as though the question had only just occurred to him.

Peters was standing in the shade, smoking. He threw a shifty, bloodshot glance back to where a stretch of water could be seen through the trees.

"Nah. It's just called the river."

The day was humid. Cicadas hummed in the canopy, and further away, far enough that they weren't a danger, a nest of wasps kept up a steady drone. Maurice was hoping that Peters was in a mood to let him swim after they had finished with this plot. Sometimes swimming was allowed, sometimes it wasn't.

"It's big, though, isn't it?"

"Eh? What are ya on about?"

"The river. It's big."

"So?"

"I just thought that big rivers were usually on maps. And if it's on a map then a cartographer must've given it a name."

Peters stared at him across the spiky tops of the marijuana plants.

"I told ya, it's not on any bloody maps. Shut up and do some work."

Cartographer. That was a good one.

Sometimes, before Maurice fell asleep in the shearing shed, he lay on his back staring up at the rafters and trying to remember big words. Apiarist, horticulturalist, somnambulant. There were others he'd come up with. He'd always been good with words. At Holland Park, he used to win prizes for spelling. Now when he remembered a good word, he stored it away so that he could pull it out when the time seemed right. He enjoyed the look of confusion that always came over Peters's face. For a satisfying moment, the big man turned into a boy sitting at the back of the class. The one who didn't have a clue what the teacher was talking about. Maurice had known boys like that. Even at good schools, there was always a dummy, a thicko, who knew how to swear and hit but was too stupid to do the work.

Illiterate. That was another word he had tucked away. He was almost certain Peters couldn't read, at least not beyond *the cat sat on the mat*. Once, Maurice had found him in the tool shed, picking his way like a blind man moving through nettles as he tried to read the instructions on the back of a bottle of liquid fertiliser. Suddenly full of bluster, Peters had thrust the bottle at him and told him to sort it out. Illiterate, though, wasn't a word he'd be stupid enough to say to Peters's face. Maurice only ever whispered that one into the dark space above his bed. Even the words he did say got him yelled at. He was called "smart arse" and a "snot-nosed little know-it-all," "Lord fuckin' muck." Sometimes there was a slap to match the insults. No, illiterate could, at the least, leave him black and blue. If Peters were drunk, illiterate might even be suicide.

Peters snuffed out his joint with spit-wet fingers. He put the remains in his top pocket and climbed over the fence. Together they finished the weeding before beginning to remove most of the larger leaves, high up on the plants, that shaded the buds. Peters had been worried that the cloud and drizzle they'd had in the last week might have encouraged mould.

Maurice didn't believe him. The river must have a name. The valley as well. And that mountain, the one that pushed like a jagged tooth above the others. Mountains always had names. Here's what he thought: Peters didn't want him to know the names, because they might help him to work out where they were. A name would be a starting point on the journey back to the road. The road would take him to a town. The town would be a way home to Hornton Street.

"Right, that's it, we're done here. How about a swim on the way back?"

"No," said Maurice. "I don't feel like it today."

When he shrugged, Peters's dreadlocks rose and fell with his broad shoulders. "Suit yaself. It's no skin off my nose."

*　*　*

When Maurice ran away for the second time, he was gone overnight. It was after midday before a grim Peters led him back past the farmhouse. Katherine came to the gate and watched. Her brother had his head lowered. His shoes and legs were caked with mud, and he didn't look at her. The three dogs ran triumphantly ahead.

When they were out of sight, she followed. From a distance she saw Peters lock Maurice inside the tool shed. She was grateful that was to be her brother's only punishment. During dinner that evening, however, Peters was sullen. It was obvious that he'd been drinking before he had arrived, and he drank more gin than usual with his meal. Even Martha was wary of him. He muttered and cursed over the cards, his anger coming to the surface in unpredictable spurts, like trapped steam through their morning porridge as it sat on the stove.

When Peters pushed his chair back so hard that it fell, Katherine kept her eyes on her cards. She listened to his heavy steps going out into the darkness. When he was gone, she went onto the veranda. She was pulling on her gumboots when Martha came to the door.

"Don't try and stop him. He could hurt you as well."

"I know. I just need to see."

Martha followed her as far as the steps. "For God's sake, girl, stay clear of him."

The air was warm. The moon was a few days off being full. Although she carried the torch, Katherine didn't need to switch it on. She was almost at the shearing shed, when she heard her brother's shouts.

Peters had dragged Maurice out of the tool shed. She

watched the large shadow labouring over the balled shape at his feet. Peters was using his belt, delivering blows that became a rhythm. At first her brother tried to roll away, but soon curled into himself and lay still. His shouts turned to groans. To silence. Peters, however, was getting louder and louder. He swore and raged in time with the blows. The leather belt hissed, slapped, and was raised high, over and over.

Finally, breathing like a draught horse, Peters lumped away toward the bus. Katherine waited until she was sure he wasn't coming back before going to her brother.

"Are you all right?" she whispered.

Maurice didn't answer. It was a long time before she was able to get him to stand. She led him into the shearing shed. He collapsed onto his bed, face down. Katherine ran back to the house, where Martha gave her medicines, including kūmarahou extract to ease the pain and reduce the swelling. When she got back, Maurice was exactly where she'd left him. His back was the worst. He lay still, only occasionally flinching or crying out as she bathed the welts. Where his skin had split, she used a bandage of softened rātā bark to stop infection.

"I *am* going to escape one day," said Maurice, so quietly she could barely hear him.

She didn't bother replying. He was a stubborn fool. She was sure that the next time he ran away Peters would beat her brother to death.

PART III

TWENTY-THREE

SUMMER, 1979-80

Martha had decided that enough clothes and sheets needed cleaning. Over breakfast she announced that today was wash day. The washhouse was behind the house, at the end of a concrete path. While Martha lit the fire, Katherine carried buckets of water from the rain barrel and poured them into the large copper that was heating over the flames. When the water was boiling, she began to feed in the clothes, not too many at once or they clotted and became unworkable.

She was only half-listening as Martha wittered about the chickens, the cows, which were both pregnant by Peters's bull, and about the weather; then the best way to treat a sore stomach, from which Katherine was suffering that morning. The water turned grey as she stirred the clothes with a long paddle. They had to be boiled for what Martha called "a good while." Katherine didn't mind how long it took. She liked the washhouse, with its heat and steam.

"You got the shits?" asked Martha.

"No."

Martha sniffed thoughtfully. "I'll boil you up some pepper-tree leaves when we're finished here."

"Thanks."

Later, she turned the handle of the wringer while Martha fed one of Peters's woollen undershirts between the rollers. It came out the other side flattened and stiff, still steaming. Martha dropped it into the wicker basket, ready to be hung on the clothesline.

"How are your hands today?" asked Katherine.

"Good as gold. This heat makes them feel just dandy."

Martha fed the rollers a faded pair of her own knickers, the cotton so thin it was almost transparent, before waggling her twisted fingers at Katherine.

"Mind you, I better be careful, otherwise they'll end up as ribbons, eh."

She mimed getting her fingers caught, and Katherine laughed.

When they finished in the washhouse, Katherine carried the basket of clothes out to the washing line and began to peg them onto the rope. That was when she noticed the blood. It was tricking in a pinkish stream down the inside of her bare leg. When she rubbed, it smeared across her palm.

"I think I've cut myself."

Martha came between the hanging sheets and looked. "You said ya tummy's been a bit tender?"

"Yes."

Strangely, Martha grinned. "You're on your rags, love. Lots of girls get it about your age."

Katherine looked at the blood on her hand. "What's that?"

"You've no idea?"

"I don't understand. Please tell me. What is it?"

"It's your period. Once a month you bleed from your fanny."

The idea was so absurd that Katherine almost laughed. This must be another of Martha's rough jokes. Martha kept on explaining as she led her over to the rain barrel and, using a bucket and a rag, helped her to clean up. When Katherine pulled down her knickers and saw how much blood there was she couldn't help crying.

"Don't make a fuss. I told you, it's normal. All girls get it."

"Did it happen to you?"

"Of course. Used to, anyway, up till a few years ago. It stops when you get to about my age. That's natural as well. Leave those to soak in the bucket. Come on with me."

With only the rag to cover herself and to stop the blood from dripping, Katherine was led into the house. Martha pointed to Katherine's bedroom.

"Grab a fresh pair of knickers from your drawer, then come to my room. I'll teach you what to do."

Although the door to Martha's bedroom was often left open, Katherine had always been forbidden to go inside. The room turned out to be as cluttered, dark, and dusty as every other room in the house. The only thing that made it different from her own bedroom were the three mirrors, mounted on hinges above the dresser. Two were narrow and rectangular and the larger one in the middle was oval. They were the only mirrors on the farm.

Martha pulled open the bottom drawer and took out a pile of grey material cut into squares. She showed Katherine how to fold them inside her knickers to soak up the blood before giving her a dozen to keep. It felt strange to have so much material pressing between her legs.

"Congratulations," said Martha.

"Why?"

"You're not a girl anymore. From now on you're a woman."

Katherine peered at herself in the middle mirror. By turning her head she could see from three different angles. Maybe it was because it had been so long since she'd seen her reflection in anything except water or window glass, but she did seem changed. Her face had lost its puppy fat. Her cheek bones were more on display. Her hair, which had only ever been trimmed since she'd arrived in the valley, was thick and hung down to the middle of her back. All the lifting and carrying had made her shoulders broad. Undeniably her breasts and hips had also changed, which made her feel slightly embarrassed.

Martha clapped her hands. "We need to celebrate!"

"How?"

"Come with me."

In the kitchen, Martha produced a dark bottle from the cupboard and poured two glasses.

"What is it?"

"Blackberry wine. Go on, you'll like it."

It smelt sweet. Although the adults drank almost every evening, Martha had never allowed her more than one or two glasses of beer. Maurice refused even that and drank only water.

Martha held up her glass. "Here's to being a woman. God help us."

They touched glasses and drank. The wine tasted syrupy but not unpleasant.

Martha grinned. "Don't look so worried. This is an important day. Drink up."

* * *

The rest of the day is a warm current carrying Katherine from moment to moment. They take their drinks and the bottle, and sit on the front step in the late-morning sunshine. Of course, Martha is talking, she's always talking, about things Katherine doesn't really need to understand, not from start to finish anyway: about the best way to brown the bottom of a pie; now about the smell of babies, and how to feed them; and something to do with a man she used to know who was a prison guard, and there was another man, a Māori bloke, with nice eyes. Although perhaps it was the same man—it's hard to keep track of Martha's thoughts. Not that it matters. Out of the wind, the sun is hot and the concrete is warm on the back of her legs. She hears herself asking questions, but all the words, Martha's and hers, seem to mix together so that the meaning is unclear. Really it's the feeling of them, the words, that's important. There are no heavy words, and nothing with edges. They're all as soft as the sunshine that's falling across the tops of her bare legs. Martha's getting to her feet, going to fetch another bottle of sweet wine from the kitchen, which Katherine thinks is a very good idea, and it seems that in the same breath Martha's back and holding not one but two bottles. Katherine reads the four letters tattooed across Martha's knuckles as her hand pours the wine with the bottle held up very high, like a magic trick or part of a show. The wine is a pretty ribbon in the sunlight, curling into the bottom of the glass. Some of it splashes up, purple-black, out onto Katherine's hand and then across the step. Martha laughs. Katherine licks her own skin and laughs, as well. She drinks and can feel the glass between her lips and the sweet wine going down her throat into her still-sore stomach, which somehow isn't a bad thing anymore but means she's changed. Not a girl. She's a woman.

Later in the day, she's laughing again—still laughing? Maybe she hasn't stopped. How strange everything is; especially walking. She must've taken off her shoes and socks because she watches her bare feet, with the slightly rounded big toes, the same as Mother's, move back and forth over the grass as though they belong to someone else. The feet lead her to Martha, who's hanging up the rest of the washing, sheets and work shirts and socks and grey undies from the basket. She helps. The wooden pegs are little tightrope walkers. Martha laughs at how funny that is and makes one trip-trap across the rope like a goat over a bridge, and then pretends he's accidentally fallen. "Fuck," she says in the peg's squeaky voice. Katherine laughs until it hurts to laugh anymore. There, that's all; the wicker basket is empty. "One, two, three"—together they heave the fork-topped pole so that the clothes are hoisted into the air. She lies on her back on the grass and looks at the flapping sheets up there with the white puffs of scurrying cloud. A moment later, the sheets are the wings of birds. Huge birds that are all talking, talking, talking in their own flappity-flap language. Martha's beside her on the grass, with her glass in her hand. She agrees that the sheets are like birds, although Katherine had thought the birds were still only in her head. It's as though her own tongue has been flapped by the wind and the words have fallen out of her mouth.

Somehow, they are in the living room now, so it must be later, although it occurs to Katherine that this is all part of the same moment when she first put the glass to her lips in the kitchen. It's the same way that the water at the top of the river is really part of the water in the bottom pool. She's sitting at the table, tracing the swirl of the grain with her finger. Martha's heating a needle over a candle flame. "You're a woman now," she says again. "There needs to be something to mark that. We have to make sure people know." Katherine nods. People do need to know that she's changed. She thinks it will hurt, but as Martha works with the needle and the ink from the snapped ballpoint pen, there's only a dull ache. She stares at the candle. The flame's never still but reaches and sinks back, again and again. There's something important about that, but she's not sure what. "There. All finished," says Martha. Katherine holds up her right hand and stretches out her fingers. The tattoo is halfway between the knuckle and first joint of her middle finger. It's a circle, joined at the bottom to a cross. According to Martha it's an ancient and powerful symbol for a woman. "What do you think?"

"Thank you."

To celebrate, they open another bottle.

There is more, which afterwards she only vaguely remembers. At some point, she throws up on the grass near the coop and watches as the chickens feed on the mess. She remembers dancing as Martha sang. The final moment that stands out from all the rest is Martha sitting on the edge of the bed. Martha's looking down at her fondly, telling her that, from this day on, she will call her Kate. It's hard to concentrate. She's warm and sleepy. Martha's still talking and her words are a flame rising and falling, and they mean something important. They're nice words, soft words, about mothers and daughters. Her reply makes Martha very happy.

TWENTY-FOUR

AUTUMN, 1980

Kate called again. "Tommy."

He turned towards her, although his expression didn't change. At least he stood still until she reached him. She dropped her flax bag onto the grass.

"There you are. I've been looking for you."

There were a few fresh bruises and some scrapes on his knees and hands, but she couldn't see anything deep or infected. Although she'd been looking, she hadn't clapped eyes on Tommy for three days. Only one of the meals she'd left in the barn had been eaten. She'd no idea where he slept on the nights when he didn't make it back to his blanket among the bales of hay. She hoped it was somewhere with some shelter. The days were getting colder. She didn't like to think of him curled into himself out in the open.

Tommy had grown even wilder lately. His hair was long and tangled. She'd tried to cut it, but he wouldn't let her. The soles of his feet were as black as bicycle tyres. Worse, he seemed to respond to her less and less.

"Let's get these off," she said gently.

Trying not to upset him by touching his skin, she shimmied off his trousers and then his underpants. Both stank of stale urine. She flicked the warmly nestled turds she discovered into the grass. Turds and piss and an occasional bruise when he lashed out were just the way things were with Tommy. She didn't mind. He was her brother. She was grateful when he stood still and stared over the top of her head as she undressed him. She moved clear just as the hooded tip of his penis twitched and he released a steady stream of piss onto the grass.

"Jesus, Tommy. Give me some bloody warning, eh?"

Still, it was better out now rather than when she had him in a fresh pair of trousers. That had happened before and it was bloody annoying. She'd experimented with an old bedsheet cut into rectangles and safety-pinned into place around her brother's waist but he'd worried it free after just a few minutes.

Peters reckoned it would make sense to let Tommy wander around naked, at least from the waist down. That way her brother could piss whenever and wherever he wanted. He could squeeze out his turds on the ground without making a mess of his clothes. But the idea of leaving Tommy to roam nearly naked, like one of the farm animals, almost broke her heart. She'd rather find him most days, at least when she was able to track him down, and change his clothes.

Tommy had stopped peeing. She took a corked bottle of kōwhai-bark antiseptic from her bag and tipped a generous amount of the yellow liquid onto a clean cloth. Moving behind her brother, she quickly and efficiently wiped the raw crack of his arse. He grunted and jumped away.

"Sorry, but you don't want it to get bad again, do you?"

She gave him a minute to forget the insult and then, with as little fuss as possible, got him into some fresh underpants and then trousers. She rolled up the old clothes and put them in a plastic bag. She'd wash them separately, tomorrow, down at the river.

"Come on, Tommy. You must be hungry. Let's go back

to the house. Food, Tommy, food."

To entice him, she handed him an oat biscuit and watched as he ate it eagerly. She began to walk, hoping he would follow.

Somewhere deep down inside the cave of the boy's mind, a flint of recognition was struck.

Katherinekatherine ...

Startled, Kate turned back. "Tommy? What did you say? Tommy?"

But it was only a flash in the dark. Her brother stared past her.

No, of course not. What she'd heard must have just been one of her brother's noises. They didn't mean anything beyond pain or fear, or, sometimes when he ate, snuffled contentment. She must have been mistaken. Tommy hadn't said her name. How could he? Poor Tommy.

TWENTY-FIVE

SPRING, 1980

Peters will punish me. But only if he finds out.

Maurice picked his way up the valley. Even after all this time, he still resented how difficult simply moving from one place to another had become, how slow. Peters sometimes called him a cripple. "Hey, Crip, get a move on." Peters also called him Cousin Lurch, and Snail, and, ironically, Speedy. Peters thought that was particularly funny.

Maurice remembered how he'd won, or at least almost won, all the sprinting races at his school's sports days. He'd been the fastest in his football team. One day, after he escaped and a proper doctor fixed his leg, he'd run fast again. Then he'd show Peters.

Passing the hives, which he was supposed to be checking, he came to the bend at the place just before the river climbed, narrowed, and became cluttered with boulders. A deep pool, twenty feet across, had formed behind a fallen tree. He laid down his crutch and knelt among the ferns, where he retrieved his hidden knife. From his pocket he took a paper bag stuffed with blue-grey lumps of slippery mutton.

Three of his four lines had been successful. Sometimes, between visits, only one or two caught anything. He'd found the nylon catgut last winter in the tool shed, balled on the top shelf, covered in dust, its existence, he hoped, forgotten by Peters. Through trial and error, mostly error, he'd taught himself how to bend nails in the vice. A rasping file created the sharp point. The hardest part had been making the barb. In the end, a nail, cut with a hacksaw, and painstakingly grooved and tied in place with nylon, worked best.

When hooked, an eel's instinct was to try and twist free. It rolled until it was spinning, churning the water. Inevitably the catgut wrapped around its head and down the body, but even when the line tightened, an eel wouldn't stop twisting. Many times he'd watched the line shorten and the nylon begin to slice into their skin. It cut deeper and deeper, as blood coloured the water. If the line was tied to a branch above the pool, an eel would sometimes twist right out of the water. Even then, it wouldn't die, not straight away. He'd seen big eels last for hours as they hung above the pool. Sometimes only the threaded beads of their spines stopped them from being cut in half.

He pulled in the lines and killed the two smaller eels, just regular soldiers, with his knife. Standing on them with one foot to keep them still, he drove the blade down through the tops of their heads. He knew better than to try and hold them with his hands. Eels were covered in clear slime that made them almost impossible to grasp. The angrier they were, the more slime there seemed to be. When they were dead, Maurice tossed the bodies into the trees. Wild pigs came in the night and ate them, bones and all.

The third eel was a lieutenant. It was as long as his leg and thick bodied. It writhed as Maurice dragged it out of the water and over to where he had cleared a patch of ground back from the pool. His spear was leaning against a tree. When he released the line the eel immediately turned its head towards the river and tried to belly away.

"Where do you think you're going?"

The eel's head turned in his direction.

He showed it the spear's three metal prongs. "You're going to die. I'm going to kill you."

The lieutenant was almost at the water when, using all his weight, Maurice thrust his spear into the spot behind the head, hard enough that two of the prongs came through into the earth. The eel bucked and coiled and swept its body from side to side. When that didn't free it, it tried the usual trick of rolling, first one way and then the other. But its body was fixed to the ground.

Squatting over the eel, Maurice used his knife. When he stood, he was holding the eel's head, two fingers lodged into the gills. His hands and forearms were slippery and pink.

Carrying the head, he made the short climb through the trees to his secret place. No one else knew about it, not even his sister. It was a large overhang, at the base of a rock wall. Small bats roosted there, during the day, but they didn't bother him.

He carefully laid the eel's head on the ledge with the others. They were lined up in order of size, so he had to rearrange them slightly. The biggest was from an eel he'd caught on the very first day he'd set his lines in the pool. At first he'd thought he'd caught the king. It wasn't until later that he had time to weigh the memories of the eel that had come right up to him that day at the edge of the river against the one he'd just beheaded. He'd realised that the king was half as large again. It was also darker, so black it had been like a hole in the water. No, he'd caught a brother or a son. So, the prince. That's what he ended up calling it.

"Look," he said, pointing now to the latest head, "look who I've got."

The prince's empty eyes stared across at him. The skull was white and almost bare. Of course he didn't expect it to speak. There were no ghosts or spirits, as Katherine stupidly believed. If for a few days the head had twitched and jiggled on the rock shelf, that had only been because of maggots and other insects eating it from the inside. That was why the black eyes had moved in his direction that day. It had only seemed to look in at him. He hadn't been fooled. He wasn't a child. Dead meant being nothing and was forever.

He went back out into the sun, where he sat with his back to the cave, wiped his hands on the grass, and looked through the treetops over the bend in the river and down the valley. Killing the eels didn't make him feel better for very long. He always thought it would, but it never did. Sometimes as he stabbed and sliced he found that there were tears running down his face. He couldn't wipe them away because of the slime and blood on his hands. He couldn't stop setting the lines, though, not yet. The eels had done an unforgivable thing.

One day, though, he would catch the king. He'd laugh as he killed it, and he would bring its head here to this place, where he would put it next to the others. After that he'd have no reason to carry on with his revenge. He was sure that would be the day he'd start to feel better.

TWENTY-SIX

EARLY SUMMER, 1980

Kate liked her new name. Short and solid, it felt like a name with roots. Since Martha had given it to her, she was treating Kate almost as an equal, someone who was reliable and competent. Even Peters had said she was a good worker. Only Maurice acted as if she were still a kid.

Once or twice a week Kate would get drunk. Not usually so badly that she threw up or passed out, but enough to relive the warm timelessness of that first time sitting on the steps with Martha. In winter she was forced to drink inside and play cards. Summer was Kate's favourite season for drunkenness. When the evenings stretched out and the air was warm and hummed and the moon was full enough to show her the way, she'd take a bottle and roam the valley alone. She still preferred the sweet blackberry wine, although sometimes she drank Peters's gin. Not for the taste, which was bloody awful. When she was drunk on gin, everything seemed to be talking to her—the grass, the trees, the river, the moon. Some nights, if she listened very carefully, she could even hear the spirits whispering among the trees.

That evening, she was drunker than usual. After dinner, she'd washed the dishes, then played a few hands of cards, before taking a bottle of gin, still half full, and setting out for the stand of flax at the head of the lake. It was one of her favourite spots. She had a shrine there.

The statue faced south so that it guarded the valley. On the way, she stopped to watch a fantail as it flittered just in front of her above a patch of gorse, catching the day's last insects on the wing. At first she'd been worried. Even in the open like this, a single fantail wasn't a good sign, especially if the bird was uncommonly dark with just a few white tail feathers, like this one. She was relieved when it was joined by another. She watched them landing for a moment, darting off, circling, cutting back, tumbling over and under each other in the air. She laughed out loud when the birds began to flicker from one place to another without needing to travel the distance in between.

When at last they disappeared entirely, she drank from the bottle and walked on. Martha had taught her to read more signs than just fantails. A hawk on its broad arc always meant good things were going to happen, though Katherine rarely managed to pick them out with her weak eyes. When, last spring, a single magpie had taken up residence near the house, she'd thrown stones at it every day until it flew away and didn't come back. A flock of pigeons flying up the valley could signal a change in the weather from good to bad if it was a sunny day. If they flew down the valley under heavy clouds, the weather was going to improve.

She'd taught herself, as well, just by watching—the best she could, anyway—and listening. The small, green rifleman, the dull warbler, the brown creeper, the tiny silvereye with its noisy twittering; they all sounded different, and each told her something. Sometimes she didn't know exactly what, because there were so many, and their messages were complicated. She was still learning.

Recently she'd been silly enough to tell Maurice about

the birds. They'd both been down at the river collecting water. She'd walked up the riverbank to talk to him and had pointed out two black dots swimming in the rapids that she was sure were ducks.

"That means the river isn't going to flood."

"That's stupid. It's just two birds. How can they mean anything?"

Kate could see that she'd made him angry. Not that his anger scared her anymore. While she'd grown bigger and stronger, her brother was still skinny. Martha said he looked as if a stiff breeze might knock him over. Besides, if she had to, she could easily outrun him.

"You may as well say this rock is a good sign," he said, scornfully.

Warily, she watched him pick up the rock he'd just prodded with the end of his crutch. He threw the rock out into the river, obviously trying to hit the ducks, but missed by a long way.

"It's all stupid nonsense. It's just made up."

"Yes," she said, trying to calm him. "You're right."

She hadn't believed it, though. The river wouldn't flood any time soon.

Now she'd reached the lake. She took another drink from the bottle and felt herself sway as though the ground were moving. She giggled. She tried not to think any more about Maurice. He spoilt things, even when he wasn't here. She didn't understand why he had to be so difficult. An eel ribboned slowly past, close to where she stood. She sat on the ground and drank until the bottle was almost empty, and watched as the world opened up. The last daylight faded, and the moon drifted clear of the mountains.

That was where she was when she saw the spirit. He walked out of the trees on the far side of the lake and came slowly towards her in the moonlight, his body glowing. He'd disguised himself as a man. He probably didn't want to frighten her. She knew what he really was, though. It was obvious; although, in the days that followed, she found it impossible to remember exactly what he'd looked like. The way he fell out of her memory must have also been part of his disguise.

He approached her, and they spoke. He sat down next to her and she shared what was left in her bottle. She did remember that. They laughed. When she tried to stand, she stumbled and fell, and he helped her.

She didn't remember walking to the big kahikatea tree. Maybe the spirit carried her. Or perhaps, like the fantails, they'd moved from one place to another in a flash, without the need to go between. The gin was finished and she was lying on the dry grass beneath the tree. When she put her hand above her head she felt the trunk with her fingertips. She was aware that he was kissing her neck and his hands were touching her. Although, of course, they weren't hands, really they were wings. She wanted to see his true shape, and may have asked him to show her, but it was hard to keep her eyes open. She wasn't afraid. She felt grateful that he'd appeared to her at last. He was warm and heavy. She was looking past his long straight hair to the branches of the tree far above her. She put her arms around him. She could feel him move. Between the branches she saw the stars.

The last thing she remembered when she woke hours later, alone and sore, was the spirit walking away. His body had glowed in the moonlight. And there, still watching her, right in the middle of his back, was an impossible eye.

TWENTY-SEVEN

5 FEBRUARY 2011

Suzanne had arranged for the family to go back to her house after Maurice's service. Everyone had said they would come, even William. "I'll pop my head in, just for a few minutes," he'd told her when she'd rung to invite him.

No one thought it worth the trouble of moving their car. They walked together, part of the same tribe in their dark suits and dresses and refulgent shoes. Despite what the BBC had predicted, the sun was still out and everyone was in an upbeat mood. Danny and George had retrieved a football from their father's car. Suzanne watched them passing it, rather skilfully, she thought, although she was no expert. Cameron and Benoît joined in, alternating between being teammates and opposition. Arthur and William trailed behind, no doubt taking turns with their monologues. She walked near the middle, the fulcrum, connected to everyone.

Suzanne saw that Astrid was keeping a close eye on the boys. Not hovering, but aware. Lately there had been some tension between Tim and Astrid. Tim had implied that it was mostly about his work, the uncertain future of his branch office, and family finances. That's all he'd told her. She knew from experience, her own and other people's, that marriages were almost always in a state of flux. Reading a marriage from the outside was close to a black art, like divining tea leaves. All she could do was include them in her prayers and hope that everything would work out.

A woman with two small dogs on leads created a bottleneck on the footpath. Afterwards, Suzanne found herself walking next to William.

"This business must be bringing up a lot of old memories," he said. "How are you feeling?"

"A little stunned. I thought I'd put it all behind me."

"Of course. How many times did you end up going back there, in the end?"

"Four. I don't regret it, though."

"Of course."

She could tell he was trying to be nice.

"Such a wild place," he continued. "It still scares me to think about those forests. I dream about them sometimes. They were so primitive. It was like stepping back in time."

"I actually came to love the bush, eventually; once I could look after myself out there."

"All I remember is feeling lost all the time. Or about to become lost."

They rounded the corner together and a gust of cold wind hit them. William tugged at the brim of his hat. She suddenly felt very fond of him.

"Do you know the memory that keeps coming back to me most often?" she asked.

"No."

"It's really got nothing to do with Julia or the children."

"I'd like to hear."

"I'm not a hundred percent sure which trip it was exactly, probably the last one. It was early evening and I was driving through this tiny little town. You know the type they have there, just a pub and a dozen houses."

"Yes." He was watching her intently. His eyes watered in the cold wind.

"There was a small wooden church with a graveyard in the front. Out of curiosity I stopped. The church door wasn't locked, so I wandered in. There were just a dozen pews, the altar, and a pulpit."

"It sounds lovely."

"Actually, no, it was cold and dusty, a bit of a wreck, really. I'm not even sure if it was still being used. I couldn't find a light switch and it was quite dark, but I sat in the front and began to pray, although the place wasn't what you'd call uplifting. That was when I realised there was a bird trapped inside—a fantail. Do you remember those?"

"Vaguely."

"I used to know the Māori name, pee-something or other. Anyway, it was fluttering around in the rafters. God knows how long it had been trapped. I couldn't just leave it to die, so I went outside and found a rock and propped open the main door. Then I sat on a bench among the gravestones and waited. After a while, it came out. It flew over my head, across the road, and into the bush. I was so happy."

She was expecting William to find her story overly sentimental. But, when she glanced over, he was looking at her fondly.

"Funny, isn't it," he said, "the things we remember when we get old?"

She smiled. "Yes, it is."

* * *

Fitting everyone into her living room was something of a squeeze. Suzanne sat in the armchair. Pride of place.

"How are you doing, Mum?" Cameron held out a plate of shortbread.

"Fine. I was just thinking that most of you never even met Maurice."

"I remember him vaguely, not much, though, just that he was a bit stuck up."

"I suppose he was."

"Anyway, it doesn't matter. We're here to support you."

Tim asked if it was all right to bring out what he called Maurice's artefacts. She didn't mind, so he fetched them from her room. People passed around the dog collar, the watch, and the notched stick. They held them somewhat reverently, turning each in their hands as though a different angle might give them an insight into its history.

Arthur was standing by the radiator. "It's a tally stick," he said, addressing no one in particular.

"Sorry, what was that?" asked Astrid, who was nearest. She was holding the stick, running her fingers over the rows of notches.

"That's a tally stick. They were common, right from the Middle Ages."

The conversation died away as people turned to listen. Even Danny looked up from his screen. Astrid passed the stick to Arthur.

"Have you seen one before?" asked Suzanne.

"I had a colleague in the history department in Edinburgh who used to collect them. His office was full of the things. He must've had at least thirty, all slightly different. These cuts here usually represent an amount that's owed by one person to another. Generally, the wider the cut, the more money. But not always."

"So it's a sort of IOU?" asked Cameron.

"Yes, exactly."

Suzanne had always imagined Arthur to have been a

diabolical teacher; a real droner. As he continued to speak, however, she saw that he could command a room. He had a certain rumpled charm. He explained that if it really were a tally stick, it would probably have been sawn in half lengthways to create two interlocking sides.

"If you had the short end, then it was you who owed the money. That's where the expression 'the short end of the stick' comes from."

"I thought that came from when people drew straws," said Tim.

"So did I," said Benoît, "to decide who is thrown out of the boat."

"Or eaten," said William.

There was laughter.

Arthur held up the stick. "No, the expression comes from these."

"Is it worth any money?" asked Tim.

"Not in itself," said Arthur. "I mean, you couldn't sell it for much. But who knows how much each notch signified, back when it was made."

"May I see?" said Suzanne.

Arthur passed the stick to Tim, who passed it to her.

"Is this the short or the long end?" she asked.

"To be able to tell, we'd need the other half," said Arthur.

Danny looked up "tally stick" on Suzanne's computer. There were lots of images. There wasn't much relevant information, though, beyond what Arthur had already told them.

* * *

It was late afternoon before people started to leave. Arthur was the first to make his excuses. When his taxi appeared, Suzanne walked him to the door. He surprised her by embracing her. She could smell the ghost of his pipe in his jacket, and his beard brushed against her cheek, as soft as baby hair. As she watched him shuffle down the path, it occurred to her that this would be the last time she'd see him. They were old. Neither of them were what you'd call fighting fit. She wondered who would claim the dubious prize of attending the other's funeral.

A short time later, Tim and Astrid left with threshold promises to visit again soon. There was talk about George's upcoming birthday. The boys both kissed her solemnly on the cheek. William went with them. They were giving him a ride to the station. He thanked her for inviting him and genuinely seemed to mean it.

When Cameron and Benoît were the only ones left, they helped her carry the dishes into the kitchen. She filled the sink and washed while Benoît dried. Cameron put everything away.

"That was interesting, about the stick," said Cameron. "What are you going to do with it?"

"I don't know. I hadn't really thought about it. Maurice's remains are being buried next week, at the family's memorial headstone. I suppose I could bury the stick with him."

"Do you want us to come?" asked Cameron.

"No. You've done enough."

Benoît touched her arm. "Are you sure?"

"I'd actually rather it was just me."

"This stick must've been important to him, I think," said Benoît. "Otherwise why would he carry it with him? So maybe it is good if it is buried with his bones."

"What do you think happened to Maurice; I mean, before he died?" asked Cameron.

She looked out the window as a squirrel flashed along the top of the brick wall in the gloom. The dark had come quickly.

"Of course, I've imagined terrible things. Evil people. They might've kept him prisoner, possibly the other children as well. Maybe they were abused, I don't know. There are cases where that type of thing has happened; children who've been kidnapped for years. But I actually prefer to imagine that a family found Maurice and kept him safe. I know that sounds naive."

"It's possible," said Benoît.

"Yes," said Cameron. "Definitely."

She could tell they were humouring her.

"Anyway, that's the story I prefer to hold onto."

Cameron gave her a quick sideways hug. "Well, we'll never know. So you're right, why not look on the bright side?"

* * *

After the boys had gone, Suzanne felt exhausted. All the chatter had drained her. The rain had arrived while they'd been doing the dishes. It fell suddenly and hard enough that Cameron had looked out the window and said, "Look at that." Although they'd planned to walk back to the church, Benoît had phoned for a taxi to drop them at their car.

She went into the living room and sat on the couch. She could hear the rain beating down. The stick—*tally stick*—was on the mantelpiece. She stared at it for a long time before she made up her mind. John's expensive watch would be buried with Maurice's remains.

Rightly or wrongly, the boy had always idolised his father. The stick, though, was too important to put beneath the ground. It could stay right where it was. When she died, it would go to Tim. He in turn could pass it on to one of the boys. Although the stick's significance was unknown, it could still serve as something beautiful and mysterious for her family to carry forward out of the past.

That decision made, she closed her eyes.

Pīwakawaka. Yes, that was it, the Māori name for the bird she'd seen in the old church.

She remembered how it had hovered and darted over her as she'd sat on the dusty pew in the near dark. Although she hadn't said anything to William, at the time the bird's appearance had seemed significant. It felt as though her prayer had miraculously been given shape. The word become flesh.

She could see the bird now. It was fluttering above her, white tail spread. She heard its tweets and the sound of its wings mingling with the spatter of the rain against the window. With her eyes still closed, Suzanne smiled.

TWENTY-EIGHT

27 APRIL 1983

Suzanne took a plastic tray from the stack and walked the length of the glass cabinets. The café offered a selection of meat pies, sausage rolls, and triangular sandwiches: egg and cheese, ham and cheese, pineapple and cheese, and cheese, with, she presumed, extra cheese. There were also huge slices of cake, cream buns, and custard squares. She chose a steak pie.

The woman waiting for her at the till wore a pale-blue apron and had the lined mouth of a heavy smoker.

"I'll bring your pot of tea over," she said, handing Suzanne her change.

"Thank you."

"Knives and forks are right there."

Suzanne carried her food to a table, next to the window. The main street of Hokitika was all but deserted. A few cars performed a slow circle around the war memorial that sat in the middle of the town's largest intersection like a misplaced mausoleum.

This was her fourth trip to New Zealand and the longest she'd ever stayed. She'd already been here a few days off a month. Since her divorce from William and her move up to London, where she got regular temping work, she was in a position to remain for as long as she wanted. Lately, though, she'd found herself dwelling on the idea that this trip might be her last. She was walking tracks she'd already been along, following creeks she'd been up (and down) before, sometimes more than once. She was crossing off things that had already been crossed off. For the first time, she felt a sense of futility. Without knowing exactly when it had happened, she'd stopped expecting to find anything new.

But the pie was good, crisp pastry, with lots of tender meat. Cameron and Tim would've accused her of being a hypocrite. *The food Stasi*, that's what Tim had called her the last time she visited his student flat.

The woman from the till arrived with Suzanne's pot of tea. "There you go."

"Thank you."

"No worries."

"Would you mind taking a quick look at a photograph? My sister and her family are missing."

The woman, whose name tag read Tina, took the photograph Suzanne held out and studied it.

"Oh yeah, right, I remember this. It was on the news a while back."

"Five years this month."

"Is that right? That long?"

"I'm afraid so."

"What was their name again?"

"Chamberlain."

The woman's head bobbed. "Yeah, yeah, that's right. I remember."

Suzanne guessed that she was about fifty but looked older, skinny rather than slim. She smelt of cigarette smoke and hairspray. She may have been beautiful when she was a young woman, but these days only her eyes were pretty without effort.

"It was big news around here. English tourists or something? Just disappeared?"

"Yes. They haven't been found yet. The woman, Julia, she's my sister."

The waitress made a sympathetic wince, like a nervous tic. "That must be tough."

"Thank you."

Suzanne had relived this conversation with only minor variations hundreds of times over the years.

"This girl here, how old would she be now?"

She was pointing at Katherine.

"She would've just turned seventeen."

"There was a girl in here, maybe a year ago, could've been her. I've a good memory for faces."

Suzanne was about to ask more questions, when the door buzzer sounded, and a noisy group of road workers came in.

"Sorry, I've gotta look after these people. If you can wait a bit, I'll come back out."

"All right. Thank you."

Suzanne finished her food while she waited, and then sat looking out at the street. On the other side of the road, a large seagull raided the rubbish bin. It was twenty minutes before the waitress returned. She held up a packet of cigarettes and a lighter.

"It's my break. Do you mind if we go outside?"

"Not at all."

Suzanne followed her onto the street and down an alley between brick firewalls. At the back of the café was a courtyard where half a dozen rubbish bags were piled in one corner. The rear wall was only waist height and on the other side was a road and then a potholed section where several large trucks were parked. Beyond that was the river mouth. Nothing about it was charming.

The waitress sat at a plastic table in the sunshine and held out the cigarettes.

"You want one, love?"

"No, thank you. I don't smoke."

"Good on ya."

Shielding the lighter from the cold breeze coming off the river, she leant into the flame and Suzanne could hear the hiss of air passing through her lips. The waitress blew smoke from the corner of her mouth.

"My name's Shelley, by the way."

"I'm Suzanne. Your name tag says Tina."

The waitress glanced down. "Nah, we all wear different ones for a laugh. We like to keep it interesting, around here."

Suzanne handed over the group photograph again, along with two blow-ups of Katherine alone.

"Do you mind if I take some notes?"

"Knock yourself out."

"You said the young woman who came in looked like my niece?"

"Yeah, I reckon. Like she would've looked by now."

"How certain are you?"

She bristled slightly. "Like out of a hundred?"

"I'm sorry. I don't mean to be skeptical, but I've had false alarms before, quite a few times. Would you say there was a strong resemblance?"

"Like I told you, I have a good memory for faces. She had the same mouth. Same eyes. The hair's the same colour too, but longer."

A sheep truck pulled in to the empty section, its tyres crunching the gravel. Both women looked over as the truck shuddered and stopped. The driver climbed stiffly down from the cab and walked away.

"I'm pretty sure she came in early afternoon. It was definitely after the lunch rush. But I'd remember her even if we'd been busy; you couldn't miss her. She was wearing these daggy old overalls and gumboots like they wear up at the freezing works. And her hair was a fright, a real bird's nest."

"So, she looked poor?"

"Or like a hippy. There's a lot of those around here. There's a happy-clappy Christian lot up by Westport as well, but she didn't look like one of them. She wasn't plain enough. And if you didn't notice her, you'd notice her baby, a real cutie."

"She had a baby?"

"Yeah."

"Was it hers?"

"I think so, yeah. A boy."

"How old was he?"

"Maybe eight or nine months, something like that. I got a bit clucky, which just shows how cute he was, eh. I've got four kids of me own, so I'm well over babies."

Suzanne shook her head. "I don't think it could be Katherine. She'd be too young to be a mother."

"It's not impossible."

Suzanne got as many details as she could. The girl had been quiet. Yes, the waitress would say she was nervous. Sure, she spoke "like people around here talk." When it was time to pay for her food she'd pulled out a bundle of twenty-dollar notes.

"I don't suppose you know if she had a car?"

She stubbed out her cigarette in the paua-shell ash-tray on the table.

"Nah, she was hitchhiking."

"Did she tell you that?"

"I saw her arrive when I was having a ciggy. Right over there." She pointed two nicotine-stained fingers at the parked trucks. "She hitched into town on a sheep truck."

TWENTY-NINE

28 APRIL 1983

Suzanne glanced around the break room at Webster Haulage. The walls were painted an insipid green, and next to the Zip on the wall, Miss December wore a come-hither smile and some of a nurse's uniform. Unwashed mugs filled the sink. The table was covered with layers of car magazines.

"I'll just go and see if Sean's back. Help yourself to a cup of tea," said the young receptionist. "There's milk in the fridge."

"Thank you."

She sat waiting, listening to the noise of trucks and voices of the men coming from the yard outside. A few minutes later a middle-aged man with thin, ginger hair entered. She introduced herself. He gripped her hand briefly, with a palm that was soft and damp.

"So, what did you want to see me about?" asked Sean Mulligan.

"I'd like to ask you about a hitchhiker, a young woman you possibly gave a ride to about a year ago."

"Oh, okay, right. I thought you were probably from Social Welfare."

"No."

"That's a relief. I'm a bit behind with my kids' payments." He grinned, embarrassed, and glanced over his shoulder at the open door. "We're not supposed to pick up hitchhikers, it's company policy."

Suzanne could hear the receptionist talking to someone on the phone. "I don't want to get you in trouble, Mr Mulligan. I'm just trying to find a missing girl."

"Like a runaway?"

"Not exactly. Her name's Katherine. She's my niece."

"Fair enough."

He closed the door before they sat facing each other over the table.

"Sometimes I pick up hitchhikers, you know, just for the company. Driving can get pretty boring and I like to find out about people's lives. A lot of them are tourists. I've met people from all over the place."

"This would've been March or April last year. It's possible you dropped her behind a café in Hokitika."

He nodded. "That's where I park up if I stop for a break."

Suzanne passed him a photograph. "That's out of date. Last year she would have just turned sixteen."

The driver took a pair of reading glasses out of his pocket and studied the photograph carefully. "Yeah, I think that's her."

Suzanne was surprised. She'd been sure he would deny any strong resemblance between the hitchhiker and Katherine.

"You think this was the girl you picked up?"

"Hang on, did she say I touched her or something?"

"No."

"Is that what this is about?"

"Really, no."

"Because, if she did, it's a bloody lie."

"It's nothing like that, Mr Mulligan. She's just missing. All I want to do is find her."

Sean Mulligan nodded slowly. Suzanne showed him several more photographs, mostly enlarged sections of group pictures, pixilated and blurry-edged, where

Katherine had been lifted from family portraits and class photographs.

"Haven't you got anything more recent?"

"Sorry, no. I wish I did."

"It's tricky to say for sure. If it's the same girl, she's changed a lot. I really didn't touch her, I swear."

"I just want to find her."

"Okay."

"Can you start by telling me exactly where you picked her up?"

"She was at Blackwater Creek bridge. That's on the highway north of Haast. It's the middle of nowhere. She was just standing there with an old army duffel bag and her baby in a thingy on her back."

Suzanne took out her notebook and wrote down the name Blackwater Creek. "Do you remember what time of day that was?"

"Earlyish, about eight or eight-thirty in the morning. She wasn't sticking her thumb out."

"But you stopped anyway?"

A shrug. "It's the middle of nowhere, and she had a baby. Actually, at first I drove past, but straight away I felt bad, so I pulled over. I figured, what else would she be doing out there except waiting for a lift?"

"And what did she do when you stopped?"

"She stood there for a little bit, just looking at the truck. I could see her in the side mirror. Then she started to walk down so I leant over and pushed open the door."

"And she climbed straight in?"

"First she had to take the baby off her back. She seemed a bit nervous."

"A young woman alone, a big truck, a strange man."

"Sure, yeah, I guess."

"What was your first impression of her?"

"I don't know. That she was a bit odd. I mean, she was wearing men's work clothes straight out of the fifties, and her hair looked as if it had never seen a brush. She certainly wasn't wearing any makeup. I'll tell you what, neither of my daughters would be seen dead looking like that."

"What colour was her hair?"

"Dark, same as this girl." He fluttered the photograph in his hand. "Actually, with her hair and skin and everything I thought maybe she was a Māori."

"So, her skin was dark?"

"Yeah, but she might've just been out in the sun a lot."

"Then what?"

"She wouldn't put the baby in the back of the cab, so she sat with it on her lap. I know that's not legal, but she had the seat belt going over both of them, so I figured it was all right. There's never any traffic cops on that stretch, anyway."

"What did you talk about?"

"It's hard to remember, exactly. I think I asked her if she wanted a ride all the way to Hoki. She said, yes, please. She was very polite, I remember that."

"Did she speak with an English accent, maybe, a bit like mine?"

"Nah, she had no accent at all."

"What else did you discuss?"

"Nothing much. I didn't push it. Some people just like to sit quietly when I give them a lift. It's a free country."

"Did she tell you her name?"

"I don't think so."

"Are you sure?"

"Sorry. It's hard to remember, a year's a long time."

"Anything else?"

"I gave her a Crunchie."

"I'm not sure what that is."

He looked incredulous. "You know, a Crunchie bar—hokey-pokey and chocolate, gold wrapper."

"Ah, right, yes." She'd seen them in petrol stations.

"I normally keep a couple in the glove box. She said she'd never had one before, but I thought she was kidding. She shared it with the baby. He made a hell of a mess. She cleaned his hands by putting them right in her mouth, which didn't seem very hygienic."

"Did you think it was her baby?"

"Sure. Why not?"

"Even though she was young?"

"My wife had our first one when she was nineteen."

Sean Mulligan remembered a tattoo on the girl's finger. Suzanne passed him her notebook, and on a fresh page he made a sketch. He thought she'd had another tattoo on the back of her wrist beneath her sleeve but only got a glimpse. The baby fell asleep, apparently. For most of the trip, the girl just looked out the window. He'd taken her all the way to Hokitika, a ride of two and a half hours. Looking slightly guilty, he admitted that, before she got out, the girl had tried to give him money.

"Did you take it?"

"She said that she didn't want to owe me anything. She went on a bit about that. She was pretty insistent, you know." He shifted in his seat. "In the end I took forty bucks, just to make her happy."

"Did she say where she was going or what she was going to do next?"

"No. She thanked me very politely. She headed off toward the main street. I never saw her again."

* * *

That evening, Suzanne sat on the bed in her motel room with her back against the pillow and sipped white wine. A map was spread next to her over the bed, with Blackwater Creek circled in red several times. In the small bathroom, the shower-head dripped. She'd closed the door but could still hear it. The curtains were open and the headlights of cars on the main road played over the walls.

She didn't believe that the young woman with the baby had been Katherine. Obviously there was a resemblance. She was sure, however, that if her niece and this hitchhiker were standing side by side, the similarities would turn out to be slight. The same hair colour. A shared curve of the jawline. Perhaps not even that much.

Before Julia and her family vanished, Suzanne had believed that people, herself included, were like cameras recording reality from slightly different angles. Now she knew that memories weren't reliable. They were shaped and folded out of assumption and supposition, put together piece by piece from what people expected to see and what they wanted to see. Even out of what they believed you wanted them to have seen. Memory and the hard facts about the past, seldom had much to do with each other.

She got up and poured herself another glass of wine and stared out into the almost-empty car park. The girl standing on the side of the road at Blackwater Creek had probably been a local, a Coaster. Most likely she'd been travelling in a car with her boyfriend or maybe her parents. There had been a blazing row. Over what? It didn't really matter. There were always things to fight about. The driver pulled over. The girl angrily leapt out, with her baby. The car took off. Maybe the driver intended to come back after everyone cooled off. Maybe not. Either way, it probably wasn't long before Sean the helpful truck driver arrived on the scene.

Taking her drink, she went outside. The bulb above the door of her unit wasn't working, but the one next door had attracted several moths. They were large enough that she could hear them rebounding off the hot glass. She stood and listened to the softly repeated thunks, as if people on the other side of the motel were playing a game of tennis.

It was time to call it quits. No one could ever say she hadn't been loyal to Julia. She'd done her very best. But, before she left the Coast for good, there was one final annoying loose thread to follow.

On the map, the nearest town to Blackwater Creek was called Rossville. She'd asked the motel's manager about it when she checked in.

"The only people living around there these days are feral," he told her, darkly. "Squatters, mostly."

She was certain nothing would come of going to Rossville tomorrow, but she'd go anyway. She had to be sure.

PART IV

THIRTY

LATE SUMMER, 1982

Maurice's fingers were clever. Turning the dried bud in his hand, he deftly snipped away the remains of the leaves with hairdressing scissors, exposing hundreds of bright pinheads like sticky dew. He was sitting in the shearing shed, at an old school desk he'd moved into the afternoon sunlight coming through the open doors. He put the bud in the shoebox on the floor, and took another from the box by his elbow. Peters had been pushing him to finish. It had been a good growing season—Peters claimed it was the best ever—and, although he'd been working for days, there were still hundreds of buds left to tidy up. At night he trimmed in his sleep, his fingers twitching beneath the blanket.

As he worked, his thoughts circled back to his sister and her baby. He never held the baby. He didn't even look at it, if he could help it. No, he wouldn't think about it. Instead, while his fingers snipped and turned, he imagined walking from room to room in their house in Hornton Street. He had a mental map. He always started at the front door. After that, he went up the stairs—twelve steps to the landing, turn right, eight more steps. One by one, he visited the bedrooms. His and then Katherine's, with the blue curtains. Afterwards, Tommy's room. He even dared his parents' room, with the big brass bed. From there, you could look out the window into the front garden.

When he was finished inside the house, he'd go out

onto the street. He would stand on the footpath under the tree near the gate. He remembered many of the neighbouring houses. There was a playground on the corner, he was sure of that, with a metal fence around it.

He could perform the same trick with a few other parts of the city. Hyde Park, where they'd often gone for family walks on a Sunday, was easy. Also Trafalgar Square down to Parliament and the bridge and the streets around the Natural History Museum.

More and more, though, when he did manage to think of something he hadn't remembered before, he wondered if he could trust it was real. He hated the idea he was inventing things. That would be no better than a lie. When he finally got back to London—and he was determined that one day he would—he was going to check he'd got everything right.

"Peters? Mate, where are ya?"

Maurice's head jerked up. He dropped the bud in his hand. The voice had been close; right outside the shed. A man. A man who wasn't Peters. That was all he could say for sure. Whoever it was called out again. Maurice had to stop himself from running outside. He wanted to shout that he was here! He was being forced to work! He didn't owe anything, not really, despite Martha's and Peters's lies. He'd demand the stranger take him away.

Still gripping the scissors, he limped without his crutch to the wall, where he put one eye to a crack in the boards, pressing his cheek into the wood. His view of the yard was restricted to a thin slice. A man moved into sight. Maurice couldn't see his face; just that he was tall and skinny. His dark jeans had mud splattered up the back of the legs. He carried a sagging backpack and a rifle on a strap over one shoulder.

"Jesus. I've told ya not to come here."

It was Peters.

"Calm down, mate."

Maurice could see the stranger, but Peters was standing out of sight.

"Look I've told ya before, ya can't just bowl up here."

"Something's happened."

"Keep ya voice down."

The man moved out of sight and the voices faded.

Maurice waited. Just as he'd thought, Peters came to the shed a short time later. He was carrying a shoebox half full of untrimmed buds, which he put on the desk. He looked around.

"How ya getting on?"

"I'm almost finished these. See."

Peters prodded the box on the floor with the toe of his boot. He picked one out and held it at arm's length.

"Yeah, this is good."

"I'd say the whole enterprise has been efficacious."

Maurice watched his face and saw him decide to let it pass. Obviously Peters had other things on his mind.

"I'll take this lot with me now. Here's some more to be going on with."

"Okay."

"You eaten?"

"I had those sausages."

"I have to go down to Martha's place a bit later. Maybe I'll bring ya back a sandwich and a couple of boiled eggs. Might be a while, though."

"All right."

Maurice waited for a few minutes after Peters left before he followed. Skirting around the back of the shearing shed took him close to the dogs, locked in their runs. All three stood and wagged their tails. They were disappointed when he offered them no more than a sniff of his hand. Bess whined and he shushed her beneath his breath.

"It's okay, girl. I'll come back later and see you."

She whined again as he moved away.

He approached the bus from the horse paddock, where there were patches of gorse he could use to hide if Peters or the stranger appeared. There was no sign of anyone. He found himself crawling the last few feet through long grass. Crouched by the number plate, he listened to the muted voices from inside. The back window was covered by cardboard taped to the inside, but after years of sun and condensation, it had curled at the edges. He peered in through a small triangle of filthy glass.

Peters was standing with his back to him, bending, doing something on the bed. The stranger was rolling a joint on the bench. His lighter flared. The man's thin face was made longer and thinner by a goatee beard that hung to his chest. He'd taken off his backpack, so Maurice could see he wore an orange deer-hunting vest over his T-shirt. When the man turned towards the open door, Maurice saw the back of the vest. Someone had painted three circles, one inside the other; a bullseye. A joke.

"Okay, good, she's all there."

"I know," said the stranger.

Peters moved aside, and Maurice saw piles of money, green notes, arranged in rows on the bed.

"Yeah, best to count it, though."

"Fair enough."

Peters lifted one of the squabs off the long bench seats. He raised the hinged lid, knelt and reached inside up to his armpit to pull out a square of plywood. A false end. One at a time, Peters produced two pillow-sized plastic bags. They were plump with finished buds. It was everything that Maurice had trimmed in the last few weeks. Peters passed the bags to the stranger, who put them carefully into his backpack.

"Right, I'll see ya again in a couple of weeks."

"I don't want ya just turning up here again, okay?"

"I already said."

"No, I mean it."

"So do I, mate."

"I'll come to your place as usual on the fourth."

"How much will you have by then?"

"Half again, maybe a bit more. Depends. Then that'll be it for the season."

"No wucking forries." When Peters didn't laugh, he said, "See ya."

Maurice slid down onto his knees and belly-squirmed into the dark space below the bus. The earth was damp and smelt of mould. Parting the grass with his hands, he watched the stranger, his pack now full, walking up the valley.

No matter how much he wanted to follow, Maurice knew he couldn't. His crutch made it impossible to move through the bush quickly or quietly. He kept watching as the man moved out of sight. He took careful note of the direction he went in, not that it meant much. It wasn't like the stranger was a bird, who'd travel in a straight line back to where he'd come from.

He could hear Peters moving around above him. Something scraped loudly, and his eyes were drawn to a metal box the size of a suitcase that was sticking out from the bottom of the bus. As quietly as he could, he pulled himself closer. Now he could see the silver lines where the box had been welded into place. When he placed his palm on the cold metal, he felt a vibration as something was placed inside.

He smiled. He didn't have to see to know what Peters was doing. He was hiding his money.

* * *

Peters put a sandwich in greaseproof paper down on the desk in the shearing shed. When he unwrapped it, Maurice saw that the bread was filled with slices of mutton, lettuce, cheese and onion relish.

"Thank you."

"No problem."

Peters cast an eye over the buds he'd delivered earlier. "What's the hold-up?"

"Some of these need a lot of work."

Peters grunted. It was undeniable, though, that some plants produced buds that were harder to trim.

"I still want 'em all done by the end of the day. Tomorrow we've got to harvest the last plants up by the waterfall."

It was an hour's walk to the waterfall. About fifty fully grown plants would have to be cut and carried back to be dried. The horse would help with the hauling, but it would still take at least two trips each way.

"Why does it matter how quickly it's done?"

"I reckon it's gunna rain most of this week. We need to get all the plants drying."

He could tell Peters was lying.

When Maurice was alone again, he kept working. He'd still be working when it was dark, but for once he didn't resent it. His fingers could do the work by themselves. That left him free to think. And suddenly there was a lot to think about.

THIRTY-ONE

LATE SUMMER, 1982

Tommy is agog. He stands in Peters's top paddock and slowly revolves, head tilted back, slack-mouthed. Above him are thousands of flashing lights. Burning raindrops. Tossed jewels. Each one reflects the afternoon sun. They're flowing like a river, heading in the direction of the bush, and back from the bush, vibrating with one urgent note.

Tommy is trying to look at all the bees at the same time, but it can't be done. There are too many. They're moving too quickly. Excited, he raises his hands to touch them. At the same time, he makes his own deep drone. Faster and faster he turns, growing louder and louder, until he's a grunting dervish, whirling barefoot across the paddock. Around and around, feet kicking up dust.

His spinning has carried him near to the hives. The bees must veer around him in order to land and take off. A single bee slips between his collar and the skin of his neck. He can feel it crawling. Alarmed, he slaps His mouth snaps shut in surprise. Stumbling over his own feet, he crashes awkwardly against the nearest hive, hard enough that the stacked boxes tilt on their base. The tower teeters, leans a fraction further, tips.

The top two boxes crash loudly onto the grass. The close thunder confuses Tommy and he stops spinning. He's lost sight of the pretty flashes. Troubled, he stares down at the boxes as an indignant objection rises about him.

When the stinging begins, Tommy prances and paws and slaps at himself. He doesn't know where the pain is coming from, just that it hurts. Legs, feet, arms, neck, cheeks, ears, nostrils; every patch of exposed skin is being attacked.

Slapping and bellowing, he begins to run. Only luck sees him head toward the river. Something is chasing him. He looks behind, but cannot see what it is. He can feel it, though, again and again, as hot needles in his skin. He can hear it. He's only twenty feet from the water when his foot sinks into a crumbling rabbit hole. There's no time to put out his hands before he hits the ground face-first.

For a moment, he lies winded. When he staggers back to his feet, blood is flowing from his broken nose into his mouth and dripping from his chin. He starts to run again, but the fall has turned him around. He's moving away from the safety of the water, now; going back in the direction he has just come from.

The bees start up again.

Tommy is almost back at the hives when he finally sinks to his knees. His face is bloating. His throat feels squeezed. Every breath is a long groan. He's still being stung, but he can't feel the barbs anymore. Rolling onto his back, he looks directly into the sun. His eyes are swelling closed. The dark edges of the world push in. For a moment, though, he's still left with the light.

Prettyshine ... pretty

* * *

It was Maurice who found Tommy the next morning. His brother was lying stiffly on his back on the grass, his face swollen. Maurice had already seen the overturned hive, but if he needed further evidence of what had happened, dozens of poison sacs were still embedded in Tommy's skin. Dead bees were tangled in his hair.

Maurice got Peters, who solemnly carried Tommy's body down to the farmhouse. Martha saw them coming and called Kate, and the two women were waiting by the time the men reached the gate.

"Poor little bugger," said Martha. "We'd better get him sorted out."

Tommy's body was laid out on a Formica table that Peters brought out onto the veranda. Martha held the baby while Kate picked the bees out of Tommy's hair. One was still moving, weakly, and she flicked it away into the garden. Dying had diminished her brother, though he'd never been more than small to begin with. She got a bucket of water and several clean cloths, along with a block of hard, yellow soap.

"Do you want to help?" she asked Maurice.

He shook his head and looked at his feet.

Kate and Martha gently removed Tommy's clothes. When he was naked, the women began to wash him. Tommy's belly was sunken and hard and Kate was ashamed to see how many bruises and scars had been camouflaged by dirt. She poured water over his hair, before lathering the soap into it with her fingers. Shielding his face with her hand, she rinsed his head clean. Filthy water ran off the Formica and onto the wooden veranda, where it slid between the cracks of the boards, onto the earth. She dried his hair with a towel and combed it back. Although she scrubbed for a long time, Kate realised that Tommy's feet would never be anything but the colour of the dirt.

Martha went inside and, as if to prove that there was

nothing she didn't have stored somewhere in the house, returned with a small pair of black trousers and a boy's shirt printed with red and yellow flowers.

"The shirt's a bit too big, but it's the best we've got."

"It's nice," said Kate. "I reckon Tommy would've liked the flowers."

"I want to do something," said Maurice, quietly.

"Here." Kate handed him a towel.

Maurice patted Tommy dry. He helped to get the trousers and the shirt on and rolled up the cuffs of the trousers so it almost looked as though they fitted.

Peters said, "I guess we bury him over with the rest? I can make a cross or something."

"No," said Kate, firmly.

Everyone looked at her and waited.

"Tommy wouldn't want to be in the dark, under the ground."

"What do you want to do, then?" asked Martha.

"He always loved the light."

* * *

The rest of the day was spent building the pyre. Peters said the easiest place for it was in the paddock behind the orchard. Despite moaning about the waste of good wood, he helped. It was his suggestion to use the old railway joists from behind the hay barn.

"Those'll make a good, solid base," he said.

Maurice and Kate watched as Peters showed them what he meant with a model made of kindling.

"You need to do it properly. Build it up like this, in layers. That way the air'll get in. D'ya see?"

"Yes," said Kate.

"It has to burn for a long time. Ya don't want it collapsing too soon."

They all worked. The joists proved to be even heavier than they looked. Martha watched the baby while she bundled dry cabbage-tree leaves into fagots. She made them until her hands were too stiff to carry on. By evening, everything was ready. Peters and Kate used the tabletop to carry Tommy who was now wrapped in a clean white sheet. The pyre was too high for Kate to get the body onto the top with any dignity, so it was Peters who laid him in place.

Kate thought that it would have been nice if Tommy had owned a special thing. A toy, perhaps. Of course, he had nothing like that. Instead, she'd hunted for things she thought he might've liked and arranged what she found around his body. There were several shards of stained glass and some bits of green and white glass from broken bottles. Reluctantly, Martha gave her a glass inkwell from the desk in the hall and three old copper coins. Kate also placed the bronze bowl from the Castle Pool shrine close to Tommy's head.

She'd wanted everything to sparkle and shine in the sun, but building the pyre had taken up the whole day, and the shadow of the ridge had already reached where they stood. The sun, though, was still on the mountains. Gently, she turned Tommy's head to see.

Never mind, the fire will make everything work.

Kate climbed down and returned to where the others were standing. She took the baby from Martha and they all watched as Peters sloshed petrol from a tin over the wood. The fumes rolled over them. When Peters had finished, he tossed the tin aside and stood back. Kate solemnly lit a candle and holding the flame away from the baby, she walked to the pyre.

"Careful, girlie. Not too close," said Martha.

As close as she dared, Kate lobbed the candle. Good luck saw it slip between the sleepers into the dry cabbage-tree leaves. There was a soft whump as the petrol ignited, and a flare from deep inside the wood. After some heavy smoke, the flames grew brighter and the smoke thinned, and the pyre burned clean. Eventually, the flames climbed to where Tommy's body lay.

Kate avoided looking at the shape of her brother. Instead, she stared at the mountains. When the sunlight left the tops, the clouds were a bright bloom. The sky gradually darkened, and soon the only light in the valley came from the burning pyre.

"Sorry about your brother," Peters said, speaking to them both. He walked away.

Martha also said goodnight. She hugged Kate and promised to help her with what needed to be done in the morning. She'd already warned Kate that the fire wouldn't burn all of Tommy's body. There'd be bones that would have to be gathered and buried.

Maurice and Kate stood together. The baby was asleep in her arms. It was easy to stare into the flames and think of nothing. It was a surprise when the pyre eventually collapsed inwards, just as Peters had planned. They stepped back as sparks and thin films of burning bark and cabbage-tree leaf rose into the night and watched them ride the shimmering column of heated air. Higher and higher, twisting and flickering, until they were burning among the bright band of stars above the valley.

"Tommy would've loved this, eh," said Kate.

Maurice stared into the flames. "I'm going to get away from here."

"When?"

"Soon. I have to do some things first."

"What?"

The firelight played over his face and he didn't answer her.

"He'll just find you and bring you back again."

"Not this time."

"He always does."

Maurice shook his head. "I'll come and say goodbye before I go."

After Maurice limped away into the darkness, Kate said a prayer. Even though her offerings hadn't been enough to save Tommy, she prayed that the spirits would look after him. She asked them to come down from the bush and take him away with them. She could almost see the spirits. There, in the corner of her eye. Tall figures, waiting patiently, wings folded behind, standing on the edge of the firelight.

THIRTY-TWO

LATE SUMMER, 1982

It was three days before Maurice ran away for the last time. Kate was woken just after dawn by tapping at her bedroom window. She left the baby sleeping in the bed. Maurice was standing outside, looking pale and serious. His face and hands were scrubbed red, and his hair was wet. After leaning his crutch against the house, he clambered awkwardly over the sill and stood by the window, fidgeting, and ignored the sleeping baby.

"Peters doesn't find me. It's the dogs, not him."

She had to lean closer to hear him.

"They'll just find you again this time."

"They won't."

"Why not?"

"I'm going to find the town," he said, suddenly fierce. "I'll tell people what happened, then I'll show them the way here so you'll be able to leave too."

He was so adamant that for a moment she believed him. She imagined strange men arriving in the valley; large, faceless figures in uniforms, coming out of the trees.

"It takes days to walk to town," she said, deliberately looking at his bad leg. "There's mountains and big rivers."

"That's just what they told you. You don't know if it's true."

"Neither do you."

"They're liars, both of them. Why don't you see that?"

"Shhh, you'll wake up Martha."

There was no arguing with Maurice when he turned goat-stubborn. The only thing she could do was let him go. Despite what he said, Peters and the dogs would find him. Most likely they'd bring him back before nightfall. The best she could hope for was that the beating he got wouldn't be too bad. It might even teach him a lesson.

"Which way will you go?" she asked.

"I'm going to follow the river to the ocean. When I get there, I'll walk north up the coast until I find the road. Or maybe I'll meet someone before then, a fisherman, or a farmer, someone anyway, who'll take me to a town."

He limped to the shelf, where Kate kept the notched stick. It was dusty and had been sitting there for so long she no longer noticed it.

"I want to take this with me."

"What for?"

"To show people. It's evidence."

"Martha hasn't even mentioned it in ages. I think she's forgotten about it."

"I still want to take it."

"Okay, I don't care."

"Here." He took a bundle of money from his pocket and thrust it at her.

"Where'd you get this?"

"I took it from Peters. Hide it. You might need it, one day."

She watched Maurice throw the stick out the window onto the grass. He climbed back out and retrieved it and his crutch. The sky was starting to blue.

"Be careful," she said.

He looked up at her. "I'll come back for you, I promise."

"Okay. I'll wait for you."

"It might only be a day or two."

"See you then."

Maurice nodded solemnly. He swivelled, almost grace-
ful, now that he was using his crutch again, and walked
away from her across the grass, the notched stick in his
free hand. She had an urge to call him back, to beg,
bully, or even blackmail him into not leaving. She was
ashamed to admit it, but her biggest fear was not that
Maurice would get lost in the bush or that, when he
was caught, he'd be badly beaten by Peters. What terri-
fied her was that he'd actually succeed in finding a
town. Then strangers really would come. They'd force
her to leave the valley. She knew it wouldn't make any
difference if she said she wanted to stay with Martha.

Full of fear, she watched her brother until he had
limped out of sight.

* * *

Maurice lay on the granite outcrop and used the binoculars he'd stolen from Peters to look through a gap in
the trees at the faded blue rectangle that was the roof of
the bus. It had been two days since he'd run away. After
saying goodbye to his sister, he'd collected his pack and
walked up the valley to this place, which he'd found
months ago. He'd already built a bivvy from old canvas
in the trees below the outcrop and stocked it with cans
of food and a bottle of water.

It both thrilled and scared him to be hiding so close.
A half-decent shout would be heard from the bus. He
imagined them talking about him down there, anxiously wondering where he might be. When all the time
he was here, watching them, laughing at them.

There'd been no movement since early the morning

before, when his sister and Martha had appeared. After they'd left, he'd watched Peters digging, and going back and forth between the bus and the shearing shed. The last Maurice had seen of Peters was midmorning, when he set out with a full pack, heading south. Today, there hadn't even been smoke from Martha's farmhouse.

He'd lied to his sister. He'd never had any intention of heading down the river. He'd tried that before, twice, and been caught both times. Not that he believed Katherine would've told on him, not at first. Once he'd been gone for a while, though, she'd get worried. She might think she was helping him, perhaps even saving him, by putting Peters and the dogs on his trail.

His plan was to wait here for at least another day. Only when Peters had figured him long gone would Maurice risk moving. He'd go north. The first river he came to he'd ignore. Eventually, he'd find one that would lead him to the coast.

The biggest risk had been stealing from Peters's bus. That had been the day before he left. He'd gambled that Peters wouldn't miss the binoculars or the hunting knife, which was only his second-best. Father's watch had been in a drawer. He'd been afraid that there'd be a lock on the hiding place in the floor, but the lid had lifted off easily. Inside was more money then he'd ever seen before. He risked taking two bundles of what he later saw were twenty-dollar notes.

Dinner that evening had been unbearably tense. Maurice kept looking at Peters for any sign that he'd discovered the theft. Peters didn't look like he knew. Even so, he might've been playing with him. He'd think it was a good joke to make Maurice sweat. When they'd walked back to the bus in the dark Maurice waited to be grabbed and shaken, accused. But when they'd reached the shearing shed, all Peters had said was a mumbled "Goodnight."

Maurice rolled onto his side on the rock and stood stiffly. There was still nothing to see, and he was hungry. He picked his way carefully down through the trees to the bivvy. A bed of pig-fern kept him off the ground and he had a blanket. The only thing his campsite lacked was a fire to cook on. Of course, he couldn't risk making smoke.

With the tip of the hunting knife, he folded back the jagged lid of a can of corned beef. Three tins of beef and two jars of Martha's bottled peaches was all the food he had been able to take without the theft being noticed. That and some apples. The trick would be to make it last until he found the town; a tin or jar each day—a little for breakfast, some for lunch, and then what was left over in the evening. Despite his promise to Katherine to be back in a day or two, he really didn't know how long it would take him to find the town.

As he ate, he found himself thinking about the dogs again.

Bess had been confused when he'd appeared outside her run in the darkness, shortly before dawn. The moon was full, so there'd been enough light to see clearly. When he unlatched the door, it didn't take any coaxing for her to come out. "Good girl." She sat waiting to see what he wanted. He stood with one leg on either side of her body, ready to clamp her in place if she tried to bolt, then ran his hand along her warm coat. He patted her head as she looked up at him. The other dogs were stirring.

Not wanting to alarm Bess, he reached around slowly and drew the knife from the sheath that was tucked into his belt. Peters sharpened all his knives using a whetstone. He often claimed the edge "could split a virgin's pube in half." When Bess saw the blade she whined, and nervously licked his hand. Maurice shifted to hold her tighter between his legs, but she was a good dog and didn't struggle. Bending, he lifted her jaw softly in his hand. He moved the knife close to the warm crook of her throat. He had no choice. Bess and the others always found him.

"Good girl. Good girl, everything's going to be fine."

It was only by building a wall in his mind between himself and what he was doing that he was able pull the blade hard across Bess's neck. A hot gush of blood covered his hand. It was then, when it was already too late, that Bess tried to struggle to her feet. He wished now that he'd held her for longer. He'd let her go too quickly. As he opened the gate to Mac's run, he could still hear her bubbling breaths and the scrabble of her claws on the hard ground.

By the time he got to Rust, the dog had known what was going to happen. Her ears were flat and she had her tail between her legs as he dragged her out of her run by the collar. He didn't blame her when she twisted her head around and tried to bite his hand. He was ashamed to remember how badly she'd died.

Maurice suddenly threw the empty tin as hard as he could into the trees behind the bivvy. He heard it strike a rock and bounce. Thinking about the dogs wasn't helping. He needed to focus on his plan. He'd watched the valley for long enough. First thing tomorrow morning, he'd pack up and leave.

THIRTY-THREE

LATE SUMMER, 1982

After Maurice left her room, Kate couldn't go back to sleep. She dressed and, leaving the baby asleep in the bed, went into the kitchen, where she began to prepare breakfast. She kept an ear out for the baby's waking sounds as she fried tomatoes and bread in dripping, and poached eggs and steamed spinach.

"What's the occasion?" asked Martha from the doorway. "Nothing. I just felt like making something nice."

"Good-oh. I'm not complaining."

Martha sat at the table and Kate served her.

"You all right, girlie?"

"Yeah, I'm fine. Thanks."

It was two hours before Peters came to the house. He didn't announce himself but sank onto the chopping block in the front yard and stared down at his boots as the chooks scratched around him. Kate saw him from the veranda. Carrying the baby on her hip, she went and fetched Martha from the garden.

"What's the matter with you?" asked Martha, standing by the gate. She brushed soil from her hands. Kate stood next to her, the joint of her bent finger in the baby's mouth.

Peters spoke from behind the veil of his dreadlocks. "He's killed the dogs."

"What?"

Martha moved closer so that she could hear, and Peters repeated himself.

"Who did?"

"The boy, who bloody else?"

Peters raised his head and Kate was shocked to see there were tears running down his cheeks into the grey of his beard. She'd never seen him cry before.

"All of them?" said Martha.

"Yeah."

"How?"

"Cut their throats."

"Jesus."

"Fuckin' oath."

"Where is he now?" asked Martha.

"How should I know?" he said bitterly. "He's buggered off."

There was a silence filled only by the sound of the chickens scratching for insects in the yard.

"I'll go and look," said Kate.

"I'll come too," said Martha.

They walked together, grim and not speaking. Pleased to be on the move, the baby wiggled in Kate's arms. He was getting heavy, but it wasn't worth moving him to her back for the short walk up to Peters's place.

"Did you know he was gunna do this?" asked Martha.

"No."

A sideways appraisal. "You sure?"

"He just said he was running away."

Kate heard the gate and, looking back, saw that Peters was following them. His head was still down and his shoulders folded forward around his chest so that he looked like a smaller man.

Kate wasn't sure if it had been Maurice or Peters who'd arranged the bodies of the three dogs in a row. They were on the grass in front of their runs, the ground black with blood. Their legs were all pointing in the same direction. Gaping necks. The smallest, Mac, was almost decapitated. Kate patted Bess's head, but it was hard and cold. Flies crawled across the blood that matted her fur and in and out of the wound on her neck and her tongue, which hung from her mouth and was covered with dirt.

Now she knew why Maurice's hair had been wet that morning, why he'd washed himself so well. Standing behind her, Martha swore loudly.

"Why'd he go and do that, then?"

"The dogs always find him."

"Yeah, but he didn't have to," said Martha, although she offered no alternative. "If Peters gets his hands on your brother, he'll kill him."

Kate looked over at Peters. He was hanging back by the shearing shed, rolling a cigarette in the shadow of the building. Martha was right, by murdering the dogs Maurice had guaranteed he'd never be able to come back to the valley. There could be no return to the ways things had been. Not for any of them.

* * *

Martha began to fret when Peters didn't appear for dinner that evening. She made Kate wait at the table, with the food in front of them still in the pots.

"He's probably just drunk," said Kate.

"Yeah, you're right."

At last, Martha sighed. "Well, we'd better not let it get cold, eh."

After dinner, they played backgammon. Martha was distracted. She kept making mistakes as she counted out her moves, and Kate won four games in a row. By the time they were ready to go to bed, Peters still hadn't appeared.

"I reckon you're right," said Martha, trying to convince herself. "He's just got pissed off his face and passed out. He'll turn up tomorrow."

The next morning, Kate left the house early, while Martha was still asleep. Kate had the baby swaddled against her back. Always in the past she'd been guaranteed a welcoming chorus of barks as she approached Peters's place. Now the silence seemed loud. No smoke came from the bus, although it was possible Peters hadn't yet lit a fire. She passed the grave, a single mound, where Peters must've buried the dogs. An empty whisky bottle sat on top of the fresh soil.

When Peters didn't reply to her call, she turned the handle and went into the bus. She'd never been inside before; there'd been no need. It was much as she'd imagined: small, dim, cluttered. Peters's own scent was there too, that heavy musk that leaked from him.

Everything smelt as though it were held together by smoke and sweat. The baby moved against her back, as if troubled.

She began to look around. The obvious answer was that Peters had gone to hunt for Maurice. His gun was gone; that was a bad sign. So was his green pack, the one he always took with him when he went into the bush.

Martha insisted on seeing for herself, when Kate told her what she'd found. Martha had woken that morning with feet more swollen than normal, so it took her longer than it had the day before to walk to the bus. For the last stretch, she had to lean on Kate.

"Pull off that cardboard. Go on, I need to see properly."

"Won't he be angry?"

"Just do it. Hurry up."

With sunlight coming through the windows, the bus seemed smaller. Martha moved around, looking at everything. She touched the empty coat hangers on the rail in the corner, making them chime faintly. Pulling open a drawer, she stirred the contents. Finally she slumped onto the edge of the bed.

"Pull back that rug."

Underneath was a metal hatch cut into the floor. When Kate dragged it aside, the space was empty.

"That prick," Martha said, bitterly.

"What was in there?"

"The money he got, selling dope. Five bloody years' worth. A third of it was mine, that was the deal."

"He might've just moved it somewhere else."

"Nah, bullshit. That bastard's not coming back. He was already spooked when ya little brother died; reckoned he'd be in deep shit if anyone found out."

"Tommy wasn't his fault."

Martha was still staring into the empty box beneath the floor. "He must've figured it wouldn't be long before ya brother showed the cops the way back here."

"Only if Maurice finds a town."

Martha's eyes flicked to Kate's face and away again. "I reckon his chances are pretty good."

Kate followed Martha outside, where they stood in the morning sunshine and she rolled Martha a cigarette. Peters hadn't taken his old horse. Hoping for an apple, it moved towards them, stopping at the fence. Looking east, up to the hills and the mountains behind, she wondered where Maurice was at that moment.

"Maybe Peters is just looking for Maurice."

Martha coughed loudly. "Nah. He's talked about Australia a few times. I reckon he'll head there. It wouldn't be hard to pay some yachtie to take him across to

Queensland or somewhere. Aussie's a big country, easy to disappear in a place like that."

"He might come back," said Kate, trying to cheer her up.

Martha spat on the ground, and Kate watched the blob of spit bubble down the blades of grass. "He's gone for good. Men, eh, girlie. They all bugger off in the end and leave ya fucked."

* * *

For the rest of the morning, Martha sat on the couch on the veranda of the farmhouse, smoking one cigarette after another and absentmindedly massaging the pain from her fingers, as she stared out across the paddocks to the river and the ridge beyond. When she was still there at lunchtime, Kate heated the leftover stew and took some out to her.

"I want you to go down to the bottom paddock and cut some flax."

Kate was surprised. "Today?"

"Soon as you can."

"What for?"

Martha clicked her tongue. "Don't argue. Just do as you're told."

Martha explained what she needed—enough flax that it would take Kate the rest of the day to cut, bundle, and carry back to the house.

"But what about Maurice and Peters?"

"That's out of our hands. All we can do is get on with things here. We'll see what happens. Now, go on, hurry up, get ready. I need that flax."

It was useless to argue. Kate fed the baby before packing some bread and cured goat meat into a bag—what would they do for meat without Peters?—along with the sharp knife she used for cutting flax. When she was at the gate, the baby again on her back, Martha called out to her.

"Make sure you get enough, eh. Don't come back before ya do."

"All right."

Halfway to the first tree, she turned back. She could just make out Martha, who was standing on the top step still watching her. Because of Kate's eyesight, Martha looked like part of the house; a column propping up the veranda, or a door. Kate looked to the sky for a bird to give her a sign. She couldn't see anything, not even a sparrow or a gull. She turned and walked on.

It was obvious that the flax was an excuse for Martha to get her out of the way. But why? When she could no longer be seen from the house, she placed her bag under a toetoe bush. The baby was sleepy and quiet as she doubled back, keeping close to the trees in case Martha was still watching out for her.

She was only just in time. As she passed the graveyard, she saw Martha making hard work of the forbidden slope behind the long-drop. She had her back to Kate as she toiled toward the trees. Strangely, Martha was wearing her good boots and embroidered jacket. Kate crouched behind a wooden grave marker that was covered in lichen, and watched. The baby started to whine and she shushed him, but he was suddenly bored and wanted to be set free.

When Martha disappeared into the trees, Kate waited several minutes before she followed up the slope. Among the trees she was afraid that the ground would open up beneath her. She chose her footing carefully, avoiding any deep piles of leaves or hollows. Although she stopped regularly to look and listen, there was no sight or sound of Martha.

For the first fifty feet, she thought she was imagining the track. Deer or pigs probably passed this way regularly. But deer didn't drag aside fallen branches. Pigs didn't cut steps into an earth bank. She was standing considering the steps, when a sound jerked her head around. A mechanical whir, at once unfamiliar and yet instantly recognisable, although she hadn't heard it in years. It came once, twice, three times before the car's engine coughed into life.

She began to move through the trees as fast as she could. She was desperate to see. The trail was now obvious, and she cut the corners and could've gone faster, except for the low branches that she was afraid might flick into the baby's face.

The trees suddenly thinned and the ground flattened. She was running out into a clearing with a large shed off to one side. A battered utility truck was driving away from her along a dirt road between the trees. The word FORD was painted on the tailgate in white. Through the rear window of the cab she could see the back of Martha's head. The truck bucked on a pothole and the head rocked.

THIRTY-FOUR

29 APRIL 1983

It took Suzanne longer than she'd anticipated to drive to Blackwater Creek. Just as the truck driver had told her, the place was in the middle of nowhere. After getting out of her car on the north side of the bridge, she flexed her back and rolled her shoulders. The road was bordered by dense bush on both sides. The bridge was about fifty feet long, a single lane spanning a shingle riverbed. She must've driven across it many times over the years. Undoubtedly at some point she'd stopped to look around, though it bothered her that she couldn't remember it specifically.

She tried to put herself in the shoes of the young hitchhiker with the baby. She still favoured the idea—her fight-and-flight theory—that the girl was a local and had either demanded to get out of a car or been unceremoniously evicted. It was the most plausible explanation.

Suzanne walked slowly across the bridge, ready to step onto the raised concrete lip if a car appeared. A truck driver coming from the south would've had plenty of time to see the girl and pull over. Sean had been on his way to the freezing works: both decks of the truck and trailer were full of sheep. Suzanne imagined the squeal of air brakes; the mixed stink of ammonia, lanolin, and fear coming from the idling truck. The girl had been brave to accept the ride. Or possibly foolhardy, depending on your point of view.

After crossing the road, Suzanne moved along the treeline. There was no scrap of litter or item of discarded clothing. Discovering that type of clue was reserved for detective novels. There was nothing to learn here.

The turnoff to Rossville was close. If the girl was a local, it was possible, although of course highly improbable, that was where she lived. Ten minutes on a narrow potholed road that twisted and cut back through heavy bush brought Suzanne to flat pastureland at the foot of two valleys. Rossville turned out to be a veneer town. Two dozen wooden shops and houses glued one deep on both sides of the road. She drove slowly. Faded signs advertised a butcher and a corner shop, although both buildings were empty. Other signs read, *For Sale. For Lease. Closed.* Although it was midmorning, there was no one around. She made a U-turn in front of the last house. The curtains were closed, and a goat stood tethered by a heavy chain on the front lawn.

The only place that appeared to be open was the pub. When she got out of the car, she could hear the fast rhythm of a generator coming from the rear of the building. Going through the door marked "Public Bar," she found herself in a large room with a wooden bar and a pool table. One wall was lined with shelves full of sacks of rice, bags of flour and sugar, salt, biscuits, tea and coffee. Next to the food were hammers, saws, drills, boxes of nails and screws, spark plugs, and other auto parts.

A tall man with grey stubble came out from the back room and stood behind the bar with his arms folded.

"I'm guessing you're lost."

"Not really. I saw the town on the map and wanted to have a look."

"Shouldn't take ya long, there's not much to look at."

"I see you're a shop as well as a bar."

"We're the one-stop shop around here."

The light above them flickered.

"Generator's playing up," said the man. "We're waiting for the electricity company to fix the lines into town. It's only been six years. Should come back on any moment." He grinned slowly.

"I'm guessing Rossville used to be bigger."

"Sure, back when the coal mine was still open. After she shut down, people couldn't even sell their places. A lot of blokes just took their families and walked away."

"Where did they go?"

"All over. Cities, mostly. Dunedin, Christchurch. A few poor bastards even went up to Auckland."

"But not you?"

"Nah, I was born here. Anyway, I've got the business." He gestured to the empty bar and the shelves. She couldn't tell if he was being deliberately ironic.

"Actually, we've had quite a few new people move to town in the last ten years or so. They can just walk into a free house, or even a farm, no questions asked. Even if there's no power or running water, it's still a home. Beats living under a motorway bridge in some shithole city. Excuse my French."

She bought a bottle of motor oil that she didn't need, before she pulled out the photograph of Katherine. The man came out from behind the bar and studied it in the sunlight coming through the window as Suzanne explained about the truck driver and the young hitch-hiker.

"I thought she might be local," she finished.

"Nah," he said, still looking at the photograph. "The Coopers've got teenagers—more than they know what to do with, the little shits—but the older ones are all boys."

"I see. That's what I thought. Thank you, anyway."

"Unless it was Martha's daughter."

"Is she about seventeen, with long, dark hair?"

He shrugged. "I dunno, I've never seen her. They live on the farm over in the next valley. I only see Martha about once a year. Mostly it's Peters that comes in to buy stuff."

"Her husband?"

Another shrug. "Dunno what the arrangement is there."

"But you think this Martha has a teenage daughter?"

"That's what she told me. She said the girl used to live up north with relatives but came down to help out on the farm. Just as well; Martha's health's not that flash. She reckoned the girl was a good worker; seemed pretty proud of her."

"Is there anything else you can tell me?"

"Yeah, a word of advice."

The man stepped closer. Suzanne saw that he had a thin scar along his jawline that ran like a firebreak through the grey stubble.

"There's normally a reason why people choose to live in the middle of nowhere with no job and no electricity. Generally speaking, it's not because they like the limelight. If I were you, I'd be very careful about rocking up out of the blue and asking a lot of questions."

* * *

The only people Suzanne saw as she drove out of Rossville were four barefoot boys, none older than eight, playing with a rugby ball on the road. They were all closely cropped, almost bald. One of them picked up the ball and they moved aside, challenging her with their eyes as she went slowly past. The smallest one had ringworm in his scalp.

Following the directions she'd been given, she turned left at the fork in the road and drove until the chipseal ended. The shingle road narrowed and climbed steeply through hillside paddocks in a series of blind corners. The land seemed disused. In places, gorse had taken over from the grass and fencelines had crumbled as the slow tide of bush crept back in. She drove carefully, worried a farmer's truck would hurtle around a corner in a plume of dust, but she encountered no other traffic before she came to the gate she'd been told about. A handmade sign warned against trespassing.

The publican had admitted that he'd never visited the farm where this Martha and her daughter lived. He'd also reiterated that she should be careful.

"There's a lot of unusual horticulture around here." He'd made a circle with his finger and thumb and held it up to his puckered lips. "People get paranoid about their crops. If you're going over there, don't go nosing around or you might get yourself shot."

Beyond the gate, which she shut behind her, two parallel ruts were all that remained of the road. At the far side of the paddock, the ruts carried on into the trees. It turned out to be a dead end, stopping after less than a hundred feet, in front of a large shed. She turned the car around before she got out.

"Hello? Is anybody here?"

No one appeared. Apart from an old utility truck that had neither registration nor licence plates, and some coiled rope hanging on the wall, the shed was empty. She'd assumed the road would take her all the way to this Martha woman's farm.

Five years ago she would probably have given up, but

that was the old her. Fetching her day-pack from the boot of the car, she checked to see everything was there. She had a first-aid kit, a change of clothes, including a waterproof jacket, enough food for two days, and a thermal blanket that would keep her warm and dry if she was forced to sleep in the bush. The air was cool among the trees, so she slipped on her good wind-breaker. She checked her compass and set off.

The shed turned out to be at the top of a ridgeline. She moved carefully down the slope, her eyes on where she placed her feet among the fallen branches. She passed another sign nailed to a tree: *Trespassers Will Be Shot*. And, in case there was any ambiguity, *Fuck Off*.

She guessed that she'd come a little over a mile when she had her first view of the valley. The flat land had been cleared except for half a dozen ancient white pines, which stood alone in the paddocks, and on the far side she saw a river. Slightly below where she was standing was a farmhouse with a long-drop toilet out the back. The sheets of iron on the roof of the house were rusted and smoke was rising from the chimney straight into the air.

The hollow sound of chopping carried to where she stood. She walked along the treeline until she could see a woman below her in the front yard. She was cutting wood with an axe, her back to Suzanne. The woman was wearing shorts and a singlet top, and her long, dark hair was tied back in a ponytail. Suzanne couldn't see her face, but she could see how broad her shoulders and back were, and that they were marked with the dark smudges of tattoos. Sleeping at a safe distance, on a rug on the ground, was a young child.

Suzanne suddenly felt foolish for coming here. Clearly this wasn't Katherine. Her niece had been a shy, bookish girl who'd attended the best school her father's money could buy. Certainly she'd been nothing like this young woman, this mother, who was using the axe with such strength and confidence. And, worse than foolish, Suzanne felt like a Peeping Tom. Her presence would be seen an intrusion. Rightly so. This valley was the woman's home; hers and her family's. The man back in Rossville had implied that they rarely left, so perhaps it was closer to being their whole world. Who was she, a complete stranger, to turn up uninvited and unannounced, to peer through the windows of their lives?

Suzanne had already turned to leave when the door to the long-drop opened. A squat woman in a singlet-top emerged less than thirty feet away, tugging at her skirt. Her legs, arms, and shoulders up onto her neck were covered in tattoos. From the description she'd been given in the pub, Suzanne knew this must be Martha.

Some instinct made Martha turn and look toward the trees. She saw the stranger, and panic flickered over her face. She glanced towards the house and back, before she turned bulldog and began to stomp up the slope.

Suzanne sighed and walked down to meet her. When they were a few feet apart, they stopped.

"Who're you?" said Martha. "This is private fuckin' property."

"I know I'm intruding. I'm sorry."

"You've got no right coming here."

"My name's Suzanne Taylor."

"So?" Martha glanced towards the house again. From where they stood, the young woman and the baby were out of sight behind the roofline but the thud and splinter of the axe and the wood could still be heard. "You'd better piss off."

"I will, but first I wondered if you'd take a very quick look at this photograph."

"Nah, just go. Go on. Fuck off." She stepped closer.

"I'm looking for someone."

"I don't give a shit. I said go."

Suzanne took the studio portrait of the Chamberlains from her pocket and held it out to the woman, who made no move to take it.

"I'm looking for a family who disappeared about four years ago. Some people told me they saw a girl on the highway near Rossville who might have been one of them. This girl here, on the right."

Seemingly against her will, the woman took three steps up the slope. Her hand reached out. For the first time, Suzanne noticed that rheumatoid arthritis had swollen the woman's joints and warped her fingers. She had to use both hands to grip the photograph. Her expression was unreadable as she studied it.

"Nah," she said at last. "I've never seen any of them."

"The young woman who's working—"

"She's my daughter."

"Of course, I understand. But do you mind if I ask, did she hitchhike into Hokitika about a year ago?"

Martha's eyes moved back and forth between Suzanne and the house. "Yeah, that's right. She went into town, but then she came back."

"Some people who saw her thought she might've been that girl there in the photograph."

"Well, she's bloody not."

"Yes, I can see that. I never really thought she was. I just had to be certain. I'm sorry to have bothered you." She reached out and took back the photograph.

"You don't look like a cop," said Martha. "Are you a private investigator or something?"

"Nothing so exotic. The children's mother, Julia, was my younger sister."

"You're family?"

"Yes."

Several conflicting emotions passed over Martha's face. "And you've been looking for them all this time?"

"I live in London, but I've been back here four times since they disappeared."

"Almost every year?"

"Yes. This is my last trip, though."

"How come?"

"I don't believe there's anyone left to find." She took a step back. "I'll leave you in peace. I'm sorry to have disturbed you."

Suzanne walked back up the slope. At the trees, she stopped and looked back. Martha was still watching her. Suzanne raised a hand in farewell and Martha replied with the same gesture.

Hidden again among the trees, Suzanne watched as Martha walked around to the front of the house. The young woman put down the axe. When she turned, Suzanne saw her face for the first time. Yes, there was a resemblance to Katherine. She could see why the truck driver and the waitress had made a mistake. But that was the extent of it, a resemblance. The young woman left the axe by the chopping block, and went into the house. She came back with two flax baskets. She joined her mother in the vegetable garden, and together they worked the earth, their bend-and-pluck-and-place rhythm unhurried yet efficient. Suzanne continued to watch, fascinated by this glimpse of lives unimagined.

The well-pecked trail of breadcrumbs that had led her from the café in Hokitika to Blackwater Creek, to the dying town, and finally to this valley, would be the last she'd follow. She had nothing left to give to the past. One day, perhaps, a hunter, or a tourist having a pee in the bushes at the edge of the road, would stumble over the rusted frame of the Chamberlains' car. Maybe some bones would still be left. That was the best she could hope for.

Although her marriage was over, she still had her two boys. And her work, her friends, her church community. Timothy and Astrid were already talking about getting married. In time there would be grandchildren she could give her energy to. Despite her best efforts, the lost would stay lost. The thought made her feel suddenly light, as if her feet might rise from the earth and she might fly up through the branches and hover over the valley, looking down.

Turning away from the farmhouse and its strange inhabitants, she set off back through the trees to her car.

THIRTY-FIVE

17 MAY 1990

Kat pushed her glasses higher on her nose with one fin-ger. She pulled the last of the weeds from the earth at the foot of the wooden cross with its single carved name, MARTHA. Her daughter was inside the house having her afternoon nap, but was old enough now to come out by herself when she woke up. Her third child, who had just turned one, was playing in the dirt among the gravestones. He was holding a crooked stick, happy as Larry to wave it around while she worked. Kat clucked her tongue at him and he smiled.

Martha had died two years ago, in the winter. During that last year, the arthritis had crippled her and she'd barely left the chair in front of the fire. She'd hated not being able to work. The pain had stolen even her knit-ting. She couldn't so much as hold a fork. In the final weeks, Kat had fed bread moistened with soup into the old woman's almost toothless mouth. It had been a good thing when a bad chest cold became worse.

After she died, Kat had gone through the drawers in Martha's room. She found nothing interesting except two short letters from a woman called Helen. "Dear Mum" was written at the top of each. There were no envelopes, though. Nothing that gave a last name or an address.

She picked up the baby, swung him to her hip and walked over to the garden. She needed potatoes for the evening meal. The sound of sawing was coming from the front yard. Aaron was replacing some of the rotten weatherboards. Her eldest was helping him. They both looked up, and Aaron raised a hand and grinned. Aaron Cooper, one of the tribe of Coopers who lived behind a corrugated-iron fence just out of Rossville. Aaron's father, known to everyone as Fridge, rode a Harley Davidson. He'd lost a leg in a crash before Aaron was born, which meant a regular sickness-benefit. The woman who lived with him was mother to the last three of his nine kids. The youngest was the same age as hers.

Kat had met Aaron on only her second trip into Rossville. He'd been in the pub, bartering with the owner over some car parts his father wanted to sell. Aaron had helped change a flat tyre on Martha's ute. Nothing much would've come of it, because they were as nervous and tongue-tied as each other. Luckily, Martha had done enough talking for both of them and a few other people as well. Before they drove away, the sly old cow had arranged a second meeting.

Aaron had quickly begun to spend a lot of time at the farm. He'd turn up on his dirt bike in the morning, offering to help with this and that, whatever needed doing. Soon, he reckoned it was easier to stay the night rather than ride all the way home. When he shifted from the spare room into Kat's bed, Martha's only reaction was to tease them both with crude jokes.

Aaron hunted, preferring his crossbow to a rifle. At least once a week, he drove to the coast to gather kai moana; spearfishing and swimming down in his wetsuit to pull crayfish from the rocks on the bottom, prising off oysters, mussels, and pāua. For cash he grew dope, in partnership with two of his younger brothers. They used the shearing shed and Peters's old sites up in the bush. It was Aaron who first called her Kat, and now she couldn't imagine being anything else.

Kat put the baby on the ground in the garden, before using the fork to turn the dark soil, revealing half a dozen white potatoes. As she worked, she found herself thinking about Maurice. Mostly she was too busy with the kids and the farm and her preparations for the new baby, already bulging her overalls, to live in the past. Sometimes, though, her brother came limping back into her thoughts.

She was sure Mo was dead. He'd promised her he would come back, and he never had. He'd been so stubborn that she reckoned only death could've kept him away. This year the Indian summer refused to end and the valley was bright and still, as it had been the last time she saw Maurice. She could imagine looking up from her work and seeing him coming towards her on his crutch. She had trouble picturing how his face would've changed. In her mind, he was still a boy and wore the same indignant scowl he always had. Of course, he'd want her to go with him. She wouldn't leave, though. Her family was here. This was home.

The baby moved onto all fours and, still clutching his stick, got unsteadily to his feet. Something had caught his attention. Kat followed his gaze past the garden, up the valley and into the sunlit grass and darker green bush. Raising a heavily tattooed hand, she shielded her eyes.

"What do you see, mate?"

He waved his stick at the blue sky. From the long grass on the other side of the fence, four magpies took to the air. As the birds flew over their heads, their warbling cries carried down the valley. "Four for a boy," said Kat, and touched her stomach. "That's a good sign eh."

The baby looked up at her and laughed. His mouth was black with dirt.

Kat turned back to the garden. She'd better get on with her work or there'd be no food on the table tonight. She had heaps to do.

THIRTY-SIX

LATE SUMMER, 1982

It was the faint shrieking of the gulls that told Maurice he was, at last, close to the ocean. He stood and listened, one hand against the papery bark of a tree. The notched stick, his evidence, protruded from the top of the pack as he strained to hear the birds again. It occurred to him that perhaps he'd only imagined the sound.

For most of the morning, he'd been following the same ridge. For the last mile or so, the ground had been rocky and dry, and the trees, almost miraculously, had thinned out. For short, welcome stretches he'd been able to travel in a straight line.

It had been three days since he left the valley. On the first day, he'd hiked north, just as he'd planned. The next valley turned out to be narrower and more heavily forested than the farm. There'd been no sign of any buildings, not even old foundations or rusted farm equipment. He'd kept walking north, heading for a saddle in the next ridge. That was where he'd spent the first night. At dawn, he'd followed a loud creek down to a river. Only then did he turn west. Instead of taking him to the coast, though, the river had betrayed him. It had flowed into rocky ravines. In the end, he'd no choice except to abandon it. He'd spent hours climbing slowly and awkwardly up through the trees, heading toward the highest point.

The second night, he'd slept under a log. The next

morning, though, his efforts had been rewarded with a view of another ridge that curved west in a long crescent. It took him half a day to reach it, but that was the ridge he'd now been following for hours. His original plan to use the river had failed, but he'd been clever and found a new way.

Snatches of brittle bird sound. He was sure this time. It was definitely gulls, and not just a small flock like the ones that sometimes fed on the paddocks in the valley. This sounded like hundreds of birds, all kwarring and kwe-arrring. Maurice took off his bag and finished the water from the bottle. He would need to fill it at the next stream he came to. Refreshed, he set off again.

After a while the birds grew louder. There was no mistaking the sound now.

"Rookery," he said.

Peters wouldn't have approved of a fancy word like that. For using it, Maurice would've been called "soft," a "poofter" or a "posh little ponce."

"It's a rookery," Maurice said again. And a third time, louder, "A rookery!"

Glancing up from his next footfall, he glimpsed a slice of blue through the trees. The ocean. It had to be. Another forty feet, and the blue widened. Framed by the trunks, the line of the horizon was touching the paler blue of the sky. The ground began to slope down. Because there was hardly any undergrowth, he was able to pick up speed. He swung himself on his crutch before shifting his weight forward, landing on his good leg and launching into the next stride. He had to keep his eyes on the spot ahead where he wanted to place his crutch. He was moving quickly.

Almost daily for who knew how long, Peters had named him "Slowpoke," "Cousin Lurch," "Snail." Now

Maurice was making a lie of those names. This was the fastest he'd gone since the accident. Perhaps he was going faster than he ever had, even before the crash. The steeper the ridge became, the quicker he was able to go. As he picked up speed—land, vault, spring, land, vault, spring—he heard another sound mingling with the cries of the birds. It was the rush, whoosh, and long pause of waves.

I'm almost there.

At any moment he'd be out of the trees and on the beach. The coast was going to be his road to the nearest town, which would definitely have a name. That was another thing he'd prove to everyone was a lie. The town would lead him to the city. The city would be his way home, to Hornton Street. To London.

Faster! I can go faster!

He'd show Peters who was a slowpoke! Could a snail move like this? Could someone named Lurch barely touch the earth? For all Peters's size and strength, and skill with his gun and knife or hammer and nails, it was him, Maurice John Chamberlain, who'd won in the end!

Faster!

He'd outwitted that grunting Neanderthal—there was another big word to confuse Peters, to shove down his fat, hairy throat! He was the one who'd defeated that farting, smelly, arse-scratcher.

That snake-headed, hairy-faced, mouth-breathing, spitting, shit-stained, green-snot-blowing ...

"Cunt!" He yelled the word as loud as he could.

But even as he put on a final turn of speed toward the growing line of blue, he couldn't help throwing a fearful glance over his shoulder. He was suddenly sure that Peters was right behind him, ready to seize him by the collar and drag him back to the valley, to snatch away his future, as if the whole escape had been nothing but a cruel joke. Peters would say that there was still a debt that had to be paid.

Faster. I have to get out of the trees.

One, two, three long strides, and he was there.

Maurice's face was split by a wild grin as he broke into the open. He'd done it! He'd escaped! He was free! Peters hadn't caught him, after all. The glare of the sun was blinding. He had a squinting glimpse of a line of surf breaking along rocks and the spread of blue water as his momentum carried him forward.

Something was wrong. The beach was somehow still beyond him. Below. There was nowhere to land his next crutch-fall. Crumbling rock. Empty air. His heart gave one hard punch and he cried out in a high voice.

The rocks below were streaked white where the gulls were nesting in their hundreds. Panicked by the boy's sudden appearance and his frightened shout, the nearest birds took off, wheeling, white and grey, tipped with red.

As Maurice fell
the dazzling sun
black and white rocks
the blue sky
and the darker blues of the ocean
melted
into one tear-stained blur.

His last indignant protest hung in the salted air alongside the sharp cries of the gulls.

ACKNOWLEDGEMENTS

A significant portion of *The Tally Stick* was written while I was the Katherine Mansfield Fellow in Menton, France. My thanks to the Arts Foundation Te Tumu Toi, and to the members of the Katherine Mansfield Trust, particularly William Rubinstein, who took such good care of us on the Côte d'Azur. Thanks for their advice on early versions of the story: Professor Patrick Evans, Mathew and Laura Nixon, and Dr Caroline Foster. I am always grateful to my enthusiastic publisher Harriet Allan and my editor Anna Rogers. Finally, I am indebted to my agents Anna Soler-Pont and Maria Cardona at Pontas Literary and Film Agency, Barcelona.

On the Design

As book design is an integral part of the reading experience, we would like to acknowledge the work of those who shaped the form in which the story is housed.

Tessa van der Waals (Netherlands) is responsible for the cover design, cover typography, and art direction of all World Editions books. She works in the internationally renowned tradition of Dutch Design. Her bright and powerful visual aesthetic maintains a harmony between image and typography and captures the unique atmosphere of each book. She works closely with internationally celebrated photographers, artists, and letter designers. Her work has frequently been awarded prizes for Best Dutch Book Design.

The cover image immediately evokes the central question of the book: What happened to the kid(s)? The wet, impenetrable woods are characteristic of New Zealand's West Coast. The cold colors and letters, starkly distinct from the image, convey the alert loneliness of being lost in the wild.

The cover has been edited by lithographer Bert van der Horst of BFC Graphics (Netherlands).

Suzan Beijer (Netherlands) is responsible for the typography and careful interior book design of all World Editions titles.

The text on the inside covers and the press quotes are set in Circular, designed by Laurenz Brunner (Switzerland) and published by Swiss type foundry Lineto.

All World Editions books are set in the typeface Dolly, specifically designed for book typography. Dolly creates a warm page image perfect for an enjoyable reading experience. This typeface is designed by Underware, a European collective formed by Bas Jacobs (Netherlands), Akiem Helmling (Germany), and Sami Kortemäki (Finland). Underware are also the creators of the World Editions logo, which meets the design requirement that "a strong shape can always be drawn with a toe in the sand."